SHOP LANDIA

A NOVEL

JIM BRESLIN

Oermead Press

Shoplandia/Jim Breslin -- 1st ed.v2
ISBN-10: 0615997813
ISBN-13: 978-0615997810

For those in the studio and those watching at home

"All happiness depends on courage and work."
- Honoré de Balzac

"You can't blame a writer for what the characters say."
- Truman Capote

ONE

··

FREIGHT TRAIN

"Hey Jake! Where are my onions?"

The eyes of show host Ron Calabrese shot right through me. "How can I make my mother's classic Italian gravy if I don't have onions?" My stomach twisted into knots. Calabrese grinned into the camera, reassuring America everything was fine.

Being chastised on live national television was a gut wrenching moment. I jumped down the steps to backstage and sprinted toward the prep kitchen.

"Jake, are you setting Calabrese up?" A voice asked through headsets.

"No. Honestly, I'm not." I replied, unsure if the person was serious or teasing. Three days into this job and I wasn't sure about anything anymore. Turning the corner into the prep room, I nearly crashed into show host Tanya.

"Whoa there, buddy."

I barely glanced at her as I sprinted into the kitchen. I had chopped the onions, pinched the garlic, scooped the tomato paste and crushed tomatoes into appropriate containers. Where had I placed the onions? I scanned the counter, but the onions had vanished.

"Did you find them?" producer Dylan asked through headsets.

"No. Damn it. They must have been tossed out. Can't he make the gravy this one time without fucking onions?"

"Whoa," a few voices called out. "Easy there, Jake. This is a family show."

"Ha," I snorted into headsets and grabbed a full onion off the counter, searched through three drawers for a sharp knife, and two more cabinets for a small bowl.

Dylan provided an update, "He's heated up the olive oil and sautéed the garlic. He's asking for onions again..."

"I'm slicing them now!" Peeling back the skin, I sliced the onion and chopped it small and thin, nearly slicing off my middle finger in the process. I imagined handing Calabrese a bowl with onions and the tip of my finger. The aroma of onion seeped into my nostrils.

"Jake?"

"I'm coming. Gimme a minute. Tomato sauce can be made without onions." Feeling a floater in front of my eye, I reflexively poked at it with my finger. Big mistake. My eyes started watering as the knife clattered into the kitchen sink. I grabbed the bowl and ran toward the set with tears streaming down my face. I stumbled past two men in suits who were casually chatting.

"No running," one of them called. I had no idea who they were so I ignored them and climbed the steps two at a time, then slowed as I entered the set.

"I've drizzled some olive oil on here and heated the pan. Hey, here's Jake now with my onions." The camera stayed on a single shot of Calabrese as he reached out his pudgy sausage fingers. I watched the monitor as my disembodied hand crept into the shot with the bowl.

Calabrese looked at me. "Jake, my mother would never forgive us if we tried to make her famous gravy without onions." With a spoon, he emptied the onions into the sizzling pan, and then inhaled deeply to show his pleasure.

My red eyes were just beginning to clear as I watched him stir. "Jake, we're missing the white wine. Seriously, can you grab the cooking wine?" He grinned at me, and then turned back to the camera and winked. I was tempted to flash him the finger I had nearly amputated but instead jumped down the steps again and sprinted past the suits.

One month ago I'd been content with my life, flirting with girls on campus and playing beer pong in my college apartment basement. I'd done everything I could to squeeze the pleasure out of my precious final college days. On the night before graduation, I climbed the fire escape onto the roof of our rowhouse and sat overlooking the little college town. I drank more than my share of Natty Lights that night, and in drunken tears, I threw myself a one-person pity party. The good life had abruptly ended and this new transition had been thrust upon me. Now, I'm a backstage minion at the beck and call of this portly show host with an ego as large as his waistline.

"You fell down the rabbit hole, eh?"

This was my introduction to Shoplandia three days before the onion incident. I had been partnered with Curtis, a gangly, shaggy-haired production assistant with glazed eyes who darted around in fits.

I just stared, unsure what I'd gotten myself into.

Curtis reached out his long, pale hand. "Dude, welcome to the live show. Do you know how we do it?"

"Not really."

"We do it all with smoke and mirrors." He waved his arms around as if he was conjuring an illusion. Curtis rocked back and forth on his feet. His blue eyes were dilated and bloodshot.

"Okay, I'm all in."

I had aimed high. Over the previous few months, I'd sent my neatly typed cover letter and resume to all the appropriate places: 30 Rockefeller Center, Black Rock, even out west to Burbank, Culver City, and Hollywood. My college roommate Thomas had been accepted into the NBC page program and was starting this same day. I was more than a little envious.

But I knew several of my classmates were still searching for anything in their discipline. Several buddies were back at their old summer gigs; waiting on tables, cutting lawns, life guarding at a pool. It looked as though I was going that route myself, but at the end of April, I stumbled onto a listing for an entry level broadcast job at Shoplandia. After a half-day of interviews, they offered me a position as a production assistant. Now, I was backstage at a television studio that sold tchotchkes, standing beside this rabbit-like creature.

"Have you watched much of the show?"

"No."

"They hire anyone these days."

I just stared, unsure if he was joking.

"Relax!" He slapped me on the shoulder. "Lighten up. Look, this place is a blast if you like living on the edge. One moment you're sweating over a computer demo that short circuits and the next moment you're getting kissed on the cheek by Florence Henderson. It's all good!"

He led me to a table with miscellaneous items organized neatly in pairs. I had the sensation I was at a yard sale. There were two karaoke machines, elastic exercise bands, oak-finished reproduction record players, jazzercise videos and over-sized doormats.

"As production assistants, we're the glue that keeps this giant machine going," Curtis said with pride. "These are the items we'll be selling today, all laid out by each hour. Our job is simple, to ensure each item is clean and operable, and on the set at the right time. Dude, I'll make you an expert. Just follow me."

He handed me a headset and an intercom box. Voices chatting about graphics, cameras, and microphones swirled around in my head.

Curtis spoke up. "Hey everyone, we have a new guy on today. Jake Meecham is starting backstage so take it easy on him."

A chorus of voices welcomed me to the studio.

"Hi Jake!"

"Welcome to the shooow!"

"Yo, dude!"

"Have him come out to the producer's desk."

I followed Curtis through the door into the cavernous arena in front of the stage. Up on the set that resembled a living room, I saw for the first time the show host I have since come to despise.

Below the front lip of the stage, in the pit where one might expect to find an orchestra, a large NASA-like command desk held an array of small camera monitors and flickering computer screens. A balding man, sporting wire-framed glasses and wearing a headset, stood at the desk studying the monitors. Behind him the room stretched out, a sea of order entry operators seated in row after row of small desks, some speaking softly into phone headsets while others knitted or read gossip magazines.

"Jake, this is Dylan. He's our producer today," Curtis said. Dylan wore jeans and a wrinkled untucked shirt. Up close, he looked to be in his thirties, and as he stuck out his hand, he smiled.

Through headsets, a voice quipped, "Any bets on how long this kid will last?"

I twisted to Curtis, embarrassed, wondering why someone would say this.

"Hey now, he's on headsets," Dylan said. "Play nice."

"They're just joking," Curtis assured me.

A voice called out, "Tell him to turn around."

Dylan pointed up to a window overlooking the studio. "There's the peanut gallery." I saw hands waving.

Two men and a young brunette woman smiled down at us.

"Hi Jake."

"Actually, that's the control room. They're not as sharp as the prime time crew, but they're okay," Dylan joked.

A chorus of hisses and boos broke out.

"Oh, was my key on?" Dylan replied. "You're the best." He took his headset off. "Do you know why we're totally live? No seven second delay here."

"Why's that?" I asked.

Dylan pointed to a series of bar charts and numbers on his computer screen. "If a product sells out, we want to move on quickly. Or if a product sucks, if nobody is buying it, I won't waste time. Your job is to always be ready with the next item."

I just nodded, trying to soak it in.

"Dylan keeps us on our toes," Curtis added.

"You bet I do."

"Time is up. Let's go," Curtis said urgently.

"So what happened to the last guy?" I asked as I followed him backstage.

"Ah, it's a long story. Don't worry about it. We have to hustle."

He handed me a bowl of M&Ms and picked up a wooden carving of a moose.

"Follow me."

I ran up the steps closely behind. When he stopped abruptly, I bumped into him, nearly spilling the candy.

"Dude, give me some space."

Up close, the current show host had gray hair and mounds of makeup caked on his sweaty, beefy forehead. He smiled into the camera and teased, "Don't go away, you won't believe what we have next."

Curtis jumped in, set the wooden moose on the table, and picked up an ionizer that had just been presented.

"Jake, this is show host extraordinaire Rob Calabrese. Rob, this is Jake. Jake is our new production assistant." Curtis grabbed the candy from me and placed the bowl on the table.

Calabrese looked me right in the eye for the first time. "Hello Jake. Welcome to hell." It was a face I'd quickly come to hate. He grabbed a handful of candy, tossed some in his mouth and grinned, and then he reached down for a second helping.

"Those are all the M&Ms we have," Curtis warned as he yanked me back to the side of the stage.

Just as a voice on headsets asked, "Ready, Rob?" Calabrese quickly flashed Curtis his middle finger and mouthed an obscenity. I glanced at the monitors and saw that as the camera clicked live, Calabrese smiled mischievously, and said, "We have so much fun behind the scenes. You won't believe this moose! You simply load this moose up with your favorite candies." Calabrese dropped the candy into the moose's neck.

"When you are looking for a treat, you do this." He lifted the moose's tail and candy trickled out the animal's ass and into the host's waiting hand. He broke into an extended hearty laugh. "Isn't this the greatest thing you've ever seen?" He held his hand out to show the bright array of colors, and then shoved them in his mouth. "Mmmm...mmm...good! All this can be yours for only $39.99!" Calabrese looked into the camera and grinned, showing a neat row of impossibly white teeth. "Want to see this again?"

The few times I had watched Shoplandia from home, I thought it was a friendly but bland form of amusement. The cheerful hosts smiled incessantly, with manicured nails and moussed hair, discussing the joys of baubles or the thrill of grilling. Now, standing a few feet from Calabrese, I realized there was truly a strange new world behind the looking glass.

Throughout my first shift, Curtis showed me the mechanics of the job: wiping down bracelets so they shined under the lights, plugging in and testing toaster ovens after cleaning the crumbs out. He stressed the importance of staying a step ahead of the producer, how to keep each host happy and how to rotate the stage. Curtis bounced through the studio like a pinball while I nipped at his heels. And then I made my first of many mistakes.

I thought a voice had cleared me to swap out a porcelain rose sculpture and I walked in front of a live camera. "Dude! Dude," the technical director yelled. "You're dogging the camera!"

The scream in my ears flustered me and I immediately backtracked through the camera shot again, exposing myself to America a second time. Once I cleared the camera lens, Calabrese stood alone with a wicked grin. He looked over and then turned back to the audience.

"That's Jake. Can we get another shot of Jake?"

I was horrified to see a robotic camera swinging my way. My hands trembled as I held the porcelain collectible. "Jake, smile! You are live." The camera stopped and the red light flashed on, indicating I was live on the air. I felt my face flush as red as the rose. I waved a limp hand and wondered if my mom was watching.

"This is Jake's first day on the job," Calabrese said, "and it may be his last." He turned my way and smirked. I tensed up with the thought of being fired, thinking of how I'd just signed a one-year lease on my apartment. Curtis darted up the steps.

"Airtime on your first day!" He patted me on the shoulder.

"Am I in trouble?"

"Don't worry about it. We all make mistakes."

"No. Seriously, am I going to get fired?"

"People don't get fired around here." He glanced at Calabrese and frowned for the first time since I'd known him. "If you do it again, and again, you might. Don't worry."

As soon as his shift ended, Calabrese slumped his fat shoulders and trudged off the set. He loosened his white shirt collar, now stained with makeup that had melted under the lights.

"Already trying to grab face time on your first day?"

I lowered my head. "I'm sorry."

Calabrese smiled and shrugged. "Hey, it's live TV." His grin quickly faded. "Don't let it happen again."

After that first day, I returned to my little efficiency apartment, threw myself onto the pull-out couch and closed my eyes, only to wake from a deep sleep forty minutes later. My shirt was soaked with sweat, and for a moment I thought the episode had been nothing more than a surreal dream. I showered and picked up some Mexican takeout from down the street. On the television, Tanya presented a terry cloth bathrobe. As I devoured a beef burrito and drank a Natty Light, I tried to piece together the rhythm behind the live show.

After dinner, restless and bored, I took a walk through the borough of Sellersburg. Couples and small groups dined outside at the restaurants and pubs along Price Street, relaxing as the sun dipped below the horizon on a cool summer night. Across the street, I caught sight of a familiar face. Curtis's shaggy blonde hair stood out as he sat at a table for four. He was with another man and two women, and they were sitting close, laughing and drinking beer, as if they'd known each other for years. They seemed so relaxed that I was suddenly overcome with a wave of loneliness as I walked back to my apartment.

I fell into a routine over the following days, learning the ebb and flow of the live show. At times, the production ran smoothly, and I worked ahead at a comfortable pace, with Curtis shadowing me. There were occasional moments such as the "onion incident," when the urgency and stress tempted me to spell check my resume. I'd build up confidence over a few days only to have it disappear in a moment of chaos, but Curtis would prop up my ego with words of advice and encourage me to keep moving forward. For all his nervous energy, Curtis proved to be a calm and collected guide, waving away tense moments and laughing at the craziness of it all.

At one point, I had set up a blender demo so the show host could make fruit smoothies. I thought I'd covered it all—laying out ice, bananas, strawberries, an empty glass and a blender. As the camera went live, I realized I'd not tested the blender and hadn't even plugged it in. Curtis witnessed the panic on my face. "What's the matter?"

As soon as I told him, he dropped to his hands and knees and crawled behind the show host, who was live on camera, and he plugged the blender in while she filled it with banana slices and ice. He returned to the far side of the set and flashed me a thumbs up just as she hit the button and the studio was filled with the joyous sound of ice being crushed.

"Thanks."

"No problem, brother. All part of the job." And then he said the words that came to haunt me. "I've got your back."

After work and supper, I usually watched television or walked through town. I tried calling my college buddy Thomas several times, hoping to plan a visit to tour 30 Rock, but his phone went to voicemail each time. During my walks, I often thought about asking Curtis if he'd want to grab a beer after work, but each time we were backstage, hustling along with the live show, I couldn't find an appropriate time to ask. One afternoon, Clancy asked through headsets if anyone wanted to go to happy hour. I was all in. When Curtis returned from the cafeteria, I called out excitedly, "The control room is heading out to the Square Bar, wanna go?"

"Oh, man. I can't today. I have plans. Thanks."

One week later, Curtis and I rotated through to the overnight shift, the graveyard shift, for three weeks. I'd only pulled an all-nighter twice in my life, both times in college. Once was to study for a chemistry exam that I failed miserably. The second time I spent with a free-spirited and sweet-voiced townie girl I'd met at a party. We spent the night sitting cross-legged in a deep conversation about her ongoing exploration of the Kama Sutra. The night dissolved into such languid, verbal foreplay that, by the time she reached out to touch my wrist at daybreak, I'd came in my pants. Needless to say, both experiences ended disastrously, and this left me on edge about staying up all night.

I decided my strategy would be to push myself through the shift on pure adrenaline. Energy flowed through my veins as the night began, but my eyes had glazed over by 4 a.m.

Two supervisors appeared in the studio just in time to give us a much-needed break. Curtis tossed his headset down on a desk. "There's an all night Quickie Mart down the road. Wanna go?"

"Yeah." I blurted out the word, desperate at a chance

to refuel. I tried to recover. "That'd be great. I'm hungry."

The security guard sat watching a sitcom from the seventies on a giant monitor as we passed him in the deserted lobby. We walked into the cool night air, which perked me awake.

"Do you party?" Curtis asked.

"Party? Yeah. I guess so."

We made our way to an orange GTO with a black stripe parked under a street lamp.

"This is yours? Sweet ride."

Curtis folded his long legs into the front seat and started the car. He slid a disc into the player and a guitar screeched from the speakers.

"This is my band," Curtis acknowledged coolly. We sat listening to some decent Phish-like jamming for a few moments before he lowered the volume.

"Dude, you're getting the job down." He reached across me into his glove compartment and pulled out a pack of cigarettes and tapped out a joint.

"I feel like I'm getting the hang of it. Thanks to you."

"Ah, no sweat. It's all part of the training."

"Seriously, I'd be lost without your help."

Curtis flicked his lighter. He lit the tip of the joint and inhaled.

I rushed to fill the awkward silence. "I am having these strange nightmares lately. They're freaking me out."

"Ah, the dreams begin." Curtis closed his eyes and smiled.

"I keep dreaming the live show is going on. And I'm

supposed to be on the stage with the next product. But I'm not. Sometimes I'm down in the cafeteria or I'm at home, but I have the headset on and everyone is telling me to switch the next product up, but I can't."

Curtis held out the joint. I took it and inhaled, held my breath for a few moments, and then exhaled before passing back the spliff.

"The voices start calling me to switch up the product, and I'm helpless because I'm not where I'm supposed to be, and the voices keep growing louder. Everyone is frustrated and they are yelling at me and I'm in a state of panic. It's like the whole show is falling apart."

Curtis inhaled the smoke for a moment and then snorted with laughter as he breathed out. This laughter spurred me on.

"And the worst part is, I wake up from the dream in a sweat and realize the live show is going on right now. Somebody is in the studio right now, switching out the next product. There is always some show host hawking something..."

Curtis raised his hand like a crossing guard. "Dude. We don't use the word hawking."

I shrugged. "Well, there's always a host selling something, and a production assistant just off camera prepping the next product. It never fucking stops."

"Stop the show, I wanna get off!"

"It's driving me a bit crazy."

Curtis blew out a smoke ring that hovered like a fog trapped between the windshield and the dashboard.

"Dude, that's the freight train. It never stops. It invades your mind like a disease. The freight train is always bearing down on you. Sometimes, I'm relaxing on a day off. All of a sudden it hits me. Bam!" He toked again.

"So you know what I mean?"

"It drives some people crazy. They can't last. After two weeks they quit. It's too much. The live show is like life. You learn to deal with it."

I mulled this over quietly.

After a few moments, Curtis added, "I've chosen to self-medicate."

We shared a few more hits, and then Curtis called out, "Quickie Mart, here we come!"

The roads were empty in the middle of the night and the street lamps cast an eerie glow. Suburban houses, set back in the rolling hills, appeared to hover in the darkness.

"So what do you think your dream job is?" Curtis asked.

I mulled this over. Throughout school, I thought I'd be a news producer or work on a sitcom. Now, my focus had been simply to understand my job as well as Curtis did. I nearly replied, *to be you*, but caught myself. Too awkward.

Curtis finally said, "I want to work in the control room, doing audio, graphics. Eventually I'd like to be a technical director. I'm just biding my time until a spot opens up."

After a few moments, the lights of the Quickie Mart came into view. Curtis pulled into the closest parking space by the front door. We were the only customers in the lot. Fatigue seeped into my bones as I climbed out of the car. Inside a young man sat behind the counter reading a magazine.

Curtis waved cheerfully. "Good morning!"

The man looked up from his magazine and nodded. I realized my shoelace was untied so I bent down. It took me four tries to tie a knot, mainly because I was distracted by a smudge on the floor in the shape of a corgi's head. After finally getting my laces tied, a process that I swear took me forty minutes, I felt the sudden craving for chocolate.

I scoured the aisles looking for the Holy Grail, perusing each shelf in search of the perfect snack. I passed over chips, cookies, and cellophane wrapped sandwiches, thinking hard about the potential of each choice, and grew disheartened as I thought nothing would satisfy my inner yearning at this ungodly hour.

As I turned down aisle three, I spied a miraculous sight. It was as if I'd heard a crescendo in a symphony hall, as if the skies had opened up and the sun shone through, directly on a family pack of Little Debbie chocolate frosted mini-donuts.

Curtis was staring in contemplation at slowly rotating dried-out hot dogs on the tabletop grill as he sipped a mammoth Mountain Dew. He hemmed and hawed, as if weighing the pros and cons of a life changing decision. With a sigh, he picked up a pair of greasy tongs and pinched each of the two remaining cauterized hot dogs off the little rollers and placed their brittle carcasses lovingly onto stale rolls. He opened the sneeze shield lid to the condiments and smeared relish, onions and ketchup across the charred casings.

"Dude, you getting caffeine?" Curtis asked.

"Uh no."

"You're going to wish you had caffeine. Did you see the Aqua Joe in there?"

"This?"

"Grab the large container. Caffeinated water."

As we paid at the counter, the door of the Quickie Mart swung open and a disheveled man appeared. He looked to be homeless, with wild unkempt hair and a beard. His t-shirt was filthy, his jeans ripped, the shoelaces on his scuffed sneakers untied. The cashier eyed him suspiciously as he made his way to the corner of the store.

Curtis and I finished making our purchases and returned to the car where I ripped open my bag of donuts. Curtis sat behind the wheel and bit into his first hot dog, keeping his eye on the homeless man inside the Quickie Mart.

"What's up?" I asked as I popped a little donut into my mouth.

"I'm thinking the poor guy has no money. Let's hang for a minute."

Curtis inhaled his first hot dog without taking his eyes off the store. He picked up his tub of Mountain Dew and sipped through the straw.

I was stoned and feeling no pain, slowly savoring each donut. I held one up to my eye so I could see the cashier through the hole.

"These things rock, want one?"

"No thanks."

"Good."

"How can you eat that stuff?"

I pointed at the seared stump of Curtis's second hot dog. "You kidding me?"

Curtis studied his charred half eaten frankfurter. "Mmm...mmm...good." He stuffed the rest of the dog in his mouth and chewed away.

The homeless man walked through the aisles as the manager watched from behind the counter. Finally, the man exited the store empty handed.

"Hey!" Curtis sprang from the car.

"What are you doing?"

Curtis talked softly to the man on the curb. I watched through the windshield, a little concerned for Curtis's safety. After a few minutes, Curtis reached into his jeans and handed the man a few dollar bills. The man nodded as Curtis returned to the car.

"Wow, you win the award for kindness."

We watched the man head back into the store, holding up the cash for the manager to see.

"We'd better get back. We're running late."

As we strolled through the lobby again, the security guard's head was down and his eyes closed. Within minutes, we were back in the studio, still flying high, switching out products and joking with the control room on headsets.

Staring into the wide-eyes of German children statu-

ettes while stoned at five in the morning was an odd experience. I checked the lineup to make sure they were in
the correct order, that each porcelain figurine matched
the description. They had cute hopeful names: Accor-
dion Boy, Best Friends Forever, Evening Angel, Holding
On To Hope and Some Bunny Loves You. The smiling
faces stared back at me as I reviewed the list. It was a bit
creepy.

Someone asked, "If you were a Hummel, which figurine would you be?"

I answered, "I'd be Umbrella Boy. Curtis could be
Some Bunny Loves You."

Melissa from the control room asked, "What would
my name be?"

"You are now Evening Angel."

"Aww, that's so sweet."

Another voice chimed through, "Aren't we selling the
Groping Show Host?"

"How about the Drunken Technical Director?"

"Imagine that, a little boy at the switcher with a quart
of Old English 800."

"I can picture it in mom's curio cabinet now."

"She'd be so proud."

I had to continually re-read the product descriptions
and felt as though I was moving in slow motion. Halfway
through the Hummel show, I let out a series of yawns
and sat down on the side of the set, ready to nod off.

"You okay over there?" Curtis asked.

"I'm exhausted."

"My friend, you are hitting the wall. Switch up Umbrella Boy and meet me backstage."

When I found Curtis in the kitchen, he was pouring a cup of coffee. "You drink joe?"

"Not often. I guess I should start if I'm going to survive this shift."

The warmth of the coffee felt good and I drank it quickly, in between switching up little figurines. But within ten minutes, my heart started pulsating out of rhythm, skipping beats here and there. My teeth jittered, and I held out my hands to see they were shaking.

"Okay, switch him up."

With quivering hands, I picked up the last figurine in the show, an extravagant piece called Sweet Harmony. I studied the four cherub faced little kids caroling by a streetlight. The price was $499. As I turned, the piece slipped out of my hands and crashed onto the floor. The streetlight cracked off and a child's head rolled across the carpet.

"Shit!"

"What was that?" a voice asked.

I picked the duplicate off the table and ran up to the set. "That coffee was strong. I have a case of the shakes."

A voice asked, "Jake, did Curtis give you a double shot?"

"What's that?"

"He makes that damn coffee with caffeinated water."

I glanced across the set and Curtis smiled at me, raising his coffee mug as if saying cheers.

I ran down the steps, picked up the broken pieces of the figurine and tried to place the broken head back on. I muttered, "I broke Harmony."

On my first morning back on day shift, I stood quietly reviewing the day's shows at the backstage table. Calabrese stood nearby, marking up notes on the next table.

A soft voice from behind asked, "Do you have jewelry for me?"

I turned to see a young brunette with blue eyes and a cute smile. Her hair and makeup looked fresh, and she wore a gorgeous green gown. The sight took my breath away. I barely managed to eek out, "I'm sorry."

"I'm Tina. I'm the model for the jewelry show. I was told to get the first few pieces to wear?"

"Oh yeah. Sure." I picked up a bracelet.

Tina lifted her arm, not to take the bracelet, but to allow me to place it on her slender wrist.

"What's your name?"

"I'm Jake." I clasped the bracelet on her wrist.

"Are you new here?"

I picked up the second piece, a necklace, and she turned around and held up her hair. "I've been here about six weeks, but I just got off overnights." I noted the curve of her neck as I clasped the necklace, and then she turned to me.

"How long have you been a model here?"

I took the emerald ring out of the plastic bag and she held out her hand. She let me slip the ring on her finger.

"I work upstairs in the office, in marketing. This is just a side job for some extra cash. Usually, I model at night but I was able to arrange my lunch break to do this show." She looked me over, as though trying to determine whether she approved of me. "It was nice to meet you."

Curtis darted over, stopping right in front of us. "Hi Tina."

"Hello," she replied flatly before turning back to me. When our eyes met, she smiled as though she was giving me a precious little gift.

"Thanks Jake," she said sweetly.

She walked through backstage and disappeared into the model's dressing area.

"She's a hottie." We turned to see Calabrese. He grinned, lowered his head and continued writing his notes.

"She is a very nice girl," Curtis corrected him.

My hand trembled in the aftermath, as it had the night I'd downed the caffeine-laced java.

As the jewelry show began, I took a few moments to check the products in the next hour's *Fun and Leisure*. Curtis appeared at my side, picked up a pair of binoculars and put them to his eyes. After a moment, he said, "I think I'm going out for a beer tonight, you interested?"

I took a breath. "Definitely, I'm up for it."

"That sounds excellent."

I made my way to the steps so I could catch sight of Tina through the doorway. Calabrese stood at a small podium, speaking directly into the camera, describing the colors in the gemstone bracelet and flirting with a female t-caller.

"Ruth from Duluth!" It didn't matter that the woman was calling from Des Moines, Iowa.

"Rob, you are a hoot!" the t-caller giggled. "I can't wait to tell Erma I talked to you! You are our favorite host."

"Oh, you are too kind," Calabrese said with a flirtatious sparkle in his eye. "Now, what did you pick up today?"

"This bracelet. It's just gorgeous."

The director punched up pre-recorded video, a tight shot of the bracelet with gemstones glimmering in the light.

"And did you pick this bracelet up for a special occasion?" While keeping his eye on the monitors, Calabrese walked over to Tina and massaged her neck and back with those pudgy fingers. She jumped at the first touch, and then bit her lip.

"Well, my grandson graduates high school this year. He's graduating at the top of his class, so I think I will wear this bracelet to his graduation."

"Congratulations Ruth! Now tell me, what high school does he go to?" The director punched up a close up of the bracelet on Tina's wrist. Calabrese stroked her hair, brought it up over her ear. Tina's eyes welled up and I held my breath. Curtis climbed the steps to the far side of the set and stared.

"He goes to school in Ames. I'm taking the bus there in two weeks. Just got my bus tickets. I'm so proud of him. He is such a good kid."

Calabrese leaned over, stuck his tongue out and

lightly licked Tina's ear. I gasped and watched Curtis take a deep breath. A voice from the control room asked, "What the hell is that creep doing?" Tina's hand began to tremble and the director punched up the pre-recorded glimmer shot. Calabrese stood up straight and grinned, amused at himself. "Well, that's so good to hear Ruth. You have a great trip now, and enjoy that bracelet. It's a stunner." The control room placed Calabrese on camera and he smiled at the women across the country who adored him.

Down at the producer's desk, Dylan was pre-occupied reviewing the script for the next hour's show. "Jake, are you ready for *Fun and Leisure?*"

I clicked on my box. "We're good to go, sir. We have all the products. Everything is checked."

"I just found out a guest for next hour isn't going to make it," Dylan noted. "Calabrese will have to sell the binoculars without him."

As the jewelry show ended, Tina quickly walked off stage left.

"Tina," Curtis called out, but she didn't stop. She was down the steps and gone. I grabbed the bracelet samples as Curtis yelled, "Rotating!" The big round pie rotated to another set that resembled a patio, and Curtis stepped up to check my work.

"Calabrese is such an ass," he said. "Jake, why don't you take your break and I'll take care of this show."

"Are you sure?"

"Yeah, I got it."

"Do you want anything from the caf?"

"No thanks."

I wanted to check on Tina. Her dressing room door was closed but I stepped up and knocked. "Tina, are you okay?"

"Who is it?"

"It's Jake."

She opened the door slightly and looked out. She'd been crying and it pained me to see her tears.

"I just thought I should check in. Are you okay?"

She nodded her head and wiped a tear from her cheek. "Yeah, I'm okay."

"Is there anything I can do?"

"No. I'm okay." She wiped her nose. "Thanks, really." She smiled sadly and closed the door.

I wanted to say more, to comfort her, but I wasn't sure what could be done. What is the company protocol? I made the trek to the cafeteria, bought a bag of chips and a soda and returned to the studio. I stopped to chat with Dylan at the producer's desk. Perhaps I could explain and see if he had any advice. I pulled up a chair and watched the show on the monitors, waiting for Dylan to finish his phone conversation.

On the air, Calabrese pulled a pair of binoculars out of the case and detailed the item number and the price. He ran through the optical specifications and other features, and talked nostalgically about the joys of bird watching.

I listened to the banter through headsets.

"Calabrese has never bird-watched in his life."

"I would not want to see Calabrese walking through

my neighborhood with those."

"Oh that's gross."

Calabrese continued his presentation, unaware that the crew was mocking him. "What's great about these binoculars is the high quality optics. Follow me."

"Follow him," Dylan called to the control room.

The director quickly set a camera to track Calabrese as he walked to a picture window with a scenic backdrop of an open field in the countryside.

"Let's take a look." Calabrese lifted the binoculars to his eyes and peered out as though catching a glimpse of the beauty of nature. The television camera zoomed in to show a tight shot of Calabrese's bulbous head peering through the binoculars. "I see a few blue jays, and over there is a cardinal." As Calabrese turned back to face the camera, he lowered the binoculars, and I gasped out loud. Two enormous smudges of black grease circled Calabrese's eyes.

"In all seriousness, these are a fine pair of binoculars," Calabrese said earnestly into the camera.

Pandemonium broke out. Headsets erupted in a series of gasps and laughter. Dylan screamed, "What the hell is that?" He leaned into the monitor. He pushed buttons and told backstage, "Get some wet paper towels quick, and a mirror. Get a mirror, damn it."

I watched Dylan push a third button to talk to the director. "Have several promo spots ready. This will take a few minutes."

The director placed a tight shot of Calabrese's pudgy face in preview and the host glanced down to see his raccoon eyes glaring under the lights. Calabrese flushed crimson, and he swiveled his head like a raging bull, looking to physically assault someone. Curtis was nowhere to be found. I sunk into my chair at the producer's desk.

"You bastards!" Calabrese slammed the binoculars onto the floor.

The phone at the producer's desk rang. "Shit!" Dylan said as he picked up the phone. "Yes."

Pause.

"I don't know."

Pause.

"It just happened." Dylan raised his voice. "I can either fix it or sit here and talk to you."

Dylan slammed the phone. "Damn VPs."

Nobody had jumped onto the set to help Calabrese. Dylan opened the drawer of the desk and grabbed a pack of cleaning wipes, sprinted up to the stage and wiped the grease marks off the smoldering host. He inspected Calabrese's eyes, placed his hand on the host's shoulder and spoke quietly. He settled Calabrese down, telling him to take several deep breaths. Within two minutes, the greasy spectacles were gone and the host was back on the air presenting a radar detector.

Dylan stepped down to the desk shaking his head in disgust.

"You were like the horse whisperer up there, settling him down like that," I said in admiration.

Mike the supervisor walked out from backstage with his hands in the air. "What happened?"

"Someone greased the binoculars."

"On purpose?" Mike asked in disbelief, looking from Dylan to me. "Did you prep the show?"

I envisioned being fired, having to call my father, being forced to move back home. "I prepped the show, but I've been on break." My voice crackled. "I'm just finishing my break now."

Mike's eyes darted back to Dylan, who simply replied, "Talk to Curtis."

"Oh shit," Mike sighed.

We turned to see a mid-level manager walking toward us.

"Let the inquisition begin," Dylan declared.

I decided to excuse myself. "I better get backstage." The last thing I heard was the manager asking, "What the hell is going on down here?"

As soon as I was through the backstage door, Curtis hustled toward me. "I'm gonna take my break now."

"What happened?" I asked.

"I don't know. The binoculars had grease rings. What am I supposed to do?" Curtis fidgeted for a second. "I'll be back after my break. Next product is set up." He tossed down his headset and disappeared through the back door.

I walked to the side of the set and watched as Calabrese sold the radar detector. When the camera moved in for a tight shot, the host turned to me with a look of disgust.

I raised my hands, palms out, and mouthed the words, "I was on break."

Through headsets, I listened to the control room crew laugh as they retold the story to those who had missed it. Someone joked about Karma. Another voice exclaimed, "Whoever did that is my hero."

"Jake, you are the man!" a voice called out. I looked up to see Clancy standing at the control room window. When Clancy made eye contact, he flashed me a thumbs up. I clicked my button. "It wasn't me. I was on break."

"They got quite a roundtable going, eh?"

At the producer's desk, Dylan, Mike, and the manager were still huddled, each taking turns talking and waving their arms. After a few moments, they split up and Mike motioned for me to meet him backstage.

"Jake?" He massaged his cheeks with his hands, trying to relieve some of the tension. "Again. Tell me exactly what happened?"

"I prepped the show, laid the products out. I was on my break when it happened."

"Did you notice any grease on the binoculars?"

"No."

"Do you know for sure they were clean?"

"As far as I know they were clean."

"Is there any reason to think someone purposely did this?"

I thought of Calabrese's tongue in Tina's ear, how she had cried and how Curtis reacted up on the side of the stage. I wanted to tell Mike that Calabrese was a pervert and that the show host deserved it, but doing so would implicate Curtis, and maybe even myself.

I replied simply, "No, not that I can think of."

"Where's Curtis?"

"He went on break."

Mike stormed off, shaking his head and muttering under his breath. I was called to the stage to switch the radar detector out with a teddy bear. Managers in suits arrived backstage in small clusters. Mike emerged from the back room twenty minutes later and called me over.

"This will be short. I just want to let you know Curtis no longer works here. We will have a new production assistant starting on Monday. I'll help out to finish the day. Give me 15 minutes. You better head back to the stage."

I froze, thinking of everything Curtis had taught me over those first few weeks. He had mentored me patiently and showed me how to stay ahead of the live show. I thought back to the first day and how Mike had referred to Curtis as "the Master."

"Oh," Mike said, "don't mention this on headsets. The peanut gallery doesn't need to know."

I turned to head to the stage, but my stomach churned as though I might throw up. The image of Curtis handing the homeless man cash popped in my mind. I'd had a chance to defend Curtis, but had been silent. I turned back to Mike.

"Can't you tell me what happened?"

Mike replied, "I'm not able to talk about it."

I placed my headset on and listened as the crew reviewed the next show. The control room folks chatted, though their voices floated as if they were off in the distance.

"What's today's special in the caf?" a voice asked.

I adjusted my headset, took a deep breath and asked, "So what's the story with Curtis? Does anyone know?"

A voice replied, "Curtis who?" Other voices chuckled.

In a louder tone, someone called out, "We have to rotate to the kitchen set." Then, more forcefully, with quickening speed, "Where is the first item for the next hour?"

"Who's rotating the set?" the director rumbled, concerned about keeping the show on track. "We have a live show to do, let's keep it moving."

As the show bore down on the crew, another voice, deafening in its roar, shouted, "Jake? Jake? Are you on?"

TWO

....

WHAT WE KNEW

We saw what happened when the camera was off air and we heard what people said when their microphones were brought down, and we had grown cynical. From the window of Shoplandia's control room, we peered out over the studio, observing the scene like federal agents without a warrant.

Below we saw the rows of order entry operators on headsets sitting in their modular cubicles. When products were selling and America was buying, the operators sat forward and intently pecked at their keyboards. When business was slow, they leaned back and conversed with their neighbors, knitted sweaters and baby blankets, or read through dog-eared copies of *People* and *Us* magazines.

The view from our perch included a massive rotating stage, which each hour spun—from a living room set to a kitchen set, or maybe from the garage set to the patio—during our top of the hour break. At the foot of the stage sat command central, the line producer's desk. When a host and producer believed they were in a private conversation, we listened in. The producers might leave their headset buttons on, or we'd put the host's mic in cue and eavesdrop. There is no privacy in a broadcast studio.

We knew the personal habits of the show hosts. We knew the timing of Karen's menstrual cycle and when Henry was hungover. Among the producers and back-stage staff, we knew who were loyal friends and who talked behind their co-workers' backs. We had opinions on who was competent, who was a team player, who was a slacker and who couldn't be trusted. We knew who received free product samples from vendors and who palmed items from the warehouse.

When one of the broadcast cameras was in our pre-view monitor, we watched Tanya wipe lipstick off her teeth with a paper towel. We watched as Frankie walked to the side of the set, threw up his hand in the scissor position to signify "cut my mic," and then squatted and passed gas. When show host Calabrese groped the young model on the set, we were voyeurs through the lens.

We could have stepped in to save Curtis but we didn't. Through the window and the preview monitors we had watched Calabrese's fingers sliding over models, order entry operators, female producers and production assistants. On the day Curtis greased Item V4863—Starling 18 X 21 Binoculars—and Calabrese lowered the product and revealed his raccoon eyes on live national television, the incident created a minor sensation. Several directors dubbed the video to their own personal reels, preserving the moment for posterity. We watched it over and over and it never failed to entertain us.

At the bar a few nights later, the binocular incident became a topic of conversation. Curtis had a good run but he had been caught. We understood. Life is not fair. Some of us thought if we couldn't save Curtis, maybe we should avenge him. Others believed Karma would even the field eventually. The space between us swelled with an awareness that we could have done something, but we didn't. We said amongst ourselves, "Someone should do something about this," and then we sipped our beers quietly as if in mourning.

After a few moments of silence, Clancy suddenly remembered a bit of news. "I heard a rumor we're going to launch a whole new campaign next week. There's going to be new promotional spots and a station I.D."

Our ears perked up. This was exciting news.

"It's supposedly an attempt to change our image," Clancy explained.

THREE

···

DAMN YANKEES

I had never seen anything like it before, it felt as though the Ringling Bros. had invaded the atrium. My boss Miles tipped me off to the event, and even though I wasn't due to be in at work until 2 p.m., I trekked in early with my coffee to see if this would live up to the hype.

Miles had left a voicemail for us producers about this new promotional campaign that Marketing VP Johnny Wake was kicking off on Friday at noon. We all loved Johnny Wake. I remember chatting with Tim Bukowski one time about Johnny's antics.

Buke said to me, "Dottie, that Johnny Wake is crazy."

I replied, "Yeah, but you know what? He is a good kind of crazy."

Buke just nodded and laughed at the truth of it. Sometimes, I think we're all a bit insane here at Shoplandia. After all, I'm the type of mom who misses her son's little league games because I'm running around a TV studio placating celebrities, coordinating makeup demonstrations and settling down show hosts during prime time. Although I love it, I'm forced to admit I have a tinge of mother's guilt. Sorry, I digress.

Anyway, in this voicemail, Miles explained the whole God Bless America hoopla, and how Johnny Wake wanted to "kick it up a notch" with our on-air presentations. Miles asked us a rhetorical question, "How do we represent America during the live show?"

Well, to me it felt like we were trying to be Eagle Scout wannabes, sucking up to big government, but whatever. As I deleted the voicemail, it struck me that we were launching an all-American product on Friday night. Coney Island hot dogs. That's pretty darn American, am I right? And then I thought about my underlying mother's guilt, how I'd missed so many of my son Zach's little league games this season, and that's when I was struck with a lightning bolt. So I left Miles a voicemail with one of my hair-brained ideas, and of course he ate it up.

This is how I found myself standing in the atrium on Friday morning, waiting for the hoopla to begin. Office workers emerged from their cloistered cubicles and stood in small clusters. The atrium at our world headquarters is shaped like a giant egg, with a skywalk splicing across the second level. Two barbershop chairs were set up by the wall, and an American flag was draped over the skywalk. As folks streamed in from the four corners of the building, the atrium filled and anticipation grew. A sets and props guy checked a rope pull attached to a black billowing curtain. The sun streamed in from the skylights as if God himself was watching over our efforts.

Precisely at 11:55 a.m., we heard a rumble from the cafeteria hallway that grew persistently intense, until four denim and leather-clad goateed bikers riding Harley Davidson motorcycles emerged slowly. An American flag wavered on the back of each bike. The audience erupted in cheers and the bikers revved their engines in response.

Just as they cut their engines, Johnny Wake appeared at a microphone, which stood at the base of the stairs. The crowd swiveled from the bikers to our illustrious Marketing VP and roared with delight. Johnny wore a pure white leather Evel Knievel-style jumpsuit, complete with red and blue stars down his sleeves and legs. Aviator sunglasses sat perched on his nose, his grin so broad that we were all instantly captivated. Johnny raised his arms in the air to calm the thunderous hooting crowd, and then he slowly took his glasses off and leaned toward the mic.

"Today, we are launching a new campaign. We are Shoplandia. We are the only shopping network wholly owned by Americans, so when the President of our United States spoke about the need to reignite the economy, we listened closely. When the President explained that it is America's duty to shop, we realized Shoplandia needed to show our stripes. Our stars and stripes that is." Johnny held out his arms again and admired his own suit. The crowd laughed and applauded. "Now I know what some of you are saying, we don't want to get all political about this, and I hear you. I hear you. But no matter what party we are in–Republican,

Democrat, Green Party, or..." Johnny smiled down at the bikers, "...even anarchists–we all know we need to do our part to bring this great country out of this rut. Are you ready to do it?"

The crowd cheered loudly. During my occasional trips to cubicle land, I often wondered if the office staff had their water laced with Ambien, but on this day, they exploded with patriotic fervor. Everyone smiled, laughed, even giggled. Someone in the crowd started chanting, "USA! USA! USA!"

Watching this, the whole absurdity of it, I couldn't help but laugh, and that appeared to be the consensus. Johnny raised his arms again to settle the crowd. Just when I thought it couldn't get any more captivating, Johnny asked everyone to hush, and as the atrium quieted, he continued.

"Okay now, so let's kick this party off with one very special guest. A true American hero. A man who is the living embodiment of our country's resiliency and a man with a big heart. Ladies and gentlemen, let's hear it for Mr. T!"

And in he strolled, *the* Mr. T, looking smaller than expected, but dripping in more gold than we had featured in the 4-hour *Gold Rush Special*. The legend's mohawk glistened as he passed through the sun's rays and hopped on-stage. He hugged Johnny as if they were long lost brothers. Mr. T raised Johnny's hand in the air, and together they struck a championship pose. Two photographers stepped in and snapped a stream of photos, and then Mr. T stepped to the mic.

"Hello great Americans! I don't have a speech prepared, except you should all be watching the one o'clock show, because I have some great hair clippers for sale. Pity the fool who passes up this great bargain!" He ran his fingers along his mohawk. People in the audience laughed. "I just want you all to get behind this campaign. America needs you. I just want to say that all of you," and he raised his hands and pointed both index fingers all around the atrium as the place grew silent, "all of you are the real A-team!"

The whole space swelled with laughter and applause. Chants of "USA! USA! USA!" echoed throughout the atrium. After a few moments, the noise abated and Mr. T humbly concluded, "God Bless America," and stepped back, making a motion for the man in red, white and blue to take the mic again.

Johnny smiled as he looked over the crowd. "If I could ask you to turn your attention to the monitor above." Heads tilted up. "Ladies and gentlemen, here is the new Shoplandia logo." The screen went white, and a few squiggly blue and red lines inched across and formed a United States flag. After a moment, two strings sprouted out to form handles, transforming the flag into a pocketbook. Underneath, a phrase faded on screen: United We Shop.

Immediately, Johnny Wake called out, "Drop the tarp!"

Heads swiveled again as the black drape fell. The new logo hung from the rafters like a basketball team championship banner.

"We are Shoplandia, and starting today, on the air and behind the scenes, we are showing our pride. Wait until you see some of the things we have planned, like during tonight's 6 p.m. show. Is Dottie Robinson here?"

A warm rush ran through my chest and I meekly raised my hand. Fingers pointed my way. Voices shouted, "Here she is."

Johnny finally spotted me, grinned and pointed, acknowledging he was putting me on the spot. "Dottie is one of our coordinating producers and she has some plans for tonight's 6 p.m. show. If you are near a TV, you want to check it out, it is sure to be an All-American moment!"

Everyone stared at me and started applauding. It was kind of embarrassing, but thank God Johnny diverted them quickly. "Warren, step up here. Show us your guns."

A manager stepped up to the mic and rolled up the sleeve of his polo shirt. "If you look closely at Warren's arm here, you might see that he has been inked. He is wearing our new logo proudly." Johnny pointed over toward the two barbershop chairs. "We have tattooing stations over there so you can get inked yourself. So step up and secure your own United We Shop tattoos!"

The crowd suddenly grew quiet. For a brief second, Johnny appeared dismayed, but then his lips parted.

"Don't worry, everyone," he announced. "These are Cracker Jack style tattoos. We're not asking you to get permanently branded. Though if you would like a permanent tattoo, if you are that committed, come see me.

And, that's not all! We have free t-shirts for you, and you, and you!" Models emerged from the four hallways and strutted through the crowd, taking the stage next to the daredevil VP. It was all too much.

After watching this spectacle, I have to admit I was a bit stunned. I'd never seen so many employees of the company laugh so much, enjoying the moment. I felt quite privileged to be working at this place, at this specific time. When I checked voicemail, Johnny had even left me a quick message. "Miles told me your plan. There's nothing that represents America like little leaguers eating hot dogs. Excellent idea, Dottie. Good luck!"

Having a few extra hours before my shift turned out to be a blessing, since my production plans for the Coney Island hot dogs were not quite finalized, and I had six other shows to prepare for. Back in the kitchen, our chef assured me he had more than enough frankfurters, buns and mustard, and that the grill on the patio had been cleaned, tested, and confirmed to be in operational order.

The food buyer, a surly, overbearing, dimwitted nobbin I'll only refer to as G, was a bit of a nag during food shows. Hired only three months ago, G's previous job as the buyer for a chain of auto goods retailers throughout Arkansas had not trained him well for the lightning speed of our digital business. G continually marveled at our sales tools, scratching his head at the feedback loop we had established with customers. This was a man who had to wait for quarterly reports to learn that five mufflers sold in Birdsong and seven brake pads sold in Pine Grove. Now he watched sales of the Sirloin and Crab Cake combo click upwards at clips of 200 boxes a minute. Our technology, our pace and our direct connection with the customer overwhelmed G like an Amish man dropped in Times Square on New Year's Eve.

At precisely 5:30 p.m., our esteemed guests arrived. The ten-year-old boys poured out of mini-vans and giant SUVs, looking resplendent in their red and white baseball uniforms with the logo of their sponsor, American Trust Co. emblazoned in blue on their chests. I rounded up the young ballplayers and lined them along the wall. My son Zach was tickled at the commotion. As the kid who only played the mandated minimum three innings each game—stuck in right field and only getting one at bat—this night gave him street cred among his peers.

Standing next to my Zach was Sammy, a kid with an all-American smile who was nearly as wide as he was tall, providing the requisite girth to stop any pitch, a backstop more than a catcher, though this kid possessed an eagle's eye and such muscle that he continually stroked the ball like a bull. Alongside Sammy, Mitchell looked like he needed a sandwich, a lanky kid with bright red hair and freckles, who hurled pitches three quarter arm, and chewed wads of bubble gum, blowing out pink bubbles until they burst across his face. The boys watched the production scene intently for about ten seconds before their behavior degenerated into fart noises and plucking the ear of the player next to them. I left them in the capable hands of our floor manager and ran inside to check in at the producer's desk and escort the official spokesman for Coney Island hot dogs out to the set.

Stan "The Man" Russell had played in the major leagues for fourteen years, mostly with the New York Yankees during their dry spell in the later sixties, before being bumped around the league for the final five lackluster years of his career. He had played ball in the era before free agency, before the big money, so he and his peers were left to squeeze a living out of their semi-celebrity status—signing autographs at card shows and pitching local car dealerships and law firms during late night commercials which aired during re-runs of B movies.

I happened to be at the producer's desk when Stan hobbled in on arthritic knees with the jumpy food buyer G. Stan had a white mop of hair and a red bulbous nose from which protruded a few flecks of white hair that were overdue for a snip with a razor. The old-timer autographed a baseball and handed it back to Dylan, who thanked him. Stan studied my face as he shook my hand with a strong grip. "Hello there, pretty lady." He held my hand just long enough to give me a lingering case of the heebie jeebies. I smelled bourbon on his breath when he asked, "Do you serve beer in the green room?"

"No Stan, we don't."

Stan twisted around, "So who decides how much airtime I get?"

Dylan replied, "That would be me."

"Do you have anything else you want me to sign?"

It was my job to march Stan into place on the outdoor set. The chef stood over the grill, tending to his craft, the smell of hot dogs wafted through the air.

As the presentation began, our host Henry held up the package of forty hot dogs. "These will last you the entire summer," he said. "Just think, you will always have some in the freezer when you get home from the pool. Just pop 'em on the grill and dinner is ready ten minutes later. You can also get this 40-pack on auto-renewal, meaning 40 hot dogs are shipped to your house every month. Mmmmmm....."

A voice from the control room asked, "Who the hell eats forty hot dogs a month?"

Oblivious to the comments, Henry continued. "Now we are so fortunate to have the American Trust Co. baseball team here to show you just how tasty these hot dogs are." He turned to the team, the kids all lined up in their adorable uniforms. The boys looked as happy as if they were on the first base line at Shea Stadium, except Mitchell flipped Sammy's hat off and Sammy responded by thwacking Mitchell in the crotch. Zach giggled and covered his mouth. Mitchell buckled over laughing, all on live television.

"The kids are up to their antics already, I think these boys are hungry. Boys, are you hungry?"

A shout of cheers emanated from behind and one kid threw his cap in the air, followed by two more.

"Okay," Henry laughed. "As we serve up some hot dogs, let me introduce you to this truly legendary baseball player who once wore the Yankee pinstripes. He's known as the Man with the Plan, Stan Russell. Stan, as a ball player who spent his 14-year career in stadiums across this great land of ours, is there anything that complements baseball like a good Coney Island hot dog?"

"No, there isn't Henry." Stan the Man held up a hot dog and looked into the wrong camera. I pointed the drunkard to the correct camera; you know, the one with the big frickin' red light on it. Stan shuffled his feet as though he was in the batter's box. "I've eaten hot dogs in every stadium from Boston to San Diego, and I have to tell you that Coney Island hot dogs are the best of the bunch."

Dylan cracked into headsets, "Stan looks as though he has downed a few dogs since retiring, eh?"

"Yeah, and a few bottles of Bud too."

After a few moments of listening to Stan drone on, Dylan sighed, "Let's tag him often when he is yammering. Nobody remembers this old-timer. We need to show the kids anyway. Are you ready with the kids?"

Each boy now nervously held a hot dog with both hands, waiting for their cue. I clicked my box on. "Kids are armed and ready."

As Henry and Stan discussed the misconception that hot dogs are fattening, the cameraman slowly worked his way down the row of ball players, briefly stopping to watch each freckle-faced kid take a bite. Each one closed their eyes and chewed away as if they were in some type of pork-induced ecstasy. The melodrama was a bit much, but they were so darn cute I let it go. Stepping carefully behind the cameraman, I held my fingers up to my cheeks, miming a reminder for each kid to smile, and to just take one bite.

Through headsets, Dylan exclaimed customers were responding. "They're eating this up," he quipped. The sales screen jumped. These adorable faces were driving the presentation, causing a tremendous spike in sales. Apparently, America loves watching little leaguers chowing down.

"That was great. Dottie, let us know when you are ready for round two," Dylan called out. "I think the less we see of Stan the better."

When I stepped in to reload, half the kids had already eaten their whole hot dog and were now restless. I motioned to the chef who lovingly prodded another round onto fresh rolls and drizzled mustard on each one. I tapped production assistant Jake on the shoulder.

"What's up?"

"I want to go check sales. Give the kids another round, but don't let them eat unless they are on camera."

Jake nodded. "No problem." The chef handed him a plate piled high with another round of hot dogs.

Inside, G had just approached Dylan and bent over the desk. I knew this must be riling Dylan, so I stopped over to run interference.

"How's it looking?"

G stared intently at the sales monitor as the camera showed the kids gorging on another round of hot dogs. The sales had spiked and hundreds of customers were waiting to chat with a live operator.

"They are loving the kids, aren't they?" G stated with the joy of a child who has just found cash in his birthday card.

"They seem to be." The truth is, there were more orders coming in than the operators could handle. Customers were starting to experience a wait, and Dylan had to give folks time to place their orders. "We'll ride the queue here, I don't want folks waiting too long."

"Can we just keep the camera on the kids the whole show?" G asked.

"Pigs get fat, but hogs get slaughtered," Dylan replied.

"Dude, we've slaughtered everything on the farm for this inventory. Stuff it down their throats. Let's pack the till, baby!"

Dylan looked up at the buyer with dismay. G was sweating and his hand kept tapping the desktop, like an addict just about to score. Dylan's stare finally sunk in and G realized he had outworn his welcome. He patted Dylan on the back and hightailed it back to the green room.

When Dylan was on his game, nobody surfed the queue like he did. He was like a baseball pitcher in the middle of a shutout or a cello player performing a solo at Radio City Music Hall. He showed the kids and the calls spiked, he'd return to Stan and give the operators time to catch up, before returning to the kids. At one point, Dylan stood, twisted around and peered out over the operators. For a second, I thought he might take a bow. All heads were down though, intently taking orders. As he worked through the inventory, Dylan threw up a quantity counter, 1807 orders taken. He wanted to go for the sell out and I could see he was going to be close.

"I'm heading back out there," I told him.

Halfway down the hall toward the outdoor set, I heard Dylan declare, "I want another pass at the kids."

"Dylan. I don't know about this."

"I'm gonna try. Come on Dottie, one more pass. We're going to sell enough hot dogs tonight to feed a third-world country."

Out on the set, the kids ate their hot dogs more slowly. A few faces seemed pained. As the camera passed down the row, Zach cringed and held his stomach. The camera passed to Sammy, who had proven to be a beast. "If anyone can pack it in, this kid can," a voice from the control room exclaimed.

Henry smiled, turned and asked Sammy, "How many hot dogs is that for you, son?"

Sammy continued stuffing the final few inches of a hot dog into his pie hole. He wasn't stopping to audibly answer this dumb man's question. Instead, he raised his left hand and lifted one finger, then two, three, four. He slowly flexed out his thumb. At the same time, Sammy's right hand finished inserting a nub of a casing into his mouth, his cheeks puffed out like a foraging squirrel. The boy's jaws hinged with the torque of a trash truck crusher and he stuck his index finger in the air to signal this was indeed his sixth foot long hot dog.

Henry's eyes widened. "Six hot dogs, do you see how good these are?"

At that moment, Sammy's mouth locked shut and his

face colored into a tint of eggshell green, and then Sammy spewed on live television. It was a tremendous sight. A fountain of muddy brick-colored beef chunks swirled with a yellow tempura and soggy chunks of white dough. The ensuing splatter on the flagstone echoed like the stream of an opened fire hydrant on a hot summer day. Years later, the clip of Sammy's projectile vomiting would be studied by Hollywood special effects experts to improve their craft in the making of the *Exorcist 7*.

"Holy crap!"

"Get off him!"

"Oh the poor kid!"

Dylan just declared, "Oh, shit."

The kids scattered, pinching their noses shut and laughing. A putrid smell enveloped us on the patio. As I cleaned off Sammy's face with a wet paper towel, Dylan exclaimed, "Those t-calls dropped faster than a mobster in cement shoes."

"Is that poor kid okay?"

"I think we just killed the goose."

The presentation wrapped quickly after that fiasco. Our floor manager escorted Henry inside, leaving me and the crew to clean up the mess. Jake squirted the slate flagstones clean with the hose. The sun set behind our colossal building. The boys closed in as I lifted the cardboard lid off of a box of brand new baseballs. Once each fresh, young face had a ball in hand, we approached Stan. "The boys here would like to get autographs."

Stan stared blankly, first at me, and then at the kids circling around him. Sammy stood in their midst with a giant wet spot across the front of his chest from being blotted with paper towels. Despite his public purging, the boy appeared to be resilient, laughing with his friends as they thumped him on the back, as though his act was a badge of courage or an American rite of passage.

"I'd like to get to a TV," Stan replied. "Do you know who's winning the Yankees game? I have some money riding on that game, and I'm ready for a beer."

Much to his dismay, the ball players closed ranks on the old-timer. Some boys smiled in anticipation, their eyes sparkling with wonder, while others looked skeptical, unsure whether they believed this old man had really ever worn the pinstripes.

There wasn't much to be said at that moment, so I bit my tongue, uncapped the Sharpie and held it out until he had no choice but to take it.

FOUR

....

BLOOPERS

When we witnessed key moments of hilarity, some-times known as bloopers, we recorded them onto our own videotapes for posterity's sake. Of course, the spewing little leaguer became an instant classic. For three days after that incident, we continually had office staff hesitantly knocking on the door of our control room, shyly asking to see the clip.

Clancy didn't turn anyone away. If he was punching the live show on the big board, he'd ask one of us to roll the tape, but usually he greeted the visitors and happily showed the video. No matter what we were doing—monitoring levels in the audio booth or double-checking prices on the product graphics—we stopped and watched the clip again, anticipating the reactions of the wide-eyed virgin viewers.

"Oh my God," a department assistant mumbled through her hand-covered mouth.

"That poor kid," a customer service rep uttered and cringed.

"Whoa, awesome!" The sports memorabilia buyer broke into howls of laughter.

We enjoyed seeing their reactions. Their brief visits broke up our monotonous routine. The best part though was when Clancy announced, "Now watch this," and played the clip slowly in reverse. The beefy chunks jumped upwards off the slate patio and arced back into the kid's mouth. Clancy would shuttle the tape forward and backward repeatedly, and we were entertained.

There's always one person who doesn't think the bloopers are funny. We played the clip one afternoon for Warren, a broadcasting manager. Clancy started the slow-motion shuffle and Warren doubled over with laughter. Dottie slipped in the door behind them and abruptly halted. Unaware of her presence, Clancy and Warren snorted with laughter. "Play it again," Warren urged. Dottie bit her lower lip and stared at the scene for a few moments. The loud slam of the control room door startled the two men, and they twisted just in time to watch Dottie stomp down the hall. We're still not sure what she was looking for.

··

FIVE

PEPPER MAN

"Come on Dad. I don't want to miss the bus again."

Warren Matthews followed his son Ryan across the patch of grass, surprised that the kid could run under the weight of his backpack loaded with books. Down the street a few children stood in a circle, their mothers huddled nearby. A rumbling pulsated through the air and everyone tilted their heads to peer at the morning sky. Ryan pointed as a helicopter flew over the neighborhood and disappeared to the west.

"Dad, is that your boss's helicopter?"

"No. I don't think it is." Warren playfully tugged his son's backpack.

"When will we get a helicopter?"

"I don't think we'll get a helicopter any time soon."

"Why not dad? Huh, why not?"

"We need a new car more than we need a helicopter."

Ryan stopped and mulled this over. Warren awkwardly waved to the mothers and they nodded briefly before returning to their conversation. In this enlightened era of gender equality, with diaper changing stations now in mens' restrooms, he still felt like an outsider at the bus stop.

"Hey, here's your bus."

The red flashers blinked as the yellow bus slowed to a stop.

"Have a good day!" Warren called.

"Okay, Dad." Ryan ran ahead, lunch box shaking at his side, and climbed into the bus.

Warren turned toward his house without giving the women a glance. He listened to the chirping birds and inhaled the crisp morning air as he passed his rusting Honda Civic in the driveway.

Inside the kitchen, Marcia loaded cereal bowls and the baby's bottles into the dishwasher.

"Yay, we made the bus today."

Without turning her head from the sink, Marcia replied sarcastically, "Wow, and the baby hasn't woken up. This is the best day ever." Warren frowned at the sharpness in her voice.

He grabbed the orange juice out of the refrigerator and drank out of the carton. Marcia didn't look at him, but busied herself cleaning dishes at the kitchen sink. She has had a rough go of it lately, he thought, with the last minute C-section nearly two months ago, and the unlikely infection that prolonged her recovery. While the physical scars were slowly mending, the more delicate issue was Marcia's deflated spirit and shortened temper. They both agreed that Marcia wouldn't return to her marketing position after the birth of their daughter Chloe, and Marcia seemed content at first. Now her long, tired days with the infant, not showering or getting out of her pajamas, along with what Warren determined must be some chemical imbalance, left her worn out with a rising sense of bitterness.

She had recently cut her hair short because the infant kept pulling at it. At first, Warren wasn't sure about the new style, but he grew accustomed to it a little more each day. Last night, he had tried to compliment her choice, and with a lost stare, she replied that she no longer knew who she was.

Marcia dried her hands on a dish towel, and then suddenly turned and stated, "I need to get away from here for a weekend, or at least a night."

"Where do you want to go?"

"I don't know. Away."

He nodded, adding up the costs of a getaway weekend. Throughout her pregnancy, they had continually calculated how they would live on one income. They took a yellow legal pad and wrote out a list titled, *Things Our Grandparents Happily Lived Without*, and underneath they scribbled luxuries such as *cell phone, Wifi, washer, dryer and central air*. When they finished their list, they laughed together, admitting they were spoiled. Despite their best efforts, unbudgeted bills arose in the first few weeks: a broken fan belt, a deposit for Ryan's summer camp and a water heater repair. They were falling short, just by small amounts, and Warren kept running numbers through his head, trying to discover a way to make up the difference. He took a deep breath and decided to reply simply.

"Sounds good to me. Let me know when and it's a date."

Without a word, Marcia started rummaging through the cabinets, pulling out her cereal box and preparing her breakfast. Warren was puzzled. He picked up his worn satchel, slung it over his shoulder and grabbed the car keys off the counter. As he opened the door, he said over his shoulder, "I'm off to work. I get to meet the great Robert Covert today. Have a good one, Hon."

"You too." She stood with her back to him, looking into the fridge.

Only as he backed up the car, replaying the conversation through his mind, did a strange thought occur to Warren. Maybe she wanted to go away without him? This possibility set him on edge for the entire drive through town.

Automobiles streamed into the Shoplandia employee lot for the start of the workday. As Warren climbed out of his rust bucket, Tony pulled his black Ford Focus into the next space and they joined the masses walking into the mammoth world headquarters.

"Are you going to the Covert presentation?" Warren asked.

"No. I just don't go for all that rah rah crap. Besides I forgot my fire walking shoes," Tony replied.

"Aw, come on. It's good in moderation. It's all mental."

"It's all brainwashing and bullshit. Sorry dude. I won't drink the Kool-Aid."

Carved out in a grassy slope by the entrance were 37 reserved spaces occupied with Jaguars, Beemers, and Benzes. The Executive Lot, reserved for the vice presidents. As the two walked along, the chirps of executives setting their car alarms interrupted the soothing songs of birds. A new Audi pulled into a reserved spot a distance ahead of them. Warren thought he recognized the man who hopped out, slid on a sport jacket and walked toward the entrance.

"Is that Ray?"

"Sure is. He got promoted. VP of Distribution. I think the announcement officially comes out today."

"No. Are you kidding me?" Warren eyed the car as they walked by. "What do you have to do to get promoted around here?"

"Not work in Broadcasting."

Warren twisted his head in surprise, but then laughed knowingly. "You spoke the truth, and the truth is harsh."

Sometimes Tony's insights cut right to the bone. A succession of Broadcasting VPs had been brought in from the outside, each one lasting an average of three or four months before they resigned, were terminated or some combination of both, with their secrets hidden securely, deep in the file room of Human Resources.

Over the past year, Tony, Warren and their five peers had endured a series of meetings getting direction from one VP after another. In May, their leader for a brief stint was a sixtyish, knee-slapping, self-absorbed Texas woman who growled like Ann Richards. Her first act was to hang a mounted snow goose on her wall, set with its white wings spread in full final glory, as if about to land on her desk. She relished in telling each wide-eyed gawker in her southern drawl that she had downed the beast on a blustery autumn morning with her 12-gauge Remington.

She set the team working on a new visual style that would empower those overlooked shoppers in the red states, "in the heart of America," to pick up their phone and order "produck," as she called it. "I want a whole new promotional campaign. I want to see women in denim nurturing their men, serving ribs and grits. I want cowboys hopping out of Ford F-150 pick-up trucks with a Toby Keith soundtrack. Our customer is Middle America!"

Over the next month, Warren, Tony and their colleagues worked on a full visual package—new graphics, station IDs, sketches on how to revamp the sets to be "aspirational but attainable." And then the goose took flight.

They took their visuals into the next VP, a twenty-something, angst-ridden, coffee-drinking Jack Kerouac hipster who took one glance and broke into a rant, asking repeatedly, "Where's the aesthetic? No, seriously, where's the fucking aesthetic?" When they played a sample of the new music the previous VP had commissioned, he tilted his head and grimaced as if his appendix had burst and declared, "Shit, people, let's get this music out of the elevator and into the fucking streets." A week later, he disappeared after flipping someone the finger out in front of the building, unaware he was in the background of a live shot for the 6 p.m. *Garden Extravaganza.*

The most notoriously shortest-lasting VP came along four months later when a Kenyan immigrant and long distance runner entered the lobby to interview for a part-time, third-shift custodian position and was mistaken for the new Broadcasting VP. He lasted two weeks in his spacious first floor office, and the rumor leaked that he was given a generous severance to tender his resignation.

This merry-go-round of Broadcasting VPs created a restlessness in those department managers who were continually overlooked for the position time and again. When HR placed an ad in *Broadcasting & Cable* for the Vice President position, using the audacious phrase, *seeking professional executive with ten years of real television broadcasting experience*, the managers and directors mutinied. The next morning the door to the vacant VP office had been taken off its hinges and replaced with a salvaged, but still operable, hotel revolving door in some type of performance art protest. CEO Creosote finally met with them to review their grievances. Throughout the ordeal, the seven managers ran their intertwined operations fairly smoothly, with minimal in-fighting, and they adopted a phrase, ending conversations amongst themselves with either a snarkiness or sigh, and uttering, "the show must go on."

Now, as Warren and Tony climbed the steps to the front entrance, Tony finally broke their reflective silence.

"That reminds me. Something funny happened yesterday. I was waiting for this meeting to start with Merchandising. It was just me and that girl Sheila from PR. She was telling me about her new dog when Bob Payne, the Merchandising VP, walked in and started listening. Well, Sheila said her dog had crapped on her living room rug over the weekend, and Payne replied with a straight face, 'Did you have the dog put down?' Well, Sheila shrieked with horror. 'No! I did not have the dog put down.' And Payne replied, 'You're not management material then.' He said it so matter of factly too! Sheila stared at him. I thought she was going to cry. After a few moments, Payne let out this little smile."

"That's awful," Warren replied, though he grinned. "Maybe I'll put a dog down today. Just so it looks good on my resume."

Just before they both reached out to open the massive glass doors, Warren caught their images reflected in the glass. Behind them, Marketing VP Johnny Wake jogged up, taking two steps at a time. Johnny called out, "Excuse me guys, I'm running late to meet Mr. Covert!" They both halted and held the doors open so the marketing guru could sprint past them.

"Thanks gentlemen!"

The live audience theatre slowly came to life as weary employees straggled in and found open seats. They fidgeted, studied their day-timers, nodded hello to co-workers, as a buzz gradually built in anticipation of the featured speaker.

The stage was transformed into a surreal gothic ca-
thedral. Massive panes of beautifully backlit stained glass
appeared to float in the air. Majestic faux limestone columns filled out the background.

"What's this for?" Warren asked as he took a seat.

Dottie responded, "The New York Boys Choir per-
forms this afternoon. We're selling their CD."

Warren nodded and smiled. He twisted and looked
up into the tiered seating. Several show hosts had come
for this event even though it was their day off. They
were dressed casually in jeans and untucked dress shirts,
sans makeup, gossiping amongst themselves. A few producers had stayed after their overnight shift. They
stretched their tired limbs and perched their coffee cups
carefully on the armrests. A few of Warren's peers bee-
lined in from their morning meeting, glad to postpone
real work for another hour.

The department staff was eager to hear world-
renowned motivational speaker Robert Covert, who was
making his Shoplandia debut to sell a six CD set, enti-
tled *Rise Above! Move Beyond!* In order to inspire excitement in the hosts, producers and managers, Covert was
giving a free private 45-minute live presentation (valued
at $499 per person) to the staff.

Senior Show Host Frankie Mack walked into the
room and smiled when he saw Warren in the front row.
Frankie turned and looked at the set, then leaned toward
Warren. "It's nice they've created a setting worthy of Mr.
Covert."

Warren smiled. He knew Frankie was a big fan of

Covert's philosophy and often listened to Covert's enigmatic CD, *Empower the Winner Within*, while he drove in for his on-air shifts. Frankie had created a pre-show ritual that he stuck to with a rigid discipline: reviewing his products, manicuring his fingernails and sitting cross-legged in a closed host dressing room while chanting the mantra, "Today I will sell out."

After the hosts and producers were seated, Johnny Wake stood at the foot of the stage, looked at the crowd with a smile of anticipation and motioned for the audience to settle down.

"I hope everyone is as excited about this special opportunity as I am. This man has counseled CEOs and Presidents, athletes and artists. His empowerment programs set the standard across the globe, and we're thrilled he is here at Shoplandia! A man that needs no introduction, so I'll simply say, ladies and gentlemen, the legendary Robert Covert."

After all the wordy foreplay, the legend appeared quietly from behind a curtain. He waved and grinned, baring huge white teeth. Warren felt the introduction was anticlimactic, until Frankie applauded and others joined in. Covert was tall with broad shoulders, like a linebacker, and he dressed smartly but casually. He stood before the room with an air of mischievous confidence.

"Good morning Shoplandia! How are you all feeling this morning?" He clapped his hands to get the blood flowing in the room. "Stand up! Everyone! Stand up!"

Covert dove right in. He told how, as an acne-faced bag boy at his local supermarket, he decided to focus on success. He weaved personal stories with results of Harvard studies, adding anecdotes from leaders such as Churchill and Gandhi to fire up the audience. Set against the stained glass, Covert roamed the stage like a preacher possessed. Warren was spellbound. After ten minutes, Covert had the audience eating out of the palm of his hand. Literally.

"Now in my weekend seminars, you may have seen me pull audience members up on stage and they actually walk on fire." A few people in the audience smiled and nodded. "Well, the fire marshal wouldn't allow us to try that here in the studio so were going to try something a little different today."

He held up a small thin red pepper and gazed at it with admiration.

"This is a Bhut Jolokia chile pepper, grown in the Assam state of India." He twirled the pepper in his fingers, as if it was a diamond. "The Guinness Book of World Records has named the Bhut Jolokia the hottest chile pepper in the world at over one million scoville units. That's twice as hot as a Habanero pepper. The words Bhut Jolokia literally translate into ghost chile, because it's been said you give up the ghost when you eat it."

Holding the pepper by the stem, he dipped it in a glass of water. He placed the pepper in his mouth and pulled out a clean stem. He munched away. A wave of gasps spread throughout the room. Producer Dylan sat on the edge of his seat. Show host Tanya cringed. Clancy took a deep breath and laughed. Host Karen closed her eyes and shuddered. Producer Buke nudged his buddy. "Dude, that's sick!"

Covert took his time chewing away. A bead of sweat formed on his brow. He walked over to the side table and grabbed his water bottle and took a swig.

"It's a little warm, but it's all about mind over matter. Just like walking over fire. Does anyone want to try it?"

Warren shot his hand in the air.

Covert pointed at him. "What's your name?"

"Warren."

"Do you like peppers?"

"I like spicy food."

"Come on up here."

Warren stood and walked out to stand by Covert.

"Have we met before?"

"No."

"Okay, good." Covert smiled. "Warren, I want you to close your eyes for a minute and listen to my voice."

Warren shut his eyes and stood there with Covert's hand on his shoulder.

"Warren, I want you to envision yourself in the frozen tundra. You are standing in a whiteout of driving snow and bitter cold. Your feet are frozen, your body is shivering in the sub-arctic temperatures. Just picture this. Let the bitter chill flow through your body."

Covert stopped and watched Warren as if waiting for a sign. The auditorium fell quiet. With his eyes closed, Warren heard a howling wind and envisioned a blustery snowstorm he'd once found himself in when stepping off a gondola in Vermont. He visibly shivered and people in the audience murmured.

Covert produced a chile from his pocket. He dipped it into the water and held it in the air for the audience to see.

"You can open your eyes." Covert handed the chile to Warren. Warren's peers stared at him. A host held her hand up to her mouth. Jake clenched his fists and gritted his teeth. Dottie covered her eyes. In the front row, Frankie's smile pierced Warren like a dare. He could see everyone watching, wincing in preparation for his bite.

He took a deep breath and bit into the pepper. The juice squirted in his mouth and he felt a lukewarm sensation. He heard gasps in the audience. After a few seconds, the temperature rose but he kept chewing. A bead of sweat trickled down his right temple. He laughed. Frankie Mack started to applaud and others joined in.

Warren waved at his fans. He felt dizzy. He sat back down in the front row. Someone reached out from behind and slapped him on the shoulder. "Way to go Warren!" Frankie patted him on the knee.

"Mind over matter," Covert said. "Nice job Warren."

The heat sank from Warren's brow to the pit of his stomach. Covert stepped back and addressed the audience. Someone handed Warren a bottle of water.

"Don't avoid the pain, but don't let it swallow you whole, don't let it consume you. You need to look at the pain, keep it in front of you, you need to fan the fires of discontent."

Warren ran his tongue between his teeth. He tried to scrape the chile heat off his tongue. He twisted the cap off the water and downed the whole bottle.

"Is your pain that you want more money? Is your pain that you want the girl of your dreams? Is your pain that you have not yet achieved the American Dream? How painful is it that you don't have what you want in life? That pain needs to permeate every pore of your skin, seep into every joint."

Warren felt a burning in his stomach, and he thought he might throw up. He took a deep breath and focused his attention on Covert's words.

"The difference between successful people and everyone else is, are you ready for this? They wanted it more. Successful people worked to find ways of acquiring wealth because they would not accept mediocrity. Most people say they want to be rich, but after they spend eight hours flipping burgers or ringing up groceries at Walmart, they go home and turn on *Dancing with the Stars* or, preferably, Shoplandia. They self-medicate with television, alcohol, marijuana or shopping."

Warren dropped his bottle cap. He didn't care though. The driving snowstorm had subsided and he sensed a moment of clarity in Covert's words as if he was standing in the sunlight on the peak of a glorious mountain.

"It's all about focus. If you want something bad enough, you need to think, night and day, about how much pain you are in that you don't have it. You need to leverage that pain in order to seize the day."

In the mens' bathroom, Warren rinsed his mouth out with water. He brushed his tongue, his teeth and the inside fleshy part of his mouth with his finger. He dabbed at his forehead with wet paper towel. Though the searing pain in his mouth had subsided, he still felt the warmth of the ghost chile.

He made his way to his cubicle and sat straight in his chair. He had always thought of his career as being like a game of checkers but he now saw clearly there was a second plane. How had he not seen this before? Most people simply did their job each day but he would focus on his career. He visualized an entire game plan, scrawling out crucial steps he would take toward not just one promotion to director, but to the step beyond, vice president. He envisioned his own VP parking space, and made a secret vow that his daily walk through the leafy lot would be his way to anchor the pain and thrust him forward.

Warren wrote *Decision-Making Criteria* on his notepad. Underneath he wrote, 1) *It will move me toward my goal of a promotion.* He stopped for a moment and reflected, then scribbled on the pad, 2) *It can be spun in a way to be perceived as being good for the business.*

Warren's single-mindedness in his approach was startling, even to himself. He reviewed his list of projects. He crossed out any project that would not fast track him to a promotion. He decided to actively seek out an executive who could be his mentor. He closed his eyes and pictured walking down the row of executive offices, mentally stopping at the office of Bob Payne, the politically astute Merchandising VP. He called Payne's assistant and set up a lunch appointment.

When Warren arrived home, Ryan ran up and threw his arms around his father, marking up Warren's white dress shirt with the red magic marker the kid clutched.

"Hey there, buddy!" Warren slid the marker from the kid's fingers.

The boy's arms were covered in red stripes like a candy cane. Warren heard the baby crying in the television room. Marcia came up from the basement stairs with a load of clothes just as the oven timer went off.

"Hey, what's for dinner?" Warren asked.

Marcia scowled. "Do you think you could help me?"

"Sure." He put his satchel on a kitchen chair and tossed the marker onto the counter. "Clothes or oven?"

Marcia thrust the laundry basket into his hands and left him standing there as she checked on the oven. He carried the basket into the television room and checked on Chloe, who laid on her back in the playpen. Ryan had drawn red circles on each of her cheeks. She resembled a Raggedy Ann doll that had come to life.

He carried the laundry upstairs and returned to the TV room with a wet washcloth to scrub the baby's cheeks. Ryan sat cross-legged on the floor watching cartoons. Marcia banged pans around in the kitchen. After scrubbing Chloe's cheeks, Warren sat on the edge of the couch. "Ryan, come here."

Ryan stood eye to eye with his father. Warren examined him for stray marks and wiped the kid's arms down. "You are only to use markers on paper. Do you understand?"

The kid nodded and turned toward the TV. Warren studied his son for a moment and then ran his fingers through the kid's hair.

As they sat down to dinner, Warren spied a brown Shoplandia box next to the sliding doors. "What's in the box?"

"Solar garden lights for the backyard."

He bit his lower lip for a second before asking with an innocent tone, "Didn't you get a box earlier this week?"

"A cookware set."

He just nodded as he buttered his roll. The truth was, since Marcia was home with the kids all day, she watched the shopping channel for hours on end. "I just have it on in the background," she had told him. Warren had seen other boxes and noticed new items in the house. A new yellow Kitchen Aid mixer appeared on the counter last week. Flameless candles flickered on the living room coffee table the week before. Here he was, working to bring money in, and Marcia was sending the money right back to the shopping channel. He thought the scenario had grown into a vicious circle, like a snake eating itself.

When the phone rang, Marcia jumped up, checked caller I.D., and announced it was her sister from Glendale.

"Let it ring," he suggested.

"I can't. We've been playing phone tag all day."

Warren sighed as she picked up the phone. "Hello?"

She hurried out of the room, leaving Warren and the kids staring at each other around the table. He took turns spoon-feeding the baby and feeding himself. The knot in his stomach would not go away. He couldn't recall the last time she asked him about his work. The pork tasted like cardboard, and he wondered if the chile pepper might have killed off his taste buds.

As they cleaned up the kitchen after dinner, Marcia realized they were out of milk and asked Warren to go to the market. After homework and baths, Marcia finally put Ryan to bed, and she walked into the television room in her pajamas and carrying a glass of wine. Warren sat in his chair with a legal pad, his mind percolating over his work, sketching out ideas on his new career strategy. The room was littered with toys.

"I'm too exhausted to clean this up," Marcia muttered as she sat on the couch, sipped her wine, and scanned through the television channels. "Oh, I booked a night away. My mom can babysit."

Warren remained focused on his notes.

"Did you hear me? I booked the Apogee Hotel."

"Oh, the Apogee. When is that?"

"Two weeks. I booked a Friday night."

"Okay."

She looked at him. "You can go, right? What's the matter?"

He looked up from his notes. "I have to start going into work earlier in the morning."

"For how long? For the week?"

"No. Indefinitely."

"I need your help in the mornings, Warren." She squinted her eyes and gulped her wine. "Getting Ryan on the bus has been a challenge, you know that."

"I know, but I need to do this. We're living paycheck to paycheck. I need to either focus on a promotion or look for a new job."

But she was stuck on the morning issues in the house. "If he misses the bus, you need to drive him so I don't have to wake the baby."

"He'll have to make the bus then. I need to focus at the office." He said it with finality, and was relieved to discover that his mild discomfort was fleeting and bearable. She shook her head, then lifted herself off the couch with her wine glass and left the room. He heard her shut the bedroom door.

Warren peeked into Bob Payne's office a few minutes before noon. Payne was on the phone but motioned that he would just be a minute. Warren nodded and stepped over to Payne's assistant.

"Hello."

"Hi." She glanced at her phone and saw the light indicating Payne was still on his call. "He's on with Creosote. He shouldn't be long."

"Thanks."

"I heard you gulped down a hot pepper the other day."

"Oh, yeah." Warren laughed, embarrassed by the assistant's attention. He blushed as though the heat had re-risen within him. His feat had made him a minor celebrity within the offices.

"I don't know how you could do it? Did it hurt?"

"No, I felt some irritation, but it wasn't too bad." He didn't divulge that later that day, after drawing up his plans, he had downed three chocolate milks and at one point, nearly curled up underneath his desk in the fetal position.

"There's the pepper man," Payne said as he patted Warren on the back like a proud father. The outward sign of affection stirred Warren, giving him the feeling he had already gained momentum in his quest.

Payne led the way to a table in the middle of the cafeteria. Warren caught people glancing their way as they set down their lunch trays. Before sitting, Payne unholstered his BlackBerry and laid it out on the table like a gunslinger. Warren reached into his pocket and placed his device down too.

Warren had steeled himself for this conversation. In the early morning at his desk, he'd thought through questions and visualized the meeting. With enthusiasm, he explained his desire for a mentor and how he hoped Payne would take him under his wing. Warren praised Payne's leadership skills, and asked forthright questions about success, productivity and efficiency. Payne seemed honestly flattered, and replied candidly about the politics involved at the upper levels. Warren felt as though the mystery of corporate life was being peeled away before his eyes.

As they wrapped up their lunch, Warren wanted to walk away with one tangible next action, so he asked,

"What practical advice do you have for someone who wants to be promoted?"

Payne picked up his BlackBerry. "This thing will either drown you or let you fly. The smartest thing I ever did was prioritize my incoming messages." He clicked through the screen and showed Warren. "I've set my BlackBerry to a special ringtone so I know when I receive an email from our esteemed CEO or the two SVPs who will likely make or break my career."

Warren smiled. "That's genius."

"I immediately respond to any of these three people. Emails from my subordinates or peers can wait."

"Don't you get urgent emails from your team?"

"I do, and they need to be answered eventually, but my employees don't write my reviews or determine my bonus." The VP smiled. Warren thought Payne had just handed him the keys to the executive bathroom.

"I've seen VPs who dedicate themselves to motivating their team to excel, but if they don't kiss the asses of the executives above them, they get nowhere."

Payne leaned in. "Creosote and these SVPs have huge egos." He held up the BlackBerry. "This little thing allows you to pucker up electronically. It makes all the difference in the world."

After lunch, Warren hustled back to his cubicle flush with excitement. He clicked through the screen and set his BlackBerry with the ringtone labeled Notifier_LightSpeed to go off any time this month's VP of Broadcasting, a burly Irishman named Seamus McGee, sent him an email.

After he set the BlackBerry, Warren sat back and waited in anticipation of an email to hear the ringtone. When Seamus suddenly appeared at his cubicle, Warren was disappointed to see him in person.

"Warren," Seamus asked. "Do you have a moment?"

"Sure."

In his office, Seamus took a seat behind his large desk. From Warren's seat, he could see outside the large paned windows into the trees. Seamus clicked his mouse for a few moments as if he had forgotten Warren was there, and then he turned to him.

"I have a special project I'd like you to work on. Your friend Covert wasn't happy with his on-air appearances a few days ago. He has specific ideas on how to present his program on the air. He's down in the green room now."

"Isn't Adam working on this project?"

"He is, but I told Adam I wanted you to assist him. Adam is frustrated with Covert and the feeling is mutual. Go down and chat with Covert. He is back on the air at 6 p.m. It's important Covert leave here today feeling good about these shows."

Warren glanced at his watch. It was just past four. "I'm on the case."

"Let me know how it goes once you meet with him."

"Okay. Will do."

As he stood to exit, Warren added, "Thanks for the opportunity," and was thrilled to see Seamus smile with surprise.

Warren entered a green room and found Covert standing at the computer watching sales numbers. Covert whirled around with a sour look on his face, but when he saw it was Warren, Covert smiled and said, "The pepper man! What's up?"

Warren laughed. "Seamus asked me to chat with you. He said you had some new ideas you want to try for the next presentation?"

Covert stood up straight from the computer. "Are you taking over for Adam?"

"Not taking over. Supplementing."

Covert walked over to the chair and sat down. He motioned for Warren to sit with him.

"Here's what I want to do."

As Warren pulled his sputtering Honda into the darkened driveway, he winced at the realization that he had failed to let Marcia notice how late he would be. Before climbing out of the car, he checked his BlackBerry and noticed she had left two voicemails. He walked in the side door to a quiet house and found a plate covered in foil waiting for him on the kitchen counter. He dropped his satchel in the corner and quietly walked room to room before climbing the stairs and peeking into Ryan's room. The kid was asleep, lying on his stomach with his legs tucked underneath him.

Warren walked into his bedroom. Marcia was reading a book in bed. The baby was asleep next to her, her tiny fists clenched.

"Hey, I'm home. Sorry. I just saw your voicemails."

"Hey," she said without looking up.

He walked around to his side of the bed and slipped off his shoes. He took the BlackBerry out of his pocket and placed it at the baby's feet, and then he sat down on top of the comforter and watched the baby sleeping peacefully. Marcia still didn't look up.

"Seamus asked me to work with Covert on his presentations." He laid back and faced the ceiling, rubbing his hands on his tired face. He wanted to garner the energy to go heat up the plate of food.

"So what's that mean, work with Covert?" she asked.

"Try new ways of taking testimonial calls."

"Does that mean you are going in early *and* working late now?"

"I'm sorry."

His BlackBerry whirred the Notifier_Lightspeed tune and he slammed his hand over it. The baby stirred and they both watched her, expecting her to wake. She moved one tiny balled hand to her mouth and remained asleep.

"Sorry," he whispered. "I'm going to heat some dinner up. Thanks for fixing a plate." He palmed the BlackBerry, and as soon as he closed the bedroom door, he clicked through and read the email from Seamus. *Covert seemed happy after the last show. Thanks.*

Even though no response was needed, he quickly typed, *No problem. My pleasure. Thanks,* and hit send.

In the early mornings, Warren turned his walk through the executive lot into his own personal suffering, as though viewing the Porsches and BMWs was walking on coals. By the time he sat in his open cubicle each morning, he had worked himself into such a rage of pain that he felt nauseous, and he used this knot in his stomach as fuel. He obsessed over how to translate his personal career plans into concrete next action steps, reviewing his meetings and projects with a critical eye.

When his ringtone sounded, Warren immediately read Seamus's messages. He often responded immediately. Sometimes he'd be in a meeting, and he'd read the message and step out. He'd clear his mind and think through a proper response before carefully pounding out a reply with his thumbs. It became clear that Seamus believed in speed. Seamus liked quick replies, particularly if he was under the gun from Creosote.

One morning, Warren logged in and found an email from covert1@covert1.com with both Seamus and Creosote copied.

Warren -

I wanted to drop a note to thank you for your creative ideas concerning my shows. Your thoughts were very beneficial in turning the show around. I appreciate all your time and effort.

Sincerely,

Robert Covert

Warren smiled. He looked around at the empty row

of cubicles, and took delight that he was the only one who came in early each day. He tapped on his desk excitedly, as if beating a drum. His quick responses to Seamus had created a funnel. The boss relied on Warren more and more, and now this email of praise, and Creosote copied as well! One word struck him. *Momentum.* He had garnered momentum and he would ride it now.

The Apogee Hotel sparkled in the sun as they pulled up in the mini-van. After a hurried departure from the house, and Marcia's two subsequent calls to her mother with remembered instructions, she finally sat back and let herself be carried away. A doorman opened Marcia's door and she stepped out onto the circular driveway. As Warren stepped out of the van, he admired the Art Museum off in the distance.

One valet took their key and another one carried their overnight bags into the hotel. They walked into the lobby and paused, overwhelmed at the opulence. A massive crystal chandelier filled the foyer and giant bouquets of white lilies sprang from a round table in the center. Colorful bouquets were tiered against the walls underneath luminous watercolors in golden ornate frames.

They checked in at the front desk and were escorted up to their room by the valet. Warren tipped the gentleman and closed the door. Marcia threw herself onto the bed and Warren opened the mini-bar.

"I wish we had time to relax before dinner," Marcia said.

The hotel's main restaurant, The Meridian, was a sumptuous oval room, bustling with tuxedoed waiters carrying silver trays. A maitre d' showed them to a table set with white linen and china. He pulled out the chair with a flourish for Marcia. Out of habit, Warren pulled his BlackBerry out of his slacks and set the device on the table.

"Would you put that away? This night is about us."

Warren stared blankly for a moment and then frowned. He picked up the device, scrolled through it, clicked a button and slipped it back into his pocket.

"Thank you." She picked up her menu with a sigh of relief. "I'm just so glad to be out of my sweatpants. It was so nice to dress up, to put on some makeup and lipstick."

"You look marvelous," Warren replied, and he watched her for a moment as she studied the menu. He thought maybe this night away would spark a renewed Marcia, and he was relieved to see her darkened mood had slowly dissipated during the drive.

After a few sips of their wine, they both sat quietly, awkwardly, taking in the small details of the extravagance. Warren felt the cool rush of the Sauvignon Blanc rush through his veins, settling in his empty stomach. He craned his neck and studied the elaborate ceiling, painted in a heavenly blue. For a brief moment, he experienced a floating sensation, as though he was watching the oval room from above, and he imagined the waiters scurrying around like ants.

"A meal without chicken nuggets and spilled milk." Marcia's voice broke the silence. "What more could I ask for?"

They ate each course slowly, savoring each bite and sipping their wine. Warren was occasionally distracted, watching the maitre d' chatting with a waiter or seating other couples.

"How is the filet mignon? Marcia asked.

He slipped a forkful into her mouth. She closed her eyes and tilted her head back. "Melts in your mouth."

She sliced a piece of salmon and placed it on his tongue. The citrus tang exploded. Warren loosened up after his second glass of wine. He reached out and touched Marcia's hand. "This was a great idea."

The waiter approached with a small menu.

"Can I interest you in some dessert tonight?" By this point, their idea of dessert was not something the waiter could satisfy.

"No thank you," they replied in unison.

As soon as the suite door slammed shut, Warren was unzipping the back of Marcia's dress while sticking his tongue in her ear. She giggled and unbuttoned his shirt slowly as they started making out in the center of the room.

Marcia reached down and unbuckled Warren's belt. She dropped his trousers to the floor with a thud. He reached down and tossed the slacks on a chair. She slid her hand across the silk boxers that she'd purchased for him at the mall, caressing them delicately before deciding they too must go.

She lay down on the bed with Warren standing over

her. He reached out and softly ran his fingers over her C-section scar, as if to reassure her everything would be okay. He slowly, rhythmically kissed her pearl white skin.

They moved in unison, taking turns, pleasing each other until he was firm and she had opened up. He entered her softly. She held onto his back, her legs wrapped around his waist, as he slowly...

"Whirr! Whirr!" His BlackBerry chimed out with the immediately recognizable ringtone of Seamus. Warren raised his head and eyed up his trousers, his tongue out like a conditioned dog, as he caught sight of the blinking green beacon calling him through the fabric.

On an overcast day seventeen years later, Warren would recall that moment while standing flat-footed in the atrium of Shoplandia with a dozen other employees, all of whom were being recognized for what their new, thirty-five year old CEO had deemed their "twenty years of extraordinary service."

Warren had held several lateral positions over the interim years, none considered a promotion, and for the last eight years he'd reported to his friend Tony. He'd watched as faces came and went: new show hosts, directors and VPs brought in for their fresh ideas, who invariably ended up buying Warren lunch and asking simple questions such as "Why do the hosts ask callers for their names?" They invariably referred to him as "an old-timer" with a nod that imparted either respect or condescension, depending on Warren's state of mind on that particular day.

That moment in the hotel room of the Apogee had actually kept him awake the night before, triggered by a conversation with his son Ryan, who had called from San Francisco where he had moved after college because of a free-spirited girl with red cascading hair and a smile that had made Warren wobble in the knees. While out west, Ryan had wedged his foot in the door at an investment firm, found a mentor and had been fast-tracked. Now, he'd been offered an opportunity, but it meant a move to Dallas, a move the girlfriend had just informed Ryan that she would not make. In a rational manner, Ryan outlined the pros and cons of his choices as if determining a retirement portfolio. Warren grunted occasionally to convey he was still on the other end of the line.

But then, the son had asked his father a startling question.

"What would you do?"

Warren's throat tightened and his forehead grew moist. He opened the glass sliding door and moved out into the cool darkness of their back patio. A tiredness overtook him, and his joints ached. He ran his hand through his graying hair, and he had not a single clue as to what advice he could give.

SIX

....

MONEY SHOT

On the morning of the show host auditions, Renee McGyver rose before dawn and made the three-hour drive to Sellersburg in her dinged up Tercel. She wore a new suit that had nearly maxed out her credit card, and this provided her with both an air of formality and an uncomfortable stiffness under the seatbelt. Working in Altoona radio had proven to be the broadcast equivalent of flipping burgers. Three years in and she was still struggling each month, living paycheck to paycheck, subsisting on beans and rice while paying off her student loans. When she first stumbled onto the posting for auditions at Shoplandia, she laughed at the thought, but then she grew curious as to what the life of a show host might entail, and if this could be her path out of post-college poverty.

College friend Marci met her under a canopy of trees in the outer parking lot of the Shoplandia world headquarters. In the distance, the sun rose over a highway bustling with morning commuters. Marci unrolled her makeup kit on the hood of Renee's car.

"They are auditioning you on camera, right?"

"That's what they told me. They are taping each audition."

"Remember, applying makeup for TV is a little different. I have some new blush that we just launched at our flagship store. It may look like too much in person."

"I'm ready. Make me over."

"Once you get this job," Marci suggested, "maybe you can get me in the door as a makeup artist."

Renee laughed. "I've got to get in the door first, but I would definitely do that." She stood looking up at the trees, a bib covering her suit, as Marci meticulously applied foundation, rouge, eyeliner, and lipstick. After three years on WALT-AM, this felt like an odd transformation, as though she was preparing for Halloween. In radio, she went in clean-faced each morning, worked in solitude in the studio, in jeans and a t-shirt. She'd never considered herself pretty, just plain, with a face that could get lost in the crowd. After a few minutes of silent concentration, Marci stepped back and admired her work. She handed Renee a mirror. The face that reflected back appeared unfamiliar and unsure.

"It's not too much?"

"On camera, you will look killer."

Self-doubt washed over Renee. She had confidence that she could host a television show, but her spirit waned when she thought too much about making a sales pitch. She recalled last night's phone conversation with her brother, and how he derisively joked, "you mean, hawking products on TV?" He made it sound so vulgar that the tendons in her neck contracted and her hands involuntarily balled into fists.

Now, she took a breath to keep from sobbing. "I don't know. Maybe this is a mistake."

The ever-positive Marci blotted the corner of Renee's eye with a paper towel. "You're gonna get this job on your natural personality, your smarts and your awesome broadcast skills. The makeup is just playing the TV game, a bit of insurance. That's all it is."

Renee smiled. "I owe you, big time."

"I want you to get this job sooo much! The mall I work at is just up the road. Just think, we can hang out, and I can say I know a celebrity. Now go in there and slay them."

Renee blew out a puff of air and clapped her hands together. "Okay, let's do it."

A line of auditionees already snaked out of the front entrance and down the steps. Renee surveyed her competition: some of the women wore conservative business suits, others sported casual dresses. Her eyes fell on a few men who resembled male models, looking sharp in jackets and ties. Other men were dressed business casual in khakis and open collar shirts. Renee checked her watch and realized the line wouldn't start moving for another half hour. Within a few minutes they were no longer the tail of the line as people gathered behind them.

A Town Car pulled up in the circle, and a buzz swept through the gathering crowd. People craned their necks and whispered, "Is it Cameron Diaz? Is it Matt Damon?" Instead, a fifty-something plump infomercial pitchman from the Bronx struggled to climb out of the passenger side, set up his little steel dolly and load it with some newfangled invention that he would pitch to a shopping network buyer.

Just as the crowd had given up on seeing anyone famous, a powder blue Bentley with New York plates pulled up to the curb. A black tied chauffeur strolled around to the passenger side rear door as the window lowered. He leaned in, conversing with the hidden passenger. After a few moments, the man opened the door and out climbed a petite, elegant woman in an immaculate red dress.

Marci squealed, "Oh my God! It's Nellie Campbell."

The Nellie Campbell of the long running soap opera *Chauncey's Circle.* The crowd cheered. Several people hurriedly pulled out cell phones and snapped photos. A second woman climbed out of the Bentley carrying a large satchel and a clipboard and stayed two steps behind the star. Nellie appeared gracious enough, pausing as if she was on the Hollywood red carpet. She smiled and waved at the well-dressed line. Renee's jaw dropped when Nellie walked right up to her and Marci with a spry smile. A wafting scent of jasmine filled the air. "What are you here for today, my dear?"

Marci blurted out, "My friend is auditioning to be a host!"

Nellie stepped back and studied Renee, as if she was mulling whether or not this young woman had the chutzpa, the killer instinct, the kahunas, to be a show host. The soap opera star finally gave an approving smile, stepped in and took Renee's hand in hers. "Well, good luck to you! Maybe we'll be on the air together someday!" The star's petite hand was as cold and limp as a raw chicken wing.

Nellie took a few steps and turned again to the adoring crowd, "Don't forget to buy my perfume which debuts today. The Scent of Amore—for that special someone in your life!"

After a few more steps, the actress swiveled yet again. "We have 200,000 bottles to move through. We need all the help we can get." The star winked and slipped through the front door.

Renee's hand trembled slightly. She looked up at the trees and focused on her breathing, steeling herself. Her lips moved as she recalled the words she had rehearsed. *When you have one of these in your hands, you will have the world at your fingertips.* She closed her eyes and imagined herself in front of the cameras, smiling and chatting casually with callers.

A few moments later, the woman who had walked in with Nellie emerged with an oval perfume bottle and began spritzing people on the wrist. While the men politely declined, several women held out their hands to experience the magic. As she worked her way down the line, a murmur spread through the crowd and the fragrance of lavender and jasmine filled the air.

After being spritzed, Marci raised her wrist and inhaled deeply. She immediately turned her head and sneezed. Startled, Renee jumped back and nearly knocked over the woman behind her. "Uh, no thanks." She waved off the spritzer. Marci let out a second violent sneeze and burrowed into her pocket for a tissue.

"Are you okay?"

Marci's eyes were red and pooling with water. "Yeah. That stuff is potent. Whoa!"

They laughed just as the line started moving up the steps. Soon, they were standing in the glistening lobby. A giant screen, as wide as the wall itself, showed a woman twirling in a long chiffon skirt. A security guard insisted Marci had to wait outside. Marci pouted for a moment, then asserted she was Renee's manager. He remained unfazed, apparently unamused. Renee finally urged Marci to go.

"I'll be fine. It shouldn't be long now."

Marci grinned. "Knock 'em dead girl."

Renee hugged her carefully, being sure not to wrinkle herself in the process. She watched Marci walk out the doors and then she took her seat next to a woman in a long purple dress and a perm. Renee studied the soaring hallway, admiring how it rose two stories with slants of sunlight streaming through glass to the lobby floor. She thought about her cramped Altoona spaces—the dingy radio studio and her shoebox of an apartment. She recalled a quote from that motivational guru Robert Covert, who she had seen last week selling his *Rise Above* program. *Don't focus on the life you currently have. Focus on the life you want to have.* She envisioned success, being on the air with Nellie, wearing elegant jewels and silk tunics, but a toxic thought drowned out the lovely image. She might have to wear those horrible holiday sweaters or actually sing karaoke. *Think positive thoughts.* She shut her eyes and imagined herself on stage with celebrities: famous designers, authors, athletes, perhaps the romance book cover icon Dmitri. When she opened her eyes, the woman ahead of her had gone into the room. Renee was next.

The small conference room was set up with a camcorder on a tripod. A woman in her mid-thirties shook Renee's hand and pointed to an open seat. A young man in his mid-twenties, dressed in a white shirt and tie, stood behind the camera and waved.

"Hi. I'm Renee." She was so nervous she didn't catch their names.

"Do you have a resume?" the woman asked.

Renee pulled papers out of her satchel and handed one over. The woman scanned it carefully and wrote notes on her clipboard.

"What are you presenting today?" the man asked.

Renee pulled out a pencil and held it up.

He grinned as if he had seen pencil presentations a dozen times already. "I'll give you a cue when to start and you'll have two minutes. Any questions?"

"No. I don't think so." Her voice cracked and she gulped. She wished she had brought a bottle of water.

The woman's head remained down, perusing the resume.

"Are you ready?"

Renee straightened herself, inhaled deeply and nodded. "Yes."

He cued her to the camera. She smiled sweetly and felt a surge within her. "Hi, I'm Renee and I have the most magnificent writing implement you could ever want. Some people will tell you this is an ordinary pencil, but it is much, much more than that. In your hand, this amazing pencil allows you to make a mark, to visualize your dreams, to leave a legacy. This Andersen number two pencil is shaped elegantly so that it fits comfortably between your fingers. One size fits all! This pleasing yellow means you'll be able to find it even when your desk is a little messy. This point is easy to sharpen and you'll surely get hours of enjoyment out of writing letters to those you love. Perhaps you'd like to start a journal to record your life's work."

She held up the pink end of the pencil. "And if you are like me, you sometimes make mistakes. Well, this handy end contains an eraser so you can basically retract what you have written. If only one could have an eraser for certain things in life! Now, think back to the most sentimental and memorable notes you have ever received, inside letters or birthday cards, and you'll recall they were handwritten. They were personal. With this pencil, you can write your own notes, document your own life, personalize cards for that special someone. Maybe write out a card for your husband or your grandkids. They'll cherish that personalized gift you give them and you'll be thankful that you picked up this pencil today."

The man behind the camera twirled his finger in little circles indicating she should wrap. She finished her thoughts, set the pencil down and leaned back. An awkwardness swelled in the room and both of the interviewers finally smiled.

"How was that?"

"Nice job," the woman moved to the door and pulled it open. "You did a really nice job." The way she said it sounded like a form letter. Renee understood they had no time for kibitzing this morning. She grabbed her bag and stood.

"Well, thank you so much for your time." She struggled to remain cordial despite her disappointment. As she was about to exit, the man called out, "Hold on a moment."

Renee swiveled.

"Let's have you present one more item. Pick something from this shelf over there and we'll give you a few minutes."

Renee studied them both. What was going on here? The man pointed to the shelf and the woman pursed her lips into a reluctant smile. Renee studied the array of items, each one accompanied by an index card in which a description had been written. There was a facial cream with a brand name she had never heard of, a pair of strapped sandals, rubber kitchen mitts, a battery operated candle, and a Precious Moments figurine. She picked up the figurine and sat, turning the big eyes of the little child so they looked into hers. The card explained the figurine was named Starry Nights, and she studied every detail. After formulating a few thoughts, she declared, "I'm ready."

In that moment of silence, she imagined herself at the starting gate of a race, and at the cue, she sprinted. She described the big round eyes on the kneeling child's face, his auburn hair, and the pattern of teddy bears on his pajamas. And then, out of nowhere, she rattled off how this would make a great gift for a little boy or for a mother who had just given birth. And although she didn't know anyone who would really desire one of these porcelain figurines, Renee claimed her sister would love Starry Nights and had a perfect spot in her living room. It was all a ridiculous white lie, but Renee was surprised at how fluently she had let it roll off her tongue. When she looked up after her two minutes, their eyes were on her. Under the table, her knees wobbled with the rush of what had just happened.

"Thanks! We'll be in touch." The woman opened the door and Renee walked into the hallway in a daze, unsure whether she had nailed the audition or simply made a fool of herself.

The process happened so quickly. Renee received the phone call a week after the audition, returned to the network for a series of interviews and a few more presentations in a quiet auxiliary studio, and then was extended an offer over the phone shortly afterwards. Between packing and arranging her move, she watched Shoplandia every free moment. She studied the hosts on the screen and admired how polished they were. Their ability to speak extemporaneously for three hours while maneuvering each product toward the camera, taking telephone calls while also listening to producers and directors was quite a feat.

Renee's first few weeks as a host in training were fresh, wondrous, and a little bit terrifying. She attended a whirlwind of meetings with buyers from different product categories. Kitchenware. Entertainment. Electronics. Fashion. Accessories. She was advised on all the trends and taken aback by the details. Nervous buyers talked about how their sales goals had been set absurdly high, and despaired that they wouldn't hit their numbers. The formal wear buyer informed her that mauve is the new black. An hour later, the casual wear buyer exclaimed denim is the new black. The food buyer declared that gourmet sausage is the new bacon and the lingerie buyer whispered that Spanx is the new tummy tuck.

For the first two months, iconic host Frankie Mack mentored Renee. She tagged along as he reviewed products backstage, met with guests in the green room, and took the stage each day to present to America. As one of the first hosts on Shoplandia, Frankie Mack offered sage advice on dealing with issues both on and off the air. He was a fatherly figure, mid-fifties, gracious and humorous behind his wire-rimmed glasses. Renee had found a tattered *New Yorker* article about the shopping network that called Frankie Mack *the Garrison Keillor of sales* for his friendly, entertaining midwestern approach. On her first day under his tutelage, they sat in the corner of the cafeteria and chatted. Frankie was dressed to go on-air, and he leaned back with his legs crossed and a bottle of cranberry juice in his hand.

"I was twelve years old when I had an epiphany," Frankie explained. "I was in Atlantic City with my folks. We were on the boardwalk when I saw a crowd of people packed tight. They were laughing. I was little and I couldn't see what the crowd was looking at, so I wedged myself through and finally nosed my way to the front." He stopped and took a swig of juice, and then adjusted his tie.

"As I popped my head out from the crowd, I saw this tall, tanned, confident salesman with a big smile demonstrating a cheese grater—the Cheez-o-matic. He had the crowd mesmerized, particularly the ladies. This salesman was showing people this cheese grater, moving his hands along gracefully, but keeping his eyes on the audience and making them laugh. The crowd was captivated. Every ten minutes or so, he'd stop his demonstration and sell nineteen or twenty kits even though twenty-five or thirty people were waving their money. And then, before selling one more kit, he'd smile and announce, 'let me show you how this works on provolone,' and he'd do another demonstration so the crowd would build again. It was amazing how he worked a crowd. It was the greatest sight I'd ever seen."

"Did you buy a Cheez-o-matic?"

"No, but I wanted one. I bugged my parents that afternoon to buy it, but they wouldn't. We were only visiting for the day, and I threw a fit." Frankie paused. "Up until that day, I thought I wanted to be the next Steve Allen or Milton Berle, but this salesman on the boardwalk was entertaining and he executed the turn. He asked for the money. People were waving dollar bills at him. That's when I knew I wanted to sell."

Renee pursed her lips.

"Uh oh," Frankie grinned. "You're a little hesitant?"

She glanced away. "I never thought I'd be in sales, you know. I was a broadcast major. I wanted to host *The Today Show*."

Frankie let out a laugh that rattled her.

"I'm sorry," he said. "I'm only laughing because I understand what you mean."

She saw he had empathy in his eyes. "We've had several folks—hosts, producers, control room folks—who come here from a local news station, or someplace like ESPN, and they have a distaste for the sales end. They just want to make television. They want to make art."

"And what happens to them?"

Frankie leaned back and reflected. "Well, some of them come around eventually. That's why hosts are brought in for six months of probation, to see if they get it." On the word "it," his fingers arced into air quotes.

Renee took a deep breath.

"Don't worry. You obviously showed promise in your audition."

Her audition. She thought about that rush she experienced, making things up on the fly, saying things she didn't believe just to quell the silence in the room. "Let me ask you. What happens when you have to sell a product that you don't believe in?"

"Every product we sell is great. What do you mean?"

Frankie replied with a straight face, but then cracked a smile and glanced around to ensure nobody was sitting behind him. He leaned in. "Honestly, there are times when I look at a product and think who the hell would want this? But I can't be judgmental on the air. I sell it for what it is. Even though I wouldn't buy the product, I simply explain the features and benefits for those who are interested." He chuckled and sat back in his seat. "Just yesterday, my mother called and asked if she should buy a certain jar of facial cream. I told her, if I loved you, I wouldn't sell you this."

She bit her lip and nodded.

"You'll be fine, Renee. You are talented, young and smart. Just give it your best shot. If you are not comfortable in six months, you can walk away."

She knew she didn't want to do that. Once she started her on-air presentations she'd surely grow comfortable. After all, she had done it once with that figurine. She had come this far, packed her bags and fled from Altoona, and she would make a go of it now, but that night while on the phone with Marci, she blurted out, "I just don't know if I have the sales gene."

Two weeks into training, the department assistant left Renee a voicemail saying she was to keep Wednesday afternoon open. She was introduced to Lawrence, the fashion consultant who worked with the hosts. He eyed Renee over in a serious manner as he circled around her, as if he was debating whether or not to purchase a piece of art. He motioned for her to slowly turn around so he could observe her from all angles, and she did so shyly, nervously.

"We have some things to work with," Lawrence declared. "Tomorrow, you and I are going to Nordstrom. We have to pick you out some suits. We have a budget of $2,000."

Renee gasped at the thought of a spending spree of that magnitude.

"I know, it's not much, but half the time you are on the air you will be wearing product we're selling anyway."

Renee laughed at her good fortune. She could definitely get used to this. Lawrence continued circling her, unaware.

"Once your contract is picked up, what is it, six months? We'll get to do some real shopping then." When he looked up at her face, there was a sparkle in his eye. She wondered if he was pulling for her or just liked to shop.

That night, Renee met Marci at Lotus Blue for shrimp low mein, and the waiter asked if they might be interested in a special prix-fixe meal—five courses of spicy cuisine. Up until recently, Renee would have considered the price obscene, but now she felt the freedom of being able to order without counting pennies or worrying about adding in a tip. Over the bottle of Chardonnay they had brought and the continual feasting on courses, Renee described her new fashion friend Lawrence and how much they were budgeted to spend on their shopping excursion the next day. When Marci's jaw opened into a jealous grin, Renee felt a swelling of pride. The two women clinked their glasses as the dim sum arrived.

The hosts were tightly packed in the conference room of their private lounge, gossiping about celebrity guests, office romances and the looming cookware recall as they waited for the quarterly show host team meeting to begin. Booming professional voices competed for attention and caught up on each other's news. This meeting was heightened by swirling speculation as to who today's mystery guest speaker might be. Renee sat in the back of the room somewhat intimidated, quietly taking in the boisterous scene. She eavesdropped on a voice whispering, "Phyllis Diller once told me not to drop names."

Joe Looter, Shoplandia's Vice President who managed the motley bunch, raised his arms and settled down the crew. To Renee's surprise, the first thing Looter did was introduce her. "I want everyone to welcome Renee to our team." All eyes turned her way and applause broke out. She blushed and gave an embarrassed wave. "Renee was the chosen one and we're thrilled to have her. For those who don't know, Frankie is Renee's mentor so she's in good hands. We're all looking forward to seeing her on air as a part of our sales team."

Looter glanced up at the clock.

"Okay, let's chat about our special guest. He will be here momentarily. You've probably heard the name Jack Burton before..."

The room exploded with superlatives and someone actually shrieked. Everyone knew who Jack Burton was.

He had created such reality TV mega-hits as *The Subordinate* and *Last Man Standing*, in which people clawed and fought with their teammates to advance to the next challenge. Each episode was full of scheming, treachery, backstabbing and lying as everyone connived to survive and win some maguffin-like prize. Jack Burton had extended his realm even further, creating a series of reality shows that had reinvigorated the careers of several miscreants and B-list celebrities by showcasing their trivial family squabbles over dirty dishes, missing car keys and who left the toilet seat up.

Looter hushed the gaggle of hosts. "Well, Mr. Burton is in the building today. It turns out he has been a fan of our channel for a while, and he has been watching. He offered to chat with us about engaging our customers."

A knocking ensued, and the door opened. Marketing VP Johnny Wake entered cautiously, smiling and waving as he made eye contact with certain hosts and then held the door open for the legendary Hollywood mogul. Jack Burton was dressed in pure Los Angeles fashion, a starched, vibrant red and white checked dress shirt with sleeves rolled up to show his tan forearms. The man was handsome enough to be in front of the camera. He sported faded jeans and cowboy boots. His stubbled face was instantly recognizable, his curly, tight cropped hair held slight streaks of gray, the kind that add character. He smiled and waved, almost sheepishly.

Looter asked Johnny Wake, "Do you want to introduce our speaker?"

Johnny grinned and started making his way to the

front of the crowded room. As he passed Renee, he placed his hand on her shoulder and joked, "Hey, it's the new girl!" Once he positioned himself at the head of the table, the show hosts fell silent.

"We've been chatting with Jack Burton about a number of possible projects, really exciting projects that have the potential to just blow up our business." He put his hands out cautiously, "and I mean that in a good way."

The hosts laughed.

"Anyway, so Jack has been here today, meeting with a few of us, and he wants to tour the studio. His theories on reality TV are really interesting, and we thought you might find them interesting too. So here he is."

Jack Burton stepped to the front of the room and patted Johnny on the back. Renee was starstruck to be breathing the same air as this famous Hollywood producer.

"Thanks for having me. I really am a fan," Burton said gracefully. "I've watched Shoplandia ever since I was an intern, hustling on the MGM lot fifteen years ago. I love that you are not actors but truly yourselves when you are on the air. That honesty you bring to the screen has inspired me. In some subtle way, you are the inspiration for reality TV."

Renee scanned the room, and was relieved to see the experienced show hosts were just as rapt.

"Obviously, this reality TV trend and home shopping are similar. It is cheap to produce, comparatively speaking. If done well, it is authentic. People deal with first world issues, and often solve these problems with real viable products. Products that make our lives better."

Burton could have been speaking Swahili and the hosts would have been grinning and nodding as if they understood. The man's creative power, track record and vast amounts of wealth held sway over the room.

"What is important in reality television is the honesty the family brings to the production. Really, it is confessional television in a way. We chat with many people about the possibility of producing a reality TV show, but once we roll the camera for a few days in their home, it becomes clear there isn't anything there. People at home want to watch folks who are mixing it up, confessing little things in their lives, revealing their guilty pleasures."

Renee glanced over at one of the senior show hosts, Karen Loftus, who sat up against the wall. She thought Karen was especially good at that sort of thing. The other night Karen told a story about trying on an outfit in the dressing room of some high-end boutique. The saleswoman told her, "You'll be fine, just put on some control top pantyhose," and Karen replied to the saleswoman, "I'm wearing control top pantyhose!" When Renee had seen that, watching from home, she gasped, for she could never tell that story on the air.

Burton continued. "My goal with our shows can be summed up in three words: water cooler conversations. That's what we strive to do, have people at work the next day asking their friends, did you see the show last night? Gossiping as though the people on the screen are their own co-workers."

Karen jumped right in, interrupting Burton. "So, let cut to the chase. What brings you to our sleepy part of the world?"

Burton bit his lip and looked at Johnny Wake. "Is the ink dry?"

The two men grinned as Johnny stepped up next to Burton.

"Does everyone know who Wainwright is?" Johnny asked.

Everyone on the planet knew who Wainwright was, Renee thought. Burton had created the country's most bankable celebrity, a marketing phenomenon. Wainwright was the daughter of a Beverly Hills divorce lawyer who first came to national prominence after full-throating the rock star Izzy in a home video gone viral. Shortly after, Burton signed her for a television series. In its third year, the reality show simply titled *Wainwright* had grown to be the most watched television show in any genre, particularly amongst girls between the ages of 13-18, according to Neilsen ratings. Only in America. Wainwright had also become an international brand. T-shirts, backpacks and costume jewelry with the ubiquitous logo—angelic wings adorning the capital letter W as if in flight—were now sold in the end caps of Target and Walmart. According to the most recent issue of Forbes, the story of the 21-year-old self-proclaimed nymphomaniac was being taught as a brand management case study in the Harvard Business School.

"Well, Wainwright is developing a line of jewelry for Shoplandia."

The hosts collectively gasped, and then cheers erupted.

Thirty minutes later, as the room cleared out, Frankie motioned for Renee to sit up at the conference table with a few of the lingering senior hosts.

"Wow! That was exciting news," she said as she sat at the big kids' table.

"Eh," Frankie replied, unimpressed.

"Aw, come on. This will bring a new caché to the channel," Tanya declared. "Wainwright has a huge following, and she can tweet about her appearances. Just think of all the press we'll get. The paparazzi follows her everywhere."

"She's definitely considered hip, modern, and relevant," Karen chimed in.

"Her face is everywhere," Calabrese inserted.

"Have you watched her show?" Frankie asked.

"I like it," Tanya replied. "It's campy, but it's fun. It's girl talk."

"I don't get it," Frankie said. "Does she have talent?"

Calabrese snorted, "You obviously haven't seen that home video. Oh, she's got talent."

Tanya slapped him on the shoulder. "You're awful."

"She is beautiful," Renee said. "I didn't know she was a designer."

"Oh, she isn't." Karen waved her arm as if brushing off the comment. "They'll just hire a whole team of designers for her, maybe give her a say in the designs."

"She'll bring in a new audience," Frankie acknowledged, "but our show appeals to good families with up-standing morals."

"Morals schmorals." Calabrese laughed. "We've got huge sales numbers to hit. We've got to keep feeding the machine. It's all good."

Frankie clasped his hands together as if in prayer. "Sometimes I wonder if we're incrementally losing our integrity..."

"The real question is..." Tanya stated with a competitive grin, "...who will get to host the show?"

Three weeks later, Renee spent the last of her days shadowing Frankie Mack during his shift. She had observed Frankie collaborating with his producers for creative demonstrations during his two-hour *Electronics Frenzy*. A desperate buyer had challenged Frankie to sell out a 900 mhz cordless phone. Renee tagged along as Frankie and producer Dottie mapped out a route that Frankie would "walk and talk," descending the steps into order entry and walking along the rows of operators. With his mic down, Frankie would speak solely through the cordless phone as he walked down the hall and into a green room, being followed by a hand-held camera-man.

As Dottie and Frankie finished their conversation in the green room, a vendor interrupted. "Hey Frankie, do you have time to chat about the fire scanner?" He spoke in a Long Island accent. "I'm really hoping to move through this inventory. This is a product that saves lives." Renee listened in as the vendor kept pushing

Frankie to use certain superlatives. "We gotta move through this inventory, man. They are threatening to return these, and I can't take it. It'll crush me."

Renee studied Frankie, surprised that he remained calm as this vendor rambled on. Frankie finally replied simply, "We'll give it our best shot." As they exited the green room, Frankie confessed out of the corner of his mouth, "Guys like him irk the hell out of me."

Once the show began, Renee sat with Dylan at the line producer's desk, listening in on a headset. Coordinating producer Dottie ran back and forth through the studio, pointing out the demonstration route to the cameraman. As Frankie began his presentation of the scanner, Dottie stopped at the desk. Dylan informed Frankie that he had a testimonial call. As soon as the caller's voice hit the air, Renee cringed. The voice had the same nasally tone as the salesman she had met in the green room. At first, she thought he must have gotten one of his Long Island friends to call in with a testimonial, but as she listened, Renee was struck with a horrifying thought. Dylan turned around to the desk where two order entry women screened the calls before patching them through to the live show.

"What's this caller's name?"

"Vince."

"Where from?"

"Huntington, Long Island."

That's when she heard Frankie say, live on the air, "Dylan, I want to take a walk right now." He approached the edge of the stage.

Dylan jumped up. "Hey, Frankie is walking off the stage. He wants to do something on the fly. Camera guys, are you ready?"

Renee held her breath. Frankie continued asking the t-caller how he used the item and the voice broke into a riff about how his sister had used this scanner, this exact scanner, to hear about a pending tornado and had ducked into her basement. "This scanner saved my sister's life. You would be crazy not to buy one for your home. And a second one for your mother's home." As the caller warbled on about how every family in America should have one, Frankie hopped off the stage and made a beeline for the green room. During this sojourn, the show host was up on camera, smiling as if nothing was wrong. The t-caller's voice grew considerably more nervous as Frankie was seen opening the green room door and turning back to the camera.

"Ladies and gentlemen, meet our t-caller." Frankie now stood in front of the sales rep who, frozen and red faced, dropped his phone down to his side. "This gentleman actually brought this product to Shoplandia. He is a vendor representative, and he has the biggest kahunas of any vendor rep we've had. Because, here at Shoplandia, our telephone calls are authentic. Unfortunately, Vince here doesn't believe that matters, he doesn't have the integrity that we do. Vince is going to learn the hard way that we expect our vendors to follow a certain code of conduct. At Shoplandia, we do not accept set-up testimonial calls. We apologize on behalf of this ill-guided vendor. Let's take a break. We'll be back after a few messages with a really great home phone."

Renee watched this unfold from the producer's desk. Dylan's phone lit up—everyone in the offices had an opinion—but he just let it ring. Dottie and Frankie were returning now from the green room, Dottie shaking her head, and confirming, "I will call the buyer right away. We're going to beat that vendor like a rented mule."

Frankie just shook his head and smirked at the guy's unbelievable audacity. Renee was flabbergasted at Frankie's on-air handling of the incident, and she was impressed with his integrity. Within minutes, suits started appearing at the producer's desk, asking questions and second-guessing Frankie's decision to call out the vendor on live television.

Renee sat next to Dylan and listened to their arguments, secretly applauding Frankie for such a bold move, wondering if she would ever have the confidence to do such a thing. A few minutes later, she felt a tap on her shoulder and turned to see Tanya leaning in to pick up a microphone pack.

"What's all the commotion here?" Tanya asked. "I heard security just escorted a vendor out of the building."

"The vendor called from the green room to give a testimonial! Frankie caught him and made an example of the guy, all live on air."

"No, really?" Tanya grinned. "You can't put anything by Frankie. God bless that man. He's the last honest salesman." She shook her head and threaded the mic through her jacket.

Dylan turned and saw Tanya. He slid his headset down. "Congratulations Tanya."

"What did I miss? What happened?"

"You didn't hear?" Dylan quipped. "Tanya is hosting the *Wainwright* show."

Tanya grinned. "This should be fun."

On the night of Wainwright's 10 p.m. debut, Renee was scheduled to go on the air the following hour. She arrived early that night, hoping to see the spectacle that was surely being created for the launch. Deep down, she hoped for the chance to meet Wainwright. The studio was bustling. The suits had come out of their offices and stayed late into the night. Wainwright appeared to have a posse more than an entourage and the halls were streaming with people Renee had never seen before. There was the diva's hair stylist, makeup artist, manager, product designers and others with titles not worthy of being mentioned. They all walked with purpose, as if their mission was critical.

Renee stopped to check in with Dylan, who was line producing a cooking show while the Wainwright mayhem swirled around him. When he saw Renee, he clicked off his headset mic. "Don't tell me, you're here for Wainwright too?"

Renee laughed. "I'm on air after Wainwright. Is that show going to be crazy?"

Dylan shook his head. "Everyone has an opinion on that show. This isn't brain surgery. Let's just put the product on the air and sell it."

Throughout the day, Renee had imagined she might meet Wainwright, either in the hall or out in the studio. She found herself rehearsing statements she might make to the diva, "You look so lovely," or "We're excited you are here and your jewelry looks fabulous." She wanted to say the right thing, the right way, make the right impression. She believed if she visualized a successful meeting, however brief, that it would become reality, just like she had envisioned a successful audition while standing in the parking lot a few months earlier.

In the host lounge, Renee spied Tanya checking her email and asked if she was ready for the debut.

"I think so."

"Did you meet her?"

"Yeah, the buyers set up a lunch meeting so we could review the lineup. I have to stop in the green room now to see her, just to make sure nothing else is new."

"Ooh, can I go with you?"

Tanya twisted her head with a wolf-like grin. "Are you a Wainwright fan?"

Renee couldn't help but laugh with embarrassment. "Well, not really. But she has created such a buzz."

Tanya turned back to her computer and closed out her email.

"I'd like to understand how she got to where she is. That's all."

"Wouldn't we all?" Tanya replied sarcastically. "Come with me."

As Tanya opened the door to the green room, Wainwright stood at the far end of the room on a cell phone with her back to everyone. She wore a leather jacket, and the sight of her made Renee feel giddy, a bit light-headed. Two extremely attractive men, dressed in suits and open collared shirts, milled around chatting quietly. A gorgeous blonde woman sat on the couch, alternately running her hand through her hair and intently typing into her phone. Renee was suddenly self-conscious about what she was wearing—a bright red, white and blue checked Duck Factory sweater that was to be the featured item in her upcoming show. She was tempted to turn and flee, but the thought of being noticed during an abrupt exit weighed on her greater than just staying frozen.

Suddenly, Wainwright's voice rose. "I don't give a fuck! I've already sold my soul for this show. Burton needs to understand I will walk after this season! That's all!" She tapped her phone shut and turned to the whole room, which now stared at her in stunned silence.

"We need to create a fucking show about the behind the scenes of the fucking show," she said with a sly ironic laugh.

Her staff tittered and the relief allowed them to return to their conversations.

"Hey there," Wainwright stepped to Tanya.

"Hi! This is Renee, she is a new show host. She is tagging along with me tonight."

"I'm on the air after your show." Renee moved to shake the celebrity's hand and was struck by how obscenely beautiful Wainwright was in person. It was as if the television cameras or tabloid photos had never captured her true essence. Wainwright smiled with feigned interest and waved her hand in a small circle before her eyes dropped down and took in Renee's sweater. For a fleeting moment, Wainwright's face grimaced like that of a toddler who had been slipped a sour candy, and after a brief uncomfortable pause, the star turned her attention back to Tanya and exclaimed, "I love how this necklace drapes on you."

As Wainwright reached out and touched Tanya's onyx beads, Renee studied the diva's face, then found herself lowering her gaze onto her supple black fitted jacket, which framed her white v-neck shirt and accentuated her perfectly rounded breasts.

"Your jacket is so beautiful," Tanya said, reaching out to touch Wainwright's sleeve.

"Isn't it? It's the second best thing they make out of lambskin." Wainwright grinned and the staff snickered at her innuendo.

Tanya unclasped her necklace and unwound it from her neck. "I adore this piece. How many times do you like to wrap it?"

"It drapes nicely any way you choose. Once it hangs down, two is mid, and three times it's like a choker."

Tanya twirled the piece and let it hang low. "It is so versatile, can go with any number of tops. I hope we have several models showing how to wear this."

"That's the money shot," Renee blurted out.

Wainwright raised her eyes at Renee. "The money shot?"

"We call it the money shot. That shot where it clicks in the customer's mind that they need it, that they decide they will pay for it."

Laughter arose from the entourage.

"Honey, where I come from, that's not the money shot. Believe me, I've performed the money shot before. That's how I got here." Wainwright reached in and lifted the necklace over Tanya's head, folded it into a choker and clasped it back on Tanya, before stepping back. Wainwright grinned and broke the silence. "The money shot? That's so cute." One of the men laughed again and Renee felt her face flush.

"If there's nothing else, we have to run," Tanya finally said mercifully. "I'll see you on the set in a few." And with that, she motioned for Renee to head out of the room.

Renee kept her distance after that. She prepared for her shift, occasionally stopped to watch Tanya and Wainwright on the television monitor, and checked sales at the producer's desk. Dylan leaned forward in his chair, his eyes darting from the sales screen to the monitor to his script. Every thirty seconds he instructed the crew.

"Let's get the quantity counter up."

"This is going to sell out. Let's get ready to move on."

A voice behind Renee called out "t-call," and the t-call light flashed on at the producer's desk. Dylan flipped a switch and relayed the message.

"We have a t-call. Hi. Who is on the air with Wainwright tonight?"

Renee admired Dylan and how he multi-tasked, juggling the show by keeping the crew moving. His phone rang and he picked it up.

Tanya and Wainwright were on air, laughing and chatting with the t-caller. Renee had turned for a moment to look out over the order entry arena when she heard Dylan explode.

"Drop the call! Drop the call!"

The t-call clicked off. A voice in the control room asked, "What was the matter?"

Tanya appeared confused. "We seemed to have lost our call. Sorry about that."

Dylan said firmly. "The t-caller said 'blow me,' right?"

Silence, then laughter swelled through the loudspeaker.

A voice from the control room corrected him. "Dude, the t-caller said 'baloney,' not 'blow me.'"

"Oh." Dylan swiveled toward Renee with red cheeks. "Well, that was embarrassing." He turned to the monitor and gave instructions to end the presentation and run a promo, and then he wrapped Tanya. As the promos rolled, he apologized into Tanya's ear. "I thought that caller said 'blow me,' but I'm told they said 'baloney.' My bad." Tanya's eyes popped wide and she covered her mouth with her hand. She glanced over at Wainwright, who was oblivious, having been swarmed by her hair and makeup artists.

Dylan flipped his key off so he was just speaking to Renee. "I must have Wainwright's home video on my mind."

At the top of the hour, Renee stood on the main stage in her Duck Factory sweater with two other color versions draped on a rack next to her. She felt relaxed on the stage now, having learned to take her time, to simply describe the details of each product. With her finger, she pointed out the stitching of the collar and the intricacy of the duck's webbed feet. She moved the second sweater to the front and repeated her description. She read the washing instructions, "Handle with care, hand wash only." She showed how the sweater hung on her, described how comfortable the 60 cotton/40 poly blend felt against her skin.

Model Cheyenne appeared at stage left in another version of the sweater, having just changed out of the hip fashion and jewelry of the *Wainwright* show. As she neared the end of her descriptions and things to talk about, Renee saw the t-call light pop on. Her producer whispered in her ear, "T-call."

"Hi and welcome to the show. Who's this?"

"This is Bobby Jo. I can't believe I'm talking on the air. I just bought this sweater." The woman's voice sounded mature and confident. "Renee, you are so adorable. I love watching you."

"Oh, Bobby Jo, that is so sweet. Thank you so much. I'm just trying my best to learn it all. Which color did you buy?"

"I bought the baby blue version. "

Renee swapped out the blue sweater to the front. The

camera zoomed in on a tight shot of the appliqué and Renee peered out over the order entry arena. Wainwright and her entourage had come out from backstage, carving a path to the green room. Dozens of order entry operators stood and poked their heads out of their cubicles, trying to catch a glimpse of the young celebrity.

"Bobby Jo, did you watch the Wainwright show?" Renee asked.

"Actually, I just caught the end of it. But I can't pull off that look, dear. This is more my style. I believe a woman has to know where to draw the line."

Renee's heart warmed and she smiled. "Well Bobby Jo, I am confident this color will be perfect for you. It's good you know what you can wear. I'm just learning myself it's so important to feel comfortable in your own skin."

"Girl, I couldn't have said it any better."

"I hope you enjoy this sweater, Bobby Jo, and I really hope we have a chance to talk again."

SEVEN

....

AMERICAN DREAM

"I've been working on this product line for two years now," Megan told us. "I've invested my life in this." Megan was the linens buyer, a tightly wound middle-aged woman who wore rimmed glasses and boxy dress suits. We were standing backstage, at a table piled high with multi-colored sheet sets, down comforters and fluffy pillows.

Three of us formed a circle around Megan. There was my favorite producer Dottie, my least favorite show host Calabrese, and me, lowly production assistant Jake.

"My boss is holding my feet to the fire on this launch," Megan said skittishly. "We've had so many bumps in the road, and of course, I'm the fall person if this doesn't work. It's too easy to go from hero to zero in this place."

Dottie smiled sympathetically. She had warned me about Megan earlier in the day. "She used to be the best buyer in the building, her sales numbers were through the roof. But then she hit some rough patches. I think she's lost her mojo."

"It's important we get the positioning right," Megan continued now. "This is our own brand. We've trademarked American Dream. You can't find these sheets at Target or Nordstrom. You can only find the American Dream here at Shoplandia. It's all about luxury. It's about staying in bed. Something I would like to do more often." Her joke fell flat, but she grinned nervously, bearing Chiclet sized white teeth.

"Wasn't this show bumped from the schedule once?" Calabrese asked.

Megan closed her eyes and shook her head abruptly. "Yeah, the goods were on the slow boat from China, but there were issues going through customs."

Dottie looked at me and pursed her lips. She had explained earlier that Megan's fall from grace began with the infamous vacuum-sealed storage bags debacle. The bags are used to store fluffy down comforters for the summer. For our on air demonstration, we bagged a giant stuffed panda, then inserted the vacuum nozzle and sucked the air out. The visual was amazing, the panda deflated to near nothing, the bag now easily stackable. According to Dottie, we sold hundreds of thousands of these bags, and customers packed and stacked their fluffy comforters tightly on closet shelves. But by autumn, the suction leaked out of the allegedly defective bags. The comforters expanded, the contents swelled like in that horror movie *The Blob* and the resulting pressure splintered and popped shelves. Customers were unable to pull out their winter bedding and some had to have new closet shelves installed in their homes.

Now, Calabrese smelled blood in the water. "Wasn't there another issue too?"

Megan huffed as though Calabrese had hung out her dirty laundry. "On first pass, the American Dream comforters didn't pass quality assurance. But we got that issue resolved."

Calabrese picked up a pillow and flipped it over. "What happened?"

Megan bit her lip and looked down at her notepad, Calabrese shot a wink at Dottie. I'd noticed that some hosts and producers occasionally liked watching certain buyers squirm, like predators circling a wounded animal. It was awful to watch, though as a relative newbie, I felt a guilty pleasure in listening to the banter.

Megan was all wound up now and spoke in bursts of words. "Well, we had to rework all the inventory because the packages labeled as king size held only full size comforters."

"Yikes! That would have been a problem," Dottie quipped.

Megan fired a look at Dottie and frowned. "Well, we caught it. So that's good."

Calabrese turned to Dottie. "Can you imagine customers ordering American Dream sheets and they don't fit the bed."

"That would have been just awful." Dottie lowered her gaze and grinned.

"So, anyway," Megan inserted flatly, "You can order the American Dream for only $78.99. The American Dream is exclusive to Shoplandia. Did I already say that?"

The final thirty minutes leading up to the debut of the show were a blur. The sets and props guys loaded two full size beds onto a set wedge that would be spun around under the lights, and those beds needed to be layered with American Dream sheets, comforters, and pillows. I jumped up on the stage and made the beds with the efficiency of a hotel maid and the effectiveness of a Marine camp sergeant.

During the tucking and smoothing, I half-listened on my headset, my mind preoccupied with preparing the show. The sheets were tight, the pillows fluffed, the headboards tightened. We stepped back five minutes before the show and agreed the set was ready. I jumped down off the bedroom wedge and walked to the side of the set. Show host Tanya had wrapped up her three-hour shift, urging customers to call in for the few remaining rolo link bracelets, and then she said her good-byes. I stood ready at the button, waiting for Tanya to step off so I could rotate the set.

"Can someone tell backstage they are going to be live on that overhead camera," Clancy asked through headsets. He had framed a shot in the preview monitor that showed the whole backstage area, where Calabrese stood reviewing his notes. Nearby, a model was looking over a table filled with neatly aligned shoes. I didn't shout a warning. Just as the camera went live, Calabrese reached over to the model's ass and rubbed it. She turned, fuming, and slapped him hard across the face. The thwack sounded like a slab of meat thumping a granite counter. She spun and exited the frame, and Calabrese actually smiled.

"You know you were live on air?" I called out.

Calabrese turned with a perplexed look and I pointed at the camera overhead. The change in his fleshy face, from a sardonic smile to a grimace of comprehension is forever imprinted on my mind. Calabrese buttoned his suit jacket and picked up his cards off the prep table. His face had turned to stone.

"Rotating set!" I shouted and pushed the button. The gears began to grind against their will and the set lurched forward.

"Does he know he was live on air?" a voice asked on headsets.

I flipped my key on. "No, he didn't, but he knows now."

Calabrese walked by without looking at me, but his nostrils flared like a bull's. His face was drained of color. He stepped up to the set as if he was walking to the gallows. "Dead man walking," someone uttered over headsets. At the center of the bedroom set, he stopped on his mark flanked by the neatly made beds. Calabrese stared at the camera waiting for a cue that would never come again.

Dylan announced into headsets, "Line up your promo spots. I don't think we'll be live again for quite some time." When I glanced down at the producer's desk, Dylan had a phone to each ear.

A tsunami of telephone calls flooded order entry. The

operators stood in their cubicles, looking for guidance on how to answer sensitive questions and nasty complaints.

Moments later, a voice from the control room called out, "Red One."

Red One - *slang, a term used to notify the entire broadcast crew that suits are in the studio or the control room. Red One acts as a signal to straighten oneself up, watch one's language and behave in a professional manner.*

Tanya sat on the producer's desk with her back to the set, holding her mic pack in her hands. It was an odd few seconds. I glanced up at the control room window and the crew stood shoulder to shoulder, noses pressed against the glass.

From the side of the set, I watched the commotion brewing at the producer's desk as Dylan chatted with the suits. All the while, Calabrese stood under the lights looking at the camera as if mentally willing it to go live.

Finally, Dylan spoke into Calabrese's ear, "We need you to step backstage."

Calabrese didn't flinch at first. The suits moved through the backstage door. As if breaking a silent tension in the arena, Calabrese put his head down and exited stage right without looking at anyone. At that moment, I knew he would never be on air again.

None of us looked him in the eye. Calabrese was a man who had brought on his own suffering. He stepped backstage and out toward the producer's desk, unbuttoning his dress shirt to remove his mic. He didn't acknowledge the suits until he nearly bumped into them. Dylan just kept his eyes trained on the monitors.

Dottie and Megan were now chatting with Tanya, trying to recap all the salient sales points of the American Dream product line in sixty seconds. Megan's arms were waving and her voice occasionally shrieked on key points. "The American Dream is exclusive."

Dylan prodded us on headsets, "We have to start the show. We've wasted too much time."

Two suits appeared backstage and asked me where they could find the model. I walked them to the dressing room. The door was ajar and the model sat talking on her cell phone. The suits stepped into her room and pulled the door shut behind them. A melancholy had settled over the place like a fog. On headsets, we only spoke when it was necessary to keep the show moving. Up on stage, Tanya ran through different colors of a sheet set and explained how the line of American Dream linens is tightly woven together.

Two weeks later, I heard rumors that Megan no longer worked at Shoplandia. Word was that she had started muttering unintelligibly at her desk, and then began wandering through the aisles of the offices, incoherently babbling such phrases as "the bar is too damn high," and "it isn't my fault." We heard whispers that some buyers had stood to watch her antics over their cubicle walls as she shouted, "it's broadcasting's fault," or "I can't be held responsible for everything."

In the cafeteria checkout line, I overheard a young assistant buyer confide to her friend, "It was so horrible. I hid under my desk because I didn't know what she would do." Her friend yanked napkins out of the metal holder. "Well, on the bright side, there's gonna be a new opening." Someone else told me that two security guards apparently calmed Megan down in the atrium that day and steered her to a small conference room. As the story was told to me, her husband arrived a short time later and escorted her to his waiting car in the roundabout, and she was never heard from again.

....

EIGHT

COVERT'S THIRD RULE

Most people don't take initiative because they haven't been told to do so.

NINE

BACKTIMING

Dylan sits on the edge of his seat at the producer's desk, waiting for the sharks. At 7:24 a.m., while sipping his turbo-coffee and reviewing item quantities, a voice-mail from his boss warns that a group of potential investors will be touring the live television studio this afternoon, so the space must be in "tip top shape." Dylan had hoped for a quiet day. Although today is Thursday, it is actually Dylan's Monday, his first day back after a few restful days where he slept in, watched television and neglected his laundry. As he deletes his voicemail, he regrets that he hasn't ironed his dress shirt.

Sure enough, as he plugs in his headset, his nostrils pick up a scent. The producer's desk smells of Lysol. His first show, *Rubies and Sapphires*, has been moved to a tiny auxiliary studio while the maintenance crew sweeps the main studio with whirring vacuums.

Dylan leads the hosts and broadcast crew through the morning with ease and grace. In moments such as this, as the live show unfolds smoothly, Dylan imagines he is conducting an orchestra. Show host Karen is in good spirits and her voice is well-tuned. The control room provides the rhythm. Clancy is operating the big board and he is a natural, experienced and in sync with Karen, one step ahead, anticipating her next thought and move, as if leading her in a dance. Although Dylan is aware they are simply selling an endless stream of items (this morning includes ionizers, hand creams, hammocks and a wood smoker), he appreciates the harmony of a well-produced show in contrast to his personal life, which has recently resembled a banging of metallic trash cans accompanied by a toddler harmonizing on a kazoo.

He traces the beginning of his funk to the moment Emme dumped him five months ago. Since then, he continually notices his knees creaking. He pulls small tufts of hair out of his brush in the mornings, and he steadily naps on gray winter days. He's two months shy of his thirty-sixth birthday. Pinned to the fridge in his apartment, his calendar only notes his shifts at the shopping network. He hasn't penciled in anything with friends or family in months.

And then yesterday, Dylan's father called from a Florida hospital. The old man had inadvertently driven a golf cart into the sand trap on the 13th hole, tumbling out and breaking his clavicle, and was now being told by some kid in a white lab coat that he may never play golf again. Dylan's father even put the doctor on the phone, who surprised Dylan with his Bronx tough-guy accent as he explained, "As you age, the healing process takes longer. One may never recover to a previous level of health."

At 1:32 p.m., two men in suits hover behind Dylan as

he monitors the live show. He is weary, but he focuses on the screen and speaks authoritatively into headsets. "Let's get a quantity counter, starting at 900."

"Copy that," the graphics operator chirps in response.

Dylan also has a phone to his right ear, half-listening as the Vice President of Planning shuffles papers, trying to decide what item to add to next hour's show since the Today's Special sold out moments before. Up on stage, country legend Willie Nelson chats with host Brandon Braxton about the country singer's new CD, which Shoplandia is selling for $19.99 plus shipping and handling charges of $3.99.

"How about you call me back once you know the item," Dylan says.

"Uh, it'll just be a minute."

The other line rings. "I have to put you on hold."

Behind Dylan, the two suits whisper back and forth. They remind Dylan of the movie *Men in Black*. They are all business. He turns and glances, wondering who the hell they are. Through headsets, Clancy asks, "What are we cutting this hour? Or are you running on Buke-time?"

Buke-time, *n. - The act of ending a show late, generally four minutes past the hour or later, due to inadequately back-timing the show and trying to slip in an extra product. Buke-time is named in honor of fellow producer Dan Bukowski, who is notorious for running his shows late.*

The clock reads 1:35 p.m. Willie has another four min-

minutes. 1:39 p.m. Working backwards from the top of the hour, Dylan slots eight minutes for the lawn ornament, due to air last. He determines he can squeeze in three more items: the battery operated callus remover, the gourmet crab cakes and the lawn ornaments.

"We'll cut the self-feeding cat bowl," he informs the crew, and then decides he'd better answer the phone, which is on its fifth ring.

"Producer's desk."

"Hey, it's the front desk. We have a fellow by the name of Dean Chrone here, says he is a guest in the next hour."

"Who?"

"Dean Chrone. Claims he flew in from Michigan."

Dylan shuffles through his papers to see if he overlooked a Chrone in the next hour, but he's not listed. Up on stage, Brandon asks Willie Nelson what new music he admires and Willie replies, "I really enjoy this young band out of L.A." Willie breaks into "Panic Switch," a song dominating the airwaves recently.

"I don't know what to tell you. I don't have the guy listed. Find out who his buyer is and ask them." Dylan hangs up the phone just as one of the men leans over and says softly, "I think we better get off this song."

Dylan swirls around so quickly that both men in their pressed suits step back in surprise. "Who are you guys?"

"We're from legal," the shorter man says.

"We don't have legal clearance for Willie to play this song."

Dylan chuckles. "You're telling me this now?" He pivots back to the monitor and closes his eyes, thinking through his options before flipping the switch to communicate with the control room. "We need to fade out of this song and go to a break. Clancy, do you have some promos lined up?"

"Sure thing boss."

"Let's bump out now." Dylan flips a second switch so he is in Brandon's ear. "We have to pop out of this song."

From the stage, Brandon raises his hands and mouths the words, "What the fuck? Are you kidding me?"

Dylan raises his hand and points his finger behind him. "These guys are from legal."

The technical director punches up a wide shot of the studio from a high fixed camera, producer's desk included, as Willie plays his soulful version of the hit. It looks like a security camera shot has captured Dylan being apprehended by two CIA agents.

"We'll run two spots and move on to the callus remover. Let's rotate that set."

As the first promo spot rolls, Brandon steps to the edge of the stage. He frowns and shakes his head, taps his mic to make sure it's not on, and then yells, "We never said goodbye to Willie."

Dylan turns to talk to the suits, to tell them this isn't the way to run a television show, that it would be wise to chat with the producer *before* the show actually begins, not in the middle of the damned song, but they have vanished. The phone rings and the caller I.D. reveals it's the Vice President of Planning. Dylan picks up the phone.

"What's the item number."

"L-5043. Pricing is coming around."

"Do you know a Chrone?"

"Chrone?"

"Some guy at the front desk. Says he is on the air next hour. He's not on my sheet."

"I got nothing."

"I told them to call his buyer. Gotta go." After hanging up, Dylan clicks the switch to talk to the control room. Up on stage, the production assistant corrals the pouting Brandon so they can rotate the set. Willie's manager, an inked, dreadlocked woman wearing a George Jones t-shirt, leads the legend backstage.

"The living room set is ready?"

"Aye aye sir," one of the production assistants confirms. The set lurches and rotates one quarter of a turn before grinding to a stop and Brandon steps on his mark. On headsets, the technical director exclaims, "Here we go, you're up." Brandon holds a plastic contraption that looks like either a curler or a tampon, which he rubs over the palm of his hand. Dylan flips a switch and reminds Brandon to solicit for testimonials.

The dreadlocked manager navigates Willie over to Dylan's desk, and Dylan whiffs the sweet smell of cannabis. "How'd we do?" the manager asks. Dylan is struck for a moment, staring at Willie, who has his guitar strapped upside down across his back. Dylan reaches out and they shake hands. "I'm Dylan. Nice to meet you." Underneath his light gray stubble, Willie has a face full of crags and the biggest blue eyes Dylan has ever seen.

"Nice to meet you," Willie responds. "Nice name."

Dylan grins and studies Willie's blue eyes, the shade of a cornflower. Calm. Serene. Content.

"Let's look here." Dylan points out the numbers to the hippie manager. "We sold 1743 units for $35,000. Not bad for this time of day." She points out the numbers to Willie and he nods politely.

On headsets, the control room beckons. "Dylan, we just got a change form for a new item being added next hour. There's a guest, Chrone."

"Copy that," Dylan replies.

"How long does it take for a callus to grow?" Clancy asks.

"I don't understand how this thing even works," the audio operator responds.

"Are calluses bad? Hey Dylan, are calluses a bad thing?"

Dylan, trying to eavesdrop on Willie and the manager, replies, "I'm off headsets for a minute."

Willie listens to the manager as she dissects the columns on the sales screen. Dylan envisions the tour bus parked along the curb outside. Sometime in the next fifteen minutes Willie will climb those steps and hit the road again.

"Where's your tour heading next?" Dylan asks.

"We're playing in Poughkeepsie tomorrow night," the manager responds.

Willie and his manager look so relaxed, not a care in the world. Dylan has the urge to say, *take me with you, please.*

A voice from behind interrupts, "How about a picture?"

It's Tamika, who works with the order entry operators. With her arms out, she motions for Dylan to step closer to Willie. "Do you mind?"

Willie just smiles as they pose. But then, in a moment before the flash pops, Dylan sees Emme walking by, giving the deluxe studio tour to the well-dressed investors. The flutter in his chest drops sharply as he notices Emme's slight paunch. She's pregnant. Emme, his ex-girlfriend, is going to have a child.

Flash!

"Okay, I got it," Tamika exclaims. She clicks through to check the image and grins.

"Thanks again." The manager reaches out her hand, which Dylan absent-mindedly shakes.

Dylan's breath knots up as though a pane of glass, lodged in his stomach, has been shattered with a hammer. *Please, really, take me with you,* he thinks, but all he can croak out is a weak "goodbye." He slowly lowers himself in his chair, and picks up the headset, but doesn't put it on. Staring at the digital clock, his stomach churns, a wave of nausea unfolds. Emme, surrounded by sharks, disappears through the backstage door. Has she made this public? His fingers count the months. Five months since she cut him from her life, quickly, cleanly, painfully.

It happened in the cafeteria, late in the day, and she had sliced him from her life with a surgical precision.

Emme had suggested they meet for coffee and she led him to the quiet corner by the window. They had been together for six months, and he had come to believe she was the one who would save him. As she sat down across from him, she cupped her hands and swept breadcrumbs off the table. Outside, rain appeared to weep from the trees and puddles dotted the walkway.

He wanted to discuss their options, but Emme had stopped him abruptly, professionally. He felt as though an HR manager was terminating him. Stumbling out of the cafeteria though, he hung onto a single word she had uttered, "hiatus," and in his mind, these letters formed of a thin string between them. From within this word had sprung hope, as though she just called for a temporary parting. In the times he thought of Emme since, he sometimes caught his lips moving, and in his breath, he had repeated the word like a mantra, hiatus.

A hand touches his shoulder and he jumps. Tamika says, "Dylan, we have a t-call, and the control room is asking for you."

Dylan nods slowly. "Thanks." He has absentmindedly wrapped the cord of his headset tightly around his index finger, causing his finger to swell and turn purple. He unwraps the cord and places his headset on, hits a button and is in Brandon's ear. "T-call."

He flips another switch. "Sorry guys, what's up?"

Basil asks, "Will we have time for the Air Purifier?"

"Uh, no." He checks his list of items. "Crab cakes next, lawn ornament will end the show."

Emme can't be more than three months pregnant. A

few weeks ago, he overheard voices in the control room mention that they saw her getting cozy at Side Bar with some guy from finance. He hadn't felt it appropriate to ask questions, to clarify. At the time, he thought it was possible he had misheard, or maybe it was a different Emme.

Someone asks through headsets if the callus remover works.

"A callus is better than a blister, right?"

"If you don't callus, you blister."

"Popping a blister feels good."

Annoyed by the banter, Dylan sets his headset on the desk and runs his hands through his hair. So many times he debated calling Emme, trying to determine if they could give it a second go. He's not been able to walk away, but he's lost his confidence and hasn't stated his case. One night, he may or may not have left her a voicemail after coming home from the Square Bar filled with liquid courage. His life was ticking away, and being with Emme had given him a sense of rolling back the clock.

A yellow paper floats down on the desk in front of him. Marvin from the planning department is walking away, but turns and waves with a quick smile. Dylan reviews the change form: a Dean Chrone has been added to the next hour.

He flips his key. "Did everyone see the change form. Third item next hour is now L3056 - Chrone Hair Restoration?" He listens for acknowledgement from the control room and the floor crew, but a shriek and sudden booming echo through the studio, as if a brawl has erupted.

Senior show host Frankie Mack darts out from backstage. He glances back over his shoulder with such a panicked face that Dylan jumps up, half expecting a pack of wild dogs to be in pursuit. Frankie's crimson face clashes with his gray pinstriped suit. His mouth is dropped open in horror as though he has just witnessed death itself.

"Dylan, what the hell is going on? I'm not selling that spray on hair crap. No way."

"What's the matter?"

Through headsets, a voice declares, "Hey, check this video out. Put this in preview so Dylan can see."

"That's the matter!" Frankie points at the preview monitor. A semi-bald head glistens under the light. Disposable paper designed in the shape of a horseshoe, or perhaps a small toilet seat, is gently taped on the man's noggin. A disembodied hand uses an aerosol can to spray in the bald spot. Bold text flies onto the screen, "No more comb-overs!" The video cuts to the face of a middle-aged male model, who confidently smiles as though all his women problems have been solved.

"Oh! My! God!" A voice from the control room gasps.

"This Chrone guy is crazy," Frankie says. From backstage, a giant, well-tanned ogre emerges wildly, shaking an aerosol can. Every few seconds, the man turns the aerosol can upside down in his beefy hand as if he's flipping over an hourglass. The man is grotesquely large and has a full healthy head of wavy brown hair. Chrone appears to be on a mission and he heads straight toward Dylan. Frankie twists toward his nemesis, but leans back and sternly warns, "Stay away from me." Half of Frankie's own bald spot has been sprayed. Frankie turns back toward Dylan. "This guy snuck up on me and started painting the back of my head. The guy thinks he's freaking Banksy!"

Chrone grins and rattles the can. "We need to finish your spot Frankie, you can't go on air like that." Frankie steps behind Dylan, using the producer as his shield. "This is an Armani suit. You ruin it and I'll sue you."

As Dylan raises his hand to halt the monster, he takes in how small his own knuckles appear on this man's chest. "Hold on a second."

Chrone stares down at Dylan like he's noticing him for the first time, and his face folds into a question mark. "Spin around a moment." The man actually steps around Dylan like a barber, admiring Dylan's bald spot. "You could use a bit of this yourself." He quickly gets off a shot at the back of Dylan's head. Dylan swipes at Chrone's arm and the aerosol can careens into a row of order entry operators, nearly striking Angela, an elderly ex-nun, as she takes an order on the phone.

"What the hell are you doing?" Chrone's grin turns sour.

"Don't you put a mark on me!"

The operators stand and stare as Chrone heads into order entry to retrieve his spray can. Dylan runs his hand through his hair and examines his palm, which looks as though he has rubbed it in shoe polish. He contemplates calling security.

"Dylan. Are we staying on this?" Clancy asks.

Dylan checks the clock and the sales. "Let's wrap this. We have crab cakes next. Right?"

"Ready to rotate to the kitchen."

Dylan flips a switch and speaks into Brandon's ear. "Wrap."

Frankie has stepped to Dylan's other side so he can keep his eye on Chrone.

"Frankie, go ahead backstage. I'll talk to this guy."

He hears the set rotate as Chrone approaches with slumped shoulders. The pungent aroma of crab and Old Bay seasoning fills the studio.

"I'm sorry, I get a bit over excited," Chrone sighs. He looks like a big mope now, and Dylan almost feels sorry for the bastard.

"Listen, you need Frankie Mack, or any host for that matter, on your side. If Frankie is mad, that won't do you any good. I suggest going backstage and telling Frankie that you're sorry."

The deflated goon nods. As he motions to head backstage, Dylan lifts the aerosol can from his hand. "It will be better if you approach Frankie without this."

Dylan holds the can to his nose. Smells like shoe polish. He drops it in the trash can and examines the screen. Braxton stands behind a stovetop wearing an apron and flipping crab cakes. "Have you eaten these crab cakes? If so, give us a call. These just smell delicious. I can't wait to eat a few. They are great by themselves or as sandwiches."

An order entry operator taps Dylan on the shoulder. "Sir, we're getting calls about the graphics." Dylan reads the panel on the left side of the screen: *L-5937 - Gourmet Crap Cakes.*

"Damn it, drop the graphics!"

"Why? What's up?" Clancy says as the graphics dissolve.

"Crap cakes? Seriously, crap cakes? Who's doing graphics?"

"Oh my gosh. I'm so sorry. Give me a minute." It's the voice of Margie. She must have returned from her break. Dylan makes a note to double-check each graphic. Margie is undependable, flighty, even on her best days.

Dylan gets in Braxton's ear. "Graphic error. Be right back up. T-call." He looks at the clock, thinking he has to get to this lawn ornament and it's already 1:49. He thinks of Emme and feels a surge in his gut before reminding himself to focus.

A woman appears by Dylan's side wearing a gardening apron. She is in her sixties, with red hair and glasses, an endearing smile, and she is cradling a brown bunny made of mud. "Do I need to get mic'd up?"

Dylan glances at the woman, then at his listing of items in the show. A guest named Dorothy Macadoo is scheduled for the lawn ornament. In headsets, he hears Braxton talking with a female caller.

"I guess you do," Dylan says. "I'm sorry. I missed that." He reaches for a microphone and asks, "Is this your company?"

"Why yes, it surely is. Macadoo's Dung Ornaments."

She is right out of a Norman Rockwell painting, with a sweet singsong voice. She carefully rests the bunny on his desk.

"Dung ornament?" He studies the brown rabbit sitting next to his papers. He pokes at it with his middle finger. The ornament is firm.

"They are made out of horse dung," Mrs. Macadoo explains. "Horse dung is the world's best natural fertilizer. Our slogan is 'Our ornaments look good in your garden, and they make your garden look good!'"

For Christ's sake, this woman turns shit into art. Dylan slides the mic onto her blouse and tells the control room it's time to wrap. He gets in Braxton's ear and does the same. After closing the segment, Braxton grabs a small plate with a crab cake and walks to the edge of the set so they can rotate behind him. "This is so good. What's next?" He lifts his fork and takes another bite.

"The ornament made of horse crap."

Braxton stops mid-chew, but eventually smiles, finishes chewing and yells out, "And my boss told me I couldn't sell shit."

Mrs. Macadoo giggles as Dylan leads her up to the set. When the camera returns live, Braxton and Mrs. Macadoo stand together on the patio set with huge smiles.

"You've heard the saying if life gives you lemons, make lemonade," Braxton exclaims. "Well, we have an extraordinary artist here who has done something similar. This is a testament to American entrepreneurial success." They run through the choices—a bunny, a gopher or a squirrel—all lined up on the table. Mrs. Macadoo explains how she started collecting and sculpting horse patties in the countryside, and now has grown the business to include a team of "horse patty picker uppers."

Dylan quips through headsets, "Sounds like my job description," and he hears a few chuckles.

Out the stage right door, Emme reappears with the potential investors and leads them to an opening where they have a clear view of the producer's desk. Dylan glances over, waiting to see if she will wave, but she is engrossed in conversation, surrounded by the sharks. The men are wearing finely tailored suits on their athletic frames and their slick hair is only out-shined by their charismatic self-confidence. Emme glances over and raises her hand in a quick wave. Dylan provides a courtesy wave back before turning toward the monitors. He recalls Buke joking about how these executive tours stop and stare at the producer's desk. "It's like we're animals on display at the zoo." Emme is just within earshot, vividly explaining how the producer manipulates time, stretches out certain items and cuts others short. She describes this in a way that makes Dylan feel as though he must be a wizard.

He turns to the monitor and his mind wanders back to one rainy afternoon in Emme's apartment. They rented a dopey movie and watched it together nestled on her sofa. The movie didn't hold their interest so they made out under the covers and ordered Chinese food. Emme was proficient with her chopsticks but he just stuck with his fork and he recalled a moment when she

looked up and had a small fleck, a sesame seed, stuck between her teeth. He had smiled, almost laughed, but caught himself. He thought it would loosen on it's own, surely the sesame seed would work its way out when she bit into her fortune cookie.

"T-call," Tamika tells the crew on headsets.

"T-call," Dylan reiterates to Braxton.

The sesame seed did not dislodge until Emme noticed it while in the bathroom and removed it herself. When she returned, she asked if he had noticed it, and he said he hadn't. She studied him for a moment as if he was a stranger. His heart plummets now, something so silly, wedged between them, and he wishes he could have a do-over for that moment. A sudden urge rises in him. He craves a breath of fresh air, a glimpse of natural sunlight after being stuck in this windowless studio for seven hours.

"Clancy, can you give me a break at the top of the hour?"

"I think I can do that, boss."

As he flips his switch off, he senses a warm touch on his shoulder. He turns to see Emme standing over him. She has broken off from the men in suits who stand clustered in the distance. "Hey, sorry to bother you."

Dylan slides his headset down around his neck and looks up into her eyes. She is as lovely as ever.

"I'm giving this tour," she nods over her shoulder, "and one guy keeps asking me the same question."

"What is it?"

"He wants to know, it's silly really, he wants to know,

does the stage only rotate one way? Can the stage rotate backwards?"

Dylan gulps. It takes him a moment to catch his breath. "Unfortunately, no. The stage only rotates one way."

"That's what I thought. Sorry to bother you. Thanks." Emme pivots as if to return to the group, but she swirls back to Dylan and leans in so close he senses her breath in his ear. "I want to be discreet about this, but I feel like you should know."

"What's up?" He leans back to see her face, but she leans in more.

"You have a brown smudge on the back of your head. On your bald spot."

Dylan bites his lip as his eyes well up. He forces a grin. "Thanks. I appreciate it." He twists toward the monitor and nods his head.

"Hi Emme." Clancy appears behind them, twirling his headset cable.

"Hey Clancy," Emme responds.

"Hey boss, are you ready for a break?"

"Oh yeah. Definitely."

"I have to go," Emme says. "They have to be back in the boardroom. Tight schedule today."

As she walks back to the group of investors, Clancy watches her. "Boss, I don't know how you let her slip away."

In the men's bathroom, Dylan stops at the mirror and studies his face, lowers his chin, and glances at his head.

He runs a paper towel under warm water and wipes it through his hair. A clump of brown paint smears the towel. He dips his index finger into the brown glob, and after a moment of contemplation, runs his finger under both eyes, marking his skin as if preparing for battle. He examines himself in the mirror for a few seconds before folding the paper towel and scrubbing his entire face clean.

In front of the building, the sky is as blue as ice. The breeze feels good against his clammy skin and his wet scalp. Willie's bus sits along the curb of the outer parking lot. He admires the road warriors milling about smoking their cigarettes. As he watches the men disappear into the bus, Willie included, Dylan ponders their life on the road, and wonders how they sustain the courage to keep moving forward. The door mechanically shuts with a low hiss and the bus glides away from the curb, heading for open water.

TEN

....

ROCKWELL

On his final overnight as a production assistant, Jake Meecham wiped down a red Kitchen-Aid mixer at seven a.m. while show host Henry sat on the product table next to 35 multi-colored teddy bears artfully arranged in pairs.

"I just don't think I'm going to see daylight ever again," Henry sulked. "I'm beginning to feel like a vampire."

Jake clipped a bowl into the canary yellow mixer. "No. Don't say that."

"Since they brought in this new host, I've been moved to overnights indefinitely. I like Renee, nothing against her, but I've been here for five years. My numbers must not be cutting it. Women want to buy from women."

It was all a bit awkward. Henry knew about Jake's pending promotion to coordinating producer, had congratulated him the week before. Now, Jake just nodded at Henry's misfortune. All he could do was commiserate. Jake and the crew liked Henry, an upstanding guy with a wife and a kindergarten-aged daughter at home. Henry didn't give anyone trouble and the crew knew they could count on him to give a positive spin when the suits swept through the studio.

"I'm sure you'll see daylight again soon," Jake reassured him.

Through headsets, Clancy asked, "Jake, are you in for Duke's Tavern? We'll buy you a beer to celebrate your last overnight?"

Jake clicked on his mic. "A celebration? Sure. I'm in. You do know I'll be back on this shift, right?"

Henry's puppy eyes widened. "Are you guys going out? At 8 a.m.?"

"Yeah, we're going to Duke's." Henry watched as Jake moved to the lime green mixer with the rag. Silence inflated the space and Jake knew he was waiting for an invitation. "Do you want to join us?"

"That might be just what I need," Henry replied with a grin. "Thanks buddy."

Henry followed Jake over to Duke's, a little blue-collar hole in the wall set over by the train tracks and a cluster of warehouses. They parked across the street in a dirt lot. Jake hopped out of his car and waited for Henry, who sat in his Acura looking around as if he might change his mind. After a moment, he climbed out of his car and followed Jake to the front door.

Inside, it was dark and peanut shells littered the floor. A bearded guy in a Communist cap stood in the corner of the bar, fondling the paddles of a classic pinball machine emblazoned with the band members of Kiss in full makeup and leather chaps. The air chimed with bells and the occasional tinny refrain of "Dr. Love."

Two postal workers sat at the far end of the bar, each with a beer mug and an empty shot glass. The dive hadn't been updated in decades. It sported wood paneled walls and a floor checked with orange and green peeling tiles. A small shaft of light shone through a blocked glass window.

"This is the greatest place." Henry took in the view. "I never even knew this was here."

Audio operator Melissa walked over. "Henry, I didn't know you were coming. Jake let you in on our little secret, eh?" The bartender placed an upside down shot glass on the bar in front of Clancy, who responded by raising his glass to salute a postal worker.

"The glamorous world of television," Jake quipped.

"Where dreams come to die," Clancy joked, before tipping back a beer.

Melissa and Clancy asked Jake about his promotion and the rumors that he had a new girlfriend. Melissa wanted to know everything, where Pam worked, went to school, who she might know.

"I met her at a bar in Sea Isle. We ended up dancing most of the night, and then we went out for pancakes the next morning."

The implications were there, but he kept much of the details to himself. He didn't mention that he had seen Pam earlier that day as she sat with her girlfriends on the beach. He had just planted his chair into the sand and there she was, her feet stretched out in the surf. He didn't disclose that he thought she was out of his league, and when she stood and sauntered back to her towel, her jet-black hair cascading over her shoulders, he had held his breath as if hypnotized.

But when Jake said the words "Pam's beach house," the crew whooped as if he'd hit the jackpot.

"It's just as easy to love a rich girl as it is to love a poor girl," Clancy said.

A grinning Melissa slapped Clancy on the arm. "Oh, cut that out."

All this focus on Jake's good fortune made him squirm. He thought he should clarify the house was just a summer rental, packed with twenty-somethings, that they were actually sleeping on a futon pad in a walk-in closet, but then Melissa steered the conversation away.

"Henry, how long have you been married?"

"Oh, me? Nine years?" Henry arched his eyes toward the ceiling. "Is that right?" His fingers flashed out as he counted the years. "Nine years next month."

Clancy laughed as Henry blushed. "It's easy to lose track, you know?"

"Are you happy?" Melissa asked. Jake drew in a breath at the directness of her question. Henry didn't blink, but he pondered this carefully, as if answering honestly was a test he must pass. "You know, most of the time I am. She's a darling girl, Anne is. A bit on the straight and narrow, which has been good for me. Sure, we have our moments. I'm sure all couples do."

But there was a quiver in Henry's voice, and Jake felt a sudden wave of agitation. The crew sipped their beers silently, and then Melissa re-ignited the conversation. "So I have a question. Is Willie Nelson coming back soon? I can't believe I missed him."

A short time later, Henry made new friends with two women who had taken seats at the end of the bar. They looked to be in their sixties, hardened by time and drink. Henry started talking them up, and he was an interesting sight still in his blue blazer with a loosened tie hanging from his neck. He stood between the two women, with an arm around each one like they were long lost girl-friends. "You may have seen me on TV..."

Next thing Jake knew, Henry had disappeared. He figured the show host had gone home, but when they walked out to their cars, squinting in the bright late morning sun, they saw Henry's Acura still parked outside. Henry was slumped across his steering wheel. The temperature was rising and this wasn't the neighborhood to be asleep in your car.

"What should we do?" Clancy asked.

"Did he drink that much?"

"I saw him doing shots with those women."

"Really?" Jake opened the Acura door and the odor of bourbon smacked his nostrils. "I don't know where he lives."

"I do." Clancy said. "I drove him home once when his car was in the shop."

Exhaustion had set in. Jake just wanted to be in his little apartment, with the shades shut and the air conditioner cranked, dead to the world for a few hours.

"How about if I scoot him over and drive him home," Jake suggested. "Can you show me the way? Bring me back to my car?"

"Sure."

It took a few minutes, but they lifted semi-conscious Henry into the backseat. Jake slipped behind the wheel and adjusted the seat. They made their way out of the borough, took one short stint on the highway, which emptied them off at the next exit. It was a glorious day, though Jake's eyelids were drooping. He cranked up the radio. Clancy navigated toward a fairly new cookie-cutter development, down a street with look-alike aspirational houses, miniaturized versions of mansions. As Jake neared Henry's cul de sac, he counted six or seven cars parked along the circle. Clancy pointed to a house that looked to be having visitors. After thinking through his options, there really was no turning back. Jake pulled into the driveway that led to a garage at the side of the house. The garage door was open but Jake didn't pull in. As he cut the engine, the sound of kids playing in the backyard came alive. Jake nudged Henry in the backseat. "Hey buddy, we're home."

Henry rolled over and groaned, spittle rolled down his cheek. "Thank you. I'm just taking a nappy now." He shifted his weight but didn't rise. Jake rolled down the window and turned the car off but left the keys in the ignition. Inside the garage was a screen door leading into the house. The thought of having to deal with Henry's wife did not appeal to Jake at that moment. As soon as a shadow appeared at the screen, Jake sprinted down the driveway, not even looking over his shoulder, and hopped into Clancy's car. As they pulled away, Jake finally twisted and watched through the rear window.

"I think they are having some kind of playgroup."

"Welcome to the neighborhood!" Clancy laughed.

A woman stepped out of the garage and walked up to the car. Clancy disappeared onto the side street just as she peered inside the car window.

"Poor Henry," Jake said with a shake of his head. "I feel like I'm back in college."

Clancy laughed and the car grew silent.

Jake closed his eyes for a moment and then opened them. "Did you ever wonder when your luck would run out?"

"What do you mean?" Clancy cranked his air conditioner.

"Henry is convinced he's been given a life sentence on the graveyard shift."

"Life isn't fair most of the time, y'know?"

Jake closed his eyes again and thought of his own string of recent good luck, both the promotion and Pamela in one summer. How long can a person's luck run?

Clancy broke the silence. "I know what you mean though. Sometimes I think I should be reading that book *When Bad Things Happen To Good People* just so I'm prepared."

"Yes! Exactly," Jake said, relieved that someone else understood.

When Jake woke up, dusk had settled in. He had two nights off before returning to the prime time shift. These rotating shifts wreaked havoc on his body. Pamela had left a voicemail but he was slow in waking himself up, wandering around his apartment, looking out the window with a glass of orange juice in his hand, feeling a bit hungry but with no sense of what he craved. His phone rang again.

"Hello?"

"Where were you?" Pamela shot back.

"Sleeping late." He rubbed his eyes. "After work this morning we went out for a beer."

"At eight in the morning?" She shrieked so loudly he held the phone out.

"Uh. Yeah. It's something we do... occasionally."

"We were supposed to have dinner tonight? With my sister? Don't you remember?"

"Oh, were we? I'm sorry. Shit. What day is today? Did you go?"

"I can't believe you did this to me."

"I'm sorry. Did you go?"

"No. I didn't fucking go! What was I going to do? Show up alone? The whole point of them inviting us for dinner was to meet you!"

"Pam, I said I'm sorry."

The silence swelled for a moment so Jake made an offer. "Give me her number. I'll call her and apologize."

"Oh, Jake. We'll just have to reschedule."

Holding the phone to his ear, Jake realized it was Pamela's intensity that intrigued and enamored him. At the beach, she was a whirlwind, gathering friends on the deck, mixing margaritas, and trying to match her room-mates up with good looking twenty-somethings who walked by on the sidewalk wearing only their swim trunks. At the bars, she was the first one on the dance floor, flowing smoothly through the crowd, surprising strangers with a quick flirty grind and a smile, before moving back to her circle of friends. Now, it dawned on him that this intensity was a double-edged sword.

And then it was September, and the days were getting shorter. Jake had started as a coordinating producer, requiring two weeks of training on day shift, and he relished this temporary daytime schedule. Pamela sometimes spent the night at his apartment. They slept with the windows open, cool air flowing through the space. He marveled at how his life had changed, how he'd become domesticated over the course of two months.

One night after dinner, Pam picked up the remote control and surfed through the channels, finally resting on Shoplandia. She watched for his reaction with a sly grin, as if she'd thrown down a humorous challenge.

Jake shook his head as he set two iced teas on the coffee table and sat next to her. The show host and the artist presented a framed print of an idyllic little thatch-roofed cottage set back in the woods. Along the side of the house, a stone path led to a footbridge that crossed a stream. It was dusk, and lights glowed from each window. The azaleas and trees were in full spring bloom, a panoramic swath of whites, pinks and purples. The whole setting was dreamlike, a cross between some dying man's first glimpse of heaven and *The Hobbit.*

"You can almost feel the mist from this little brook," the artist proclaimed.

"Yet it seems so cozy inside this little house," the host added.

"We don't call this a house, we call this a home," the artist corrected him.

"Yes, and you can have this amazing piece of art in your home for only $149.99...."

They watched the screen for a few seconds, then Pam said, "My sister has some paintings like these. She has one in her living room and a couple in her dining room. What's his name?"

"Jonas Gotlade, the painter of night."

"It's so beautiful, it's my dream house," Pam said.

Jake laughed, but then noticed Pam intently studying the cottage.

"It's so adorable isn't it?" She sighed. "I want a house like that some day." She leaned into his chest and stared at the television as if in a trance. Jake wrapped his arm around her shoulder and held her close. For Jake, it appeared to be the perfect moment.

"Maybe someday," he said.

Pamela's sister's house did not remind Jake of a Jonas Gotlade painting. The house was made of tan vinyl siding with the garage facing the small front yard. Bikes were strewn on the grass and the net had been ripped from the basketball rim. The boys had drawn chalk outlines of themselves, giving Jake the illusion the driveway was a murder scene. Two boys chased a smaller one out of the garage and pinned him down on the lawn. The little one was both screaming and laughing as the older boys tortured him, holding a worm over his face and chanting "open wide." As Pamela and Jake walked up the driveway, they all turned and stared at the strange guy with Pam. The little one squirmed and slipped out of their grasps.

"Hey guys, how are you all doing?" Pamela was all smiles, talking as if they were toddlers and not the pre-teen terrors Jake had just witnessed. It was obvious the boys were not amused.

"Who's that?" the middle one asked, pointing his finger. He ran the back of his hand across his snotty nose.

"This is Jake. He's my new friend. We came over for dinner."

"Our mom is in the backyard."

They found Carol on the back deck smoking a cigarette. When Pamela called out "hi," her sister jumped nervously.

"You caught me!" She stubbed out the cigarette on the railing and dumped it into a red Solo cup. "I'm trying to quit, honestly." Jake followed Pam up the steps onto the deck and Carol shook Jake's hand.

"Pam, you're right. He is cute." Carol winked, then sipped from her wine glass. Jake noticed a resemblance between her and Pam, though the ten years difference in age, and assuredly raising the three boys, made her look tired. She was wearing a purple knit top that Jake recognized as one of Shoplandia's own brands.

"Let's get you a drink." Carol opened the sliding door and the scent of nicotine followed them inside. Toys and video games were scattered across the family room. As they stepped into the fluorescent-lit kitchen, garlic wafted through the air. "That smells great," Jake said admiringly. He and Pam stood right by the doorway, and he noted several kitchen gadgets were ones they sold on the shopping channel. Pam's sister peeked into the oven and shut it again.

"I hope you like Italian food. I'm baking a lasagna."

"I love lasagna."

Carol leaned back on the counter. "So Pam tells me you are a producer at Shoplandia?"

"Well, yeah. Actually I just got promoted. Just started."

"A TV producer, so glamorous." Pamela stroked his arm as if he were her cat.

"So do you work with the celebrities? I want to hear some juicy gossip."

Jake smiled, hoping to let the issue pass.

Pam said, "They have that painter you like! He was on last night."

"That's where I got those prints. Off the TV."

Jake asked, "Do you shop a lot with Shoplandia?"

Carol downplayed it. "Ah, I pick up things here and there. I used to like HSN, and the Q. But now I stick with Shoplandia."

"Jake was just working with Willie Nelson a few

weeks ago!" Pam inserted.

"Oh man! Really? I love Willie."

"He was nice. He's very laid back."

"Because he was stoned. Tell me he was stoned. Am I right?"

"I can neither confirm nor deny that." Jake said with a grin.

"Do you want beer or wine?"

"A beer."

Pam chimed in. "I'll take wine."

Carol opened the fridge and handed Jake a beer. "So let me ask you. When they put those numbers up on the screen that say five thousand people ordered, is that real?"

"Yep, that's real."

She shook her head. "That's amazing. Oh, I have so many questions for you."

The youngest kid stumbled into the kitchen and stared at Jake.

"Ralphie, did you say hi to Jake?"

The kid wore a striped long sleeve shirt and had brown smudges on his cheeks. He must have been about six years old. He came over and took Jake's hand without saying a word.

"Oh, he wants you to see his new bike."

The little boy led Jake through a laundry room and into the garage. The boy pointed at his bike, but then he led Jake back into the house, into the family room. The boy stopped at a large and fairly dirty fish tank. There were angelfish and goldfish darting about, about a dozen in all. The boy just pointed. "Fish."

"I see that." Jake squatted down to the boy's height. He listened as the two sisters chatted in the kitchen.

"Oh, he's a cutie."

"And he has so much potential," Pam remarked.

The boy's fingers followed one goldfish with bulging eyes. "Fish." Jake watched the one fish dart back and forth. He wondered if the fish made any progress, if it was content trapped in this tank. And then the boy deserted him.

Jake walked into the dining room as he listened to the sisters banter back and forth. The table was set for dinner, with a white linen tablecloth and china place settings. The boys' plates were tightly packed onto one side. He was admiring a few family photos on the dining room wall, interspersed with a Jonas Gotlade print, when he heard a hefty voice shout, "I'm home." He glanced into the kitchen and witnessed Carol step up and kiss this large bear of a husband. He wore a blue dress shirt with the sleeves rolled up and the shirt had come untucked at some point. His yellow tie hung a little too low under his belt. "Jake, this is Ted. Honey, this here is Jake, Pamela's new boyfriend. It's okay to call you her boyfriend, isn't it?"

Jake stepped forward. "Why yes. Hi, nice to meet you. Thanks for inviting me."

"I had nothing to do with it," Ted replied as he shook Jake's hand with his meaty paw. And then he smiled to let Jake know he was joking. "Any friend of Pammy's is a friend of ours." He looked over at Pam and winked.

"How you doing there, little sis?"

They called the kids and Carol instructed everyone where to sit, with the little one climbing over his brother to take the middle seat. Jake wondered if the kid who had held the worm had washed his hands. Carol laid out the salad and disappeared back into the kitchen. They passed around a basket of warm rolls. The father and three sons moved about, slicing the pad of butter and adjusting their silverware. Jake sipped his beer and Pam put her hand on his thigh under the table. He reached down and held her hand for a moment just as Carol returned with a giant casserole dish of steaming lasagna. The aroma of tomato and garlic filled the room. Jake was struck with a sentimental feeling at the sight of it all. Ted had each son pass over his plate and he provided each with generous portions. Carol took her seat at the other end and then asked dutifully, "Do we have everything?"

Jake realized he was indeed hungry and he helped himself to some salad, and then dumped a heaping of lasagna on his plate. The first bite scalded the roof of his mouth and he gulped down some beer.

"Carol is quite the shopper," Ted announced. "She is keeping your business on the air."

Carol shot back, "Cut it out Ted." But she was smiling. "You watch your fish tank for entertainment and I watch my shopping show." She turned to Jake as if she owed him an explanation. "I like to pick things up and it's fun to watch. I like when you have the celebrities on air. And I like some of the hosts.

"Who's your favorite?" Jake asked with interest.

"Tanya is great. She is so funny. And Frankie Mack is very good."

"Do you watch Henry?"

"Oh, is he the one with brown hair?"

"Yeah."

"He is okay. But I loved Calabrese. What happened to him?"

Jake nearly choked on a piece of roll and Pamela tapped her hand on his back.

"Oh, dear. Are you okay?" Carol asked.

The three boys giggled and Ted told them to be quiet.

Jake's cheeks flushed red. He reached for a sip of beer, mainly to stall until he could think of a response. He breathed out. "I'm sorry. It just went down the wrong windpipe. I don't know what happened to Calabrese. It was all hush-hush."

"He was entertaining." Carol replied. "Oh, and that new girl is adorable."

"Renee?"

"Yes!"

Ted perked up. "Wait, you have Wainwright on the air, right?"

"Yes we do."

"Oh man, what's she like?" he asked with a smile and a nod.

"Ted. The boys are right here."

The oldest boy realized he missed something. "What?

What's going on?"

"Nothing dear. Finish your dinner."

When the kids started squirming Carol suggested they go play and she would call them in for dessert. The women stood to clear the plates away. Jake rose to help but Ted motioned for him to stay seated. A few minutes later, the smell of coffee floated into the dining room. Ted declared, "So that Shoplandia was a hell of an idea. Man, I'll tell you. The guy who started that—it's like printing money."

"It's pretty profitable I guess."

"I have an idea for a product. I should pitch it."

Carol floated in to gather more plates. "Oh Ted, don't talk about that silly idea."

"It's not silly. There's a real use for this. I think many people would want it."

Jake grinned. Carol left with the dirty dishes. Ted rolled up his sleeves and leaned in. "It's an idea I've had for years to help people clean their fish tanks. I just need to get some prototypes made."

Just to be polite, Jake asked, "What is it?"

Ted leaned back and grinned. "I don't know if I should tell you. You're sly." And then in a louder voice, he yelled to the kitchen. "This guy is sly. Wants to know my million-dollar idea. He'd probably go pitch it as his own, having the inside track and all."

Carol appeared with a stack of plates. "Ted, he's not going to steal your idea."

Jake's faced warmed. "I'm not in that side of the business, product development. You develop it and get it in the door at Shoplandia, and I'll help you sell it on air."

Ted nodded as if thinking over the possibilities, as if dreaming he was making a fortune. One of the boys shouted to his brothers in the backyard. Ted suddenly stood and stretched his arms out, then sat back down. "So you know those woods where your studio is?"

"Yeah?" Jake thought it a silly question.

"Well, I grew up here in Sellersburg. Carol and Pam are from a few towns over, but I grew up right in the borough. Back when I was in high school that was all fields and woods. This is before they built all those corporate parks, those giant glass enclosed buildings. It was part of a farm, called Out of Reach Farm. Odd name. We used to go back there at nights, you know, drinking beer or taking girls back there for kicks. It was great. You could have bonfires. Nobody would bother you. They were fun times."

Carol walked in carrying a Brooklyn cherry cheesecake. "What are you talking about now?"

"That field behind Out of Reach Farm. Remember the night you and I went back there? You were still in high school, weren't you?"

Carol blushed. "Oh Ted, that was so long ago. We were just kids." She started slicing the cheesecake.

"Do you recognize this?" she asked Jake.

"I sure do." Jake smiled. "We had a Brooklyn Cheesecake show two weeks ago."

Pam appeared at the doorway. Carol asked, "Sis. Can you call the boys in?"

"I remember going back into that field." Ted had a faraway look in his eye. "We'd cut the car lights and it was so dark. The highway wasn't there yet. It was so dark you could see the stars."

Pam's voice could be heard outside calling the kids.

"The black sky. That sky was infinite," Ted recalled.

Carol set a slice of cheesecake in front of Jake. Pam walked in just as Carol was about to set a slice at her seat. "I don't want any." Pam waved her off. "Really, Carol. I don't want a slice." She sat next to Jake, placing her hand on his thigh again. "I'll just take a few bites of Jake's."

ELEVEN

···

DAY OF THE DEAD

It was my favorite holiday, Halloween, and I had co-ordinated a family friendly moment to unfold on Shoplandia. Over the past two weeks, I had envisioned what success would look like. Show host Frankie Mack was going to invite eight little goblins onto the set, drop pre-packed cellophane candy bags into each trick-or-treater's basket and show the kids on their way, creating a dash of fun in between our monotonous stream of sales pitches. Unfortunately, what started as a simple premise had been poked at from nearly every depart-ment in the building.

First, the lawyers insisted each child have a notarized release signed by both their parents and school princi-pals. Then, the Vice President of Merchandising over-heard a department assistant excitedly boast that her 6-year old daughter would appear on the air as a fairy princess. The cold-hearted bastard shot off an email openly questioning whether airtime should be spent on something as frivolous as the joy of costumed children.

My boss's boss fired back, copying CEO Gordon Creosote, writing, *these moments represent the brand as* much as the logo on our shipping boxes. These moments show we have retained the spirit of our humanity. He also volleyed a live grenade, suggesting the merchants focus on their jobs instead of trying to produce the live show from the backseat.

When Buke heard about the controversy, he declared, "Dottie Robinson, you have created a Frankenstein." I'd spent every spare moment shuffling paperwork, trading emails and retrieving panicked voicemails from parents and school administrators. At times, I nearly abandoned the whole idea, but something deep inside kept me moving forward. In addition to brightening up the live show, I had a single selfish reason. I wanted to see my son dressed in his Halloween costume.

Shortly after putting my headset on and hustling to the green room, the real mayhem unfolded. The audio operator called me out on headsets.

"Dottie, have you seen Frankie Mack? His mic is still turned off."

I glanced at the clock. He was due on air in five minutes. "I've not, but I'll track him down." Finding errant show hosts was part of my "other assorted duties" as a coordinating producer.

As I swiped my access card and entered the hallowed sanctuary known as the show host lounge, an uneasy quietness swept over me. The canary yellow walls were lined with framed photos showing an array of beautiful show hosts. Each photo featured a coiffed, airbrushed host holding out a popular product as if personally communing with a customer. A silver necklace dripped from Tanya's outstretched fingers, Henry flipped a single fried egg with an exclusive fry pan. Wearing her apron, Karen held her cookbook, the cover of which showed a photo of Karen herself, smiling in her kitchen.

The clock read 3:57 p.m. Crap. Senior show host Frankie, the most dependable of the bunch and due on air in three minutes, was nowhere to be found.

"What am I? A freaking babysitter?"

The silence was eerie as I made my way past the workstations. At this time of day, I expected to hear the perpetual chirping of hosts. They congregate behind closed doors in their private spaces, checking email, cracking jokes, gossiping about celebrity guests as if they were friends.

"Frankie?"

I tiptoed along the row of darkened dressing rooms and saw light spilling out from the final door. When I leaned into the doorway, I spotted Frankie sitting rigid, gazing into his mirror. He wore a black pinstripe suit, an orange tie and a white starched dress shirt. He held a makeup puff in his right hand.

"Frankie Mack! It's show time. You're on the air in less than five minutes."

I stepped into the dressing room and studied Frankie's expressionless face in the mirror. I touched his shoulder and a chill coursed through my fingers. Frankie didn't flinch. He remained stiffly perched in his chair.

"Frankie." I placed my palm firmly on his suit jacket and shook. Frankie didn't budge.

"Oh, Frankie." A sobbing welled up from the deepest pit of my stomach. "Oh, fuck." I drew a deep breath, stepped back, reached for the phone and dialed security.

"Norm, it's Dottie. We need an ambulance in the host lounge. It's an emergency."

I studied Frankie's reflection in the mirror. He sat balanced in the chair, his back straight as a telephone pole. The phone clicked off but I continued holding it to my ear.

"Poor Frankie."

I recalled recently meeting Frankie's wife and two young sons. Just two weeks earlier, Frankie had sneaked the boys into the green room to meet their hero, baseball legend Cal Ripken. I called Joe Looter, the VP who corrals the show hosts. His assistant Lorraine picked up on the second ring.

"Looter's office."

"Hi, it's Dottie. Where's Looter?"

"Getting a cup of coffee."

"He's needed in the host lounge. It's an emergency. You'd better track him down."

I studied Frankie again, hoping for some sign of movement, as if this were an optical illusion. Frankie wasn't moving anywhere. His handwritten notes rested tidily on the table in front of him. Just an hour or so earlier, he had been reviewing the operations manual for a sausage maker and joking how he was going to show his sausage on live television.

Tears welled up. I wiped my cheeks, and then realized I better call the line producer. I summoned my strength to sound commanding. "Dylan, Frankie is not going to make his shift. He's sick. Tanya will have to stay for at least an hour. I'm tracking Looter down now to see who can go on afterward."

Dylan sighed. "What? Tanya has plans after her shift. She's going to be pissed. What's wrong?"

"Frankie is sick. Dylan, this isn't good. I'll stop by in a few minutes once I have an update." I hung up the phone and stood at the doorway. The only sound was my own heart thumping in my chest. Frankie had been a mentor, not just to me, but also to Dylan and the crew. He was the face of the network, the host who didn't mince words, who acted with integrity and earned the trust of our customers. We often joked he was the last honorable salesman.

Suddenly, the door burst open and Norm from security charged in like a rhinoceros.

"He's in here."

Norm stopped at the door to the dressing room. "Come help me."

He stood at Frankie's side. "Let's put him on the floor." I didn't want to, but I moved forward slowly and placed my arm underneath Frankie.

"One, two, three." We lifted in unison. Norm kicked the chair, which rolled back and pinged against the wall. We lowered Frankie flat. Norm straightened out his legs and started administering CPR.

I felt nauseous, a bit faint, with an urge to escape the host lounge. I stumbled out to the studio desk, the cool air bringing a slight sense of relief. The intern sat typing away on the computer.

"Hey." I leaned on the counter in an attempt to act casual. "Frankie Mack is sick. Can you let the guests know they'll be working with Tanya?"

"What's wrong with Frankie?"

I wasn't about to declare Frankie's death to an intern. "Not sure. An ambulance is on the way but I don't want to alarm the guests. Can you talk to them? Apologize for me."

Looter walked breezily down the hall carrying a cup of coffee, as if he didn't have a worry in the world. I waved him over, swiped my badge against the pad, and led him into the host lounge. As soon as the door shut behind us, I blurted out, "Frankie Mack is dead." My voice cracked on the last word.

Looter's mouth dropped open like a catfish. "What? You're kidding, right?" He placed his coffee on the table and I led him to the dressing room. Norm and a young security guard were applying CPR. The door opened and two paramedics rushed in, escorted by a third security guard. They hustled past us and knelt, checking for any signs of life.

I tapped Looter on the shoulder and led him back to the conference room. "We have Tanya staying on for another hour, but we'll need someone after that. We're telling guests and the crew that Frankie is sick."

Looter stared blankly. I had to wave my hand in front of his face to bring him back.

"Joe. We'll need a host for five p.m."

Looter finally nodded. "Five p.m. I'll get something figured out."

When we returned to the dressing room, Frankie's body had been placed on a stretcher and his dress shirt was torn open. Tubes protruded from his mouth and a paramedic had paddles on his chest, trying to shock him back to life. Norm had stepped into the shadows, running his hand through his hair with a nervous energy.

I bit my nails and mumbled, "Lord help us," hoping for a miracle to occur. When Norm glanced over and our eyes met, he shook his head. A moment later, the senior paramedic made the call. "Radio back, let them know we've ceased efforts."

I exhaled and then recalled where I was, in the middle of my work shift, with a live TV show going on just through the other side of the wall.

"Shit. I need to tell Dylan."

When I entered the studio, the normal bustle of employees caught me off guard. Order entry operators were on the phone up-selling spatulas to customers who had just ordered their 8-piece Iron Chef Cooking Set. Two engineers discussed flesh tones while color balancing a camera. Production assistants giggled as they walked by. I went to shush them, out of a combination of habit and respect for the dead, but realized the live show was on the outdoor set. I paused at a monitor and watched Tanya and a guest, flipping juicy half-pound burgers on the grill in the fading sunlight.

I rolled a chair up to the producer's desk and sat on the edge. When I tapped Dylan, he turned anxiously, as though he had been waiting forever for an update. He clicked a button and urgently dropped his headsets.

"Someone just said Frankie is being wheeled out on a stretcher? What the hell is going on?"

"Frankie Mack is dead." I tried to smile, as I often did while relaying something unbelievable, but I just broke down. I placed my face in my hands and leaned forward so the order entry operators wouldn't stare.

Dylan gulped and turned away. We often shared laughs about the remarkable events that occurred behind the scenes. We regularly dealt with misguided stunts that guests tried to pull or on air gaffes made by the crew. But those were issues that producers could rectify, that we could settle ourselves, or shoot back to the offices to follow due process. This was entirely different.

I let out a breath. "Looter has to call Frankie's wife. The rumors will be swirling soon." My eyes turned from Dylan to the monitor where the live show ticked away. The show proceeds no matter what, but it didn't feel right. A handheld camera focused on sizzling burgers as the guest exclaimed, "Now, this is living!" The cameraman stepped back and slowly raised the camera to show Tanya and the guest standing at the grill. Behind them, in the distance, two paramedics wheeled the stretcher with Frankie Mack's dead body across the screen.

"Oh shit."

Headsets exploded with voices.

"What the hell is that?"

"Is that Frankie Mack?"

"Is Frankie dead?"

Dylan swiped at his headset and commanded, "Get off that shot. Please put up a close up."

The voices talked over each other in confusion.

"Oh my God!"

"Dylan, what is going on?"

"That was Frankie Mack?"

Dylan responded briskly. "Frankie is sick. We don't know exactly what's up right now."

The phone at the desk rang and the caller ID revealed it was the office of the CEO.

"Oh, shit."

As Dylan picked up the phone, a buzz of voices slowly swept across order entry. The phones were lighting up. Operators answered hundreds of calls with questions from curious and dismayed customers who had seen a body wheeled across the background. I stood and observed the sea of commotion.

Dylan spoke into the phone with his head down. "It was an accident. We didn't know they were wheeling him out of the building." I listened, relieved I wasn't having this conversation with the CEO.

"Um, the person on the stretcher was Frankie Mack."

Silence.

"Yes, sir. That's what I've been told. Dead, sir."

Silence.

"He was supposed to be on the air this hour. Tanya is doing this show. Looter is finding a host for next hour."

Silence.

"That would be helpful, sir. Thank you."

Dylan slowly hung up the phone. "Creosote didn't

know."

I nodded.

"He's going to get Johnny Wake to work up a plan on how to handle this."

My cell phone rang and I answered quickly. Looter said, "I have Henry rushing in here but he won't be ready for air until six. We need Tanya to stay for one more hour."

"Ugh." I cupped the phone. "Can Tanya do another hour?"

"Does she have a choice?" Dylan replied. He looked at the products for the show and cringed. "Does he know we have a two-hour cooking show?"

Before I could relay the question, Looter responded. "I know. Nobody can make it in that quick. I don't think we have a choice."

"We'll tell her. We'll let you know if it's a problem."

Dylan twisted the knob and the headsets came alive to voices conversing in the control room.

"I need a break."

"What are we going to do?"

"I feel sick."

The crew continued punching up shots, following the host's actions, moderating the audio levels, matting graphics. Going through the motions.

Someone started to sob, though I wasn't sure where it was coming from.

"Listen," Dylan said into his headset, "We'll get some information as soon as possible. Let's focus on the show right now. Let's keep the ship afloat."

"Should we go off the air?"

"Maybe we should just roll the emergency tape?"

Dylan reiterated. "No. Just focus on the show please. We have PR coming down to provide a game plan."

"Dottie?" a voice asked over headsets.

"What's up?"

"Who is the host for next hour, and do we have any candy for the kids?"

"Give me a minute." I clicked off my mic. "I better head backstage. Are you telling Tanya about next hour or am I?"

"I guess I better do it. I'll just say he is sick."

I nodded somberly. "When she gets off air, I'll break the news. Are you okay?"

Dylan looked pale. He loosened his tie. "Frankie Mack. I can't believe it."

"Dylan, are we getting to the plug-in scentscape?" a voice asked through headsets.

He reviewed his papers and glanced at the clock. "No, we're running out of time."

"How true it is."

As I headed backstage, conversations flowed through headsets. Someone in the control room accidentally left their mic on and I eavesdropped on snippets, a combination of shock and sadness. I had a sinking feeling the crew might mutiny.

A fledgling production assistant named Kim leaned on one of the tables, listening on a headset and staring off into the distance. Her eyes were watery and red, and she lifted a tissue to her nose. As I stepped close to her, she turned to me with her eyes glazed, as if she didn't recognize me.

"Are you okay?"

"He was just backstage..." She shook her head in disbelief.

"I know he was." My eyes misted up and I wrapped my arms around her.

Clancy from the control room turned his key on. "Hey Dylan, shouldn't we cancel the show?"

"We can't just stop the show," Dylan replied.

"Someone just died."

"Clancy, that's not confirmed," Dylan said tersely.

A silence pulsated through headsets and swelled until I couldn't take it any longer. I removed my arm from around Kim and flipped on my key. "Look, this situation sucks. Okay? Nobody is more upset than Dylan and me. But what the hell are we supposed to do? Announce it on the live show? His wife doesn't even know yet. Christ, his mother watches the show. She's probably wondering where he is."

Dylan chimed in, using a more reasonable tone. "Please just focus on keeping the show together. The suits will figure out what we should do down the line."

I welled up, overcome with a combination of grief and remorse that I'd just blown up at the crew. I briskly walked out from backstage with my head down, through bustling order entry and into the hall. Maybe the crew was right. How do we proceed as if nothing happened? Was I handling my friend's death as just another obstacle to the live show? I ducked into an empty green room, snuck into the bathroom, placed my headset on the counter, and promptly burst into tears, short and spasmodic. After crying for a few moments, I grabbed some tissues and asked, "Who am I anymore?"

I sniffled and took a few deep breaths before placing my headset back on.

"Dottie, you have some visitors."

"I'll be right out."

I checked my face and wiped my nose. When I stepped into the hall, the first of the trick-or-treaters had arrived, a tall figure dressed in a black cloak and wielding a scythe. He was accompanied by his mother.

"Kyle, say hi to Dottie, the nice woman who is putting you on TV. Dottie, this is my son Kyle."

As the hooded figure slowly twisted around, his scythe nearly sliced my jugular. His face was covered with a rubber mask that recalled a Munch painting, and he fumbled while removing it. Underneath was an acnefaced kid with braces who was on the cusp of being too old to trick-or-treat.

The kid groaned, "Hi."

"Kyle nearly didn't come today," his mother said. "He thinks he is too old for this, but I didn't want him to miss this chance to be on TV. His grandparents are watching in Portland, Oregon."

"Hi Kyle. You arrived earlier than expected."

The doors burst open and a stream of trick-or-treaters swarmed into the hall. Several younger children held the hands of their parents. A tiny girl was dressed in a pink tutu and ballet slippers, her hair pulled back in pigtails. There was a white-sheeted ghost, a Merlin-like wizard and a horned red devil holding a pitchfork who kept poking at a young fairy princess. At the end of the line I spotted my son Zachary, dressed as a race car driver, and my husband Bryce, wearing his dress shirt and slacks, having picked up our son directly after work. I motioned for the group to move to one side so as not to block the entire hallway.

"Hi everyone. You all look so great, thanks for coming." I patted Zach on the head and smiled at Bryce. I explained the game plan, talking mainly to the parents, who were distracted, studying each passing person as if hoping to see a celebrity. Bryce's eyes drifted as a thin, leggy model strutted by. I reminded the children they needed to be quiet in the studio and we would be ready to go in just a few minutes. As I stepped over to chat with Zach, Bryce's smile faded.

"Are you okay?"

"It's been a rough day." I wanted to pull him aside and confide in him, possibly get a hug, but I knew I'd fall apart in his arms and create a scene. Instead, I waved my hand at the kids and their parents. "Come, follow me!" They tagged along, a whole line of costumed children trailed by their parents, as we made our way to the studio. When we turned the corner, Zach yelled out, "Dad! Look! It's a Christmas tree!"

"It sure is," Bryce replied.

A team of set dressers had taken over the living room like busy elves. Two men were assembling an artificial

Christmas tree that must have been fifteen feet tall. Two women in elf caps unpacked boxes with holiday props: garland, snow globes and ornaments with framed photos of each host. The kids excitedly pointed out the tree and the stockings hung from the mantel as if they were experiencing Christmas morning for the first time. A few mothers laughed nervously and nodded their heads.

"Excuse us," a voice called from behind. "We need to place this wreath directly above the front door." Artie, the supervisor for sets and props, handed a wreath to one of his crew.

"Hold on a minute!" I shouted. My arm began to twitch. "Artie, we have to chat." I started nervously tapping a pencil against the palm of my hand.

"Okay, give me a minute." He directed one of the elves to unpack a box and place the wrapped presents under the tree.

I swiveled to the parents. "I'm sorry, give us a moment." A few mothers had already wandered to the product tables, where they were eyeing up silver jewelry. I stared at the children all lined up in Halloween costumes with a Christmas tree in the background. The pencil snapped in my hand.

Bryce stepped over. "Take it easy dear. Are you okay?"

"I can't believe this. I've been working on this for two weeks and they put a fucking Christmas tree up on me."

As Artie handed the wreath off and walked toward me with his shoulders slumped, I realized the poor guy looked as frazzled as I felt. His dress shirt hung out and was marked by a black smudge on his collar. His mussed up hair was adorned with a single strand of tinsel. This poor sight reminded me that we were in this together. I pulled Artie through the door that leads to the warehouse, so as not to have the conversation in front of his crew, the kids or the parents.

"Artie, we are due to trick-or-treat on this set during this show. We can't bring trick-or-treaters onto the set if it is all dressed up for Christmas. It will look ridiculous."

Artie rubbed his face with both hands. "Dottie, Christmas kicks off November first. I'm under orders to have all the sets totally Christmasized by midnight."

Christmasize (v.) *the act of creating garish Christmas spirit through television production to maximize holiday sales. The commercialization of the Christian holiday by installing props, snow, and candy cane graphics, etc., by November 1.*

"I've been working for two weeks to bring these kids in here to trick-or-treat. As soon as they get their candy, we'll get off this set and let you Christmasize it, Hanukkah-size it or even Kwanzaa-size it. Damn. I don't care. It's still October, let us celebrate Halloween first. Artie, I've been planning this for weeks."

Artie drew in his breath. "Look Dottie, do you know how many times I've seen my six-year-old daughter trick-or-treat on Halloween? Never. I'm always stuck here putting up the damn Hanukkah bush."

I smiled, a show of empathy. "I'm sorry Artie. I know. It sucks. Damn, if I'd known I would have asked you to bring your daughter in." A silence fell between us. "Look,

I worked on this for two weeks. These parents had to get legal clearances signed by principals to get these kids on the air. The paperwork was insane. I've promised these parents their kids will go on air, but putting them on a Christmas-themed set will make us all look silly, don't you think?"

Artie looked off in the distance, mulling it over. I was worried he might break under the stress. "Can you keep your guys busy on another set for twenty minutes. That's all I'm asking for. Then it's all yours." I looked into his eyes, willing him to work with me.

"Twenty minutes," he responded.

"Twenty minutes, maybe less."

Artie spun to head out to the set and direct his crew. I raised my hand to pat him on the shoulder and express my thanks, but decided to hold off.

Instead, I hustled out to update Dylan and get this trick-or-treat episode crossed off my list. At this point, I wanted the whole night to be over with. Tanya stood under the lights of the front set, which was rotated to the kitchen. Standing next to her was a Frenchman named Jacque, wearing a white chef's coat, whisking a pot. Tanya held up a small round plastic container and gave out the item number and the price of Jacque's Rendered Duck Fat.

"How is Tanya holding up?" I asked.

Dylan swiped his headset off. "She's a bit tired. We just brought her coffee and cookies from the green room. Turns out she hadn't eaten before her shift. Oh, and of course she knows absolutely nothing about cooking and hasn't reviewed the products or met the guests. Other than that, we're doing awesome."

I tried to force a smile. "This has been the day from hell. When can we do this trick-or-treating? Christmas is breathing down our neck here."

As Dylan studied his sheet of items in the show, a silence settled over the studio.

Up on the set, Tanya ran through her guest's credentials. "Jacque owns the four star restaurant Le Bleu in New York City, and is considered chef to the stars. Perhaps you've seen his show on the Food Network." The chef smiled at the camera as Tanya launched into her first question.

"Tell me how you get your duck fat. How do you liposuction a duck?"

Jacque turned and stared at her.

Headsets exploded. "She didn't just ask that, did she?"

I closed my eyes and shook my head.

"Our duck fat is the best in the world," Jacque finally replied tersely in a French accent. "It can be used to make anything taste better and is actually healthier than butter."

"Let's trick-or-treat out of this product, get it done." Dylan determined. "At this point, I just want to get Tanya off the air."

Ten minutes later, the center of the set was de-Christmasized. Boxes of ornaments and decorations sat to the side of the cameras, with only narrow pathways leading to the set. The mammoth tree had been dragged as far to the side as possible. I clicked my headset on. "Don't shoot this too wide. The tree is off stage left. We don't want to confuse the holidays."

The trick-or-treaters lined up behind the front door of the living room, huddled together tightly against the faux backdrop of a field. After providing last minute directions, I left them in the capable hands of the production assistants and dashed out to the producer's desk to watch with Dylan.

As they rolled the final promotional spot, a floor manager navigated Tanya to her mark in the living room. When the camera came up live, Tanya promoted her shows for the next day as the audio guy triggered the doorbell sound effect.

"What's that noise in my ear," Tanya asked, looking off camera.

"It's the doorbell," Dylan replied in her ear. He clicked off his mic and threw his hands up in the air.

"Oh, the doorbell," Tanya repeated with surprise and broke into a giggle. She'd crossed the threshold of exhaustion and was punchy now. Tears streamed down her cheeks. Each time she attempted to speak, she was overcome with giggles again.

"Why, who could be at the door?" She asked in mock surprise. Tanya is a terrible actor. She stepped back to the door and opened it. "Oh, look. Trick-or-treaters."

Led by the teenaged grim reaper, the trick-or-treaters streamed in and lined up. The bowl of candy sat right off to Tanya's side, but she still asked, "Where's the candy?"

Dylan spoke in her ear, "To your left."

Tanya looked down at the large orange plastic bowl overflowing with specially marked trick-or-treat bags. "Oh the candy is right here!" She giggled again, a long, continuous belly laugh that led to another round of tears flowing down her cheeks. "I'm sorry. I apologize." She dabbed at the tears on her cheeks with her fingers.

She slowly walked down the line, with her back to the camera, stopping to ask each trick-or-treater his or her name. Since the kids were not mic'd up, all we could hear was a low, muddled response.

"Christ, this is terrible television," the technical director huffed. He took control of a different camera and zoomed in to show just the trick-or-treaters. The camera panned across the grim reaper, the race car driver, the ballerina, the fairy princess. They were adorable, innocent kids, some smiling, others nervous, each one patiently holding out their bag for a treat.

"We have to hurry this up," I said. Half the building wanted to squash the idea and now Tanya has turned the trick-or-treating into a farce. I held my breath, anticipating the phone to ring any moment.

When the scene ended, I felt no joy, just a sense of relief. "Well, that was worth it." Dylan instructed Tanya to walk stage right to present the Ottoman 2000 Juicer. Once the camera was off the kids, two production assistants escorted them off the set. The smallest ones ran to their mothers holding out their trick-or-treat bags and smiling.

Feeling the need to exit the studio, I escorted the trick-or-treaters out to the main lobby and shook hands with the grinning parents as they said goodbye. Bryce and Zach hung back.

"Take it easy tonight. Relax. I'm worried about you," Bryce said.

I leaned in to give him a quick kiss and slipped my hand into his. "Don't worry dear. I'll call you." I patted Zach on the head. "Nice job out there. Have fun trick-or-treating tonight."

At 5:59 p.m., I stood on the edge of the set waiting for Tanya to finish her prolonged shift. As the show ended and the promotional spot rolled, Tanya's smile faded. She tapped her mic to ensure it was brought down.

"Well, that was a cluster-fuck. What the hell is going on? I had a meeting scheduled with the jewelry buyers for Gold Bonanza. Tacking on two hours at the last minute. Christ!"

"Tanya." I calmly guided her by the arm, and my quiet demeanor caught her off guard.

"What? What happened?"

I walked her out of the high traffic area and glanced around. A few production assistants sat on the prep tables, watching from a distance.

"Five minutes before your shift ended, I found Frankie Mack in the host lounge. He's dead."

"You're joking."

"I wish I was."

She stepped back with her hand to her mouth. "Oh, God help us." Her eyes welled up with tears.

"Only the crew knows right now. Well, and the suits.

Looter has called Frankie's wife."

At 9 p.m., once we'd settled into a three-hour jewelry special, I informed the crew I was taking lunch. I sat down in the break room, a windowless, claustrophobic space with a row of vending machines that rattled out sugary sodas and salty snacks. On the opposite side of the room, a bulletin board held meaningless company memos. The formica tables were littered with the day's newspapers, opened to the sports and gossip pages. The air reeked from someone's bag lunch tossed in the trash can. Hanging from the ceiling, a silent television displayed a model wearing a delicate necklace on her fair, elegant neck.

With a sigh of exhaustion, I pulled my brown bag out of the fridge and sat at one of the three barren tables. The day was a blur. I placed my head on the table and closed my eyes for a moment, letting my mind drift off in a half sleep.

A distorted set spins in perpetual motion. A gurney stands front and center. A blue-haired woman in North Dakota gasps as she hears of Frankie's death. The grim reaper smiles at my husband and son. I push forward through the order entry arena, like a camera carried by a steadicam operator. I float through the producer's desk where Dylan toils. The front skirt of the rotating stage splits apart. Underneath the set, cloaked in darkness, the gears grind and lurch forward. A furnace slides closer, the orange glow visible through the small plate glass. I pick up a rag, unlatch the cast iron door and watch as flames consume a beating heart.

The slam of the break room door frightened me out of my slumber. Standing before me was Jake, recently promoted to coordinating producer and my relief at midnight.

I bolted upright. "Shit, you scared me." I glanced around. "I must have dozed off. I'm so glad to see you."

"I just heard about Frankie." Jake pulled up a chair and sat. "I can't believe it. Is it true you found him?"

I nodded. "It was horrible."

"I can't imagine." We sat in silence for a few moments, until Jake finally spoke.

"I was just thinking about something Frankie did this past summer when we were in Arkansas doing a remote. After the show, the whole crew went to eat at some southern rib restaurant. I bet there was eleven or twelve of us, and I was sitting next to Frankie. The crew had been teasing me about being the new guy, you know how it is..."

I nodded.

"Anyway, they were great ribs, the best I have ever had. After dinner, the waitresses all started clapping and singing some type of birthday song and they came to our table. I looked around to see whose birthday it was but they put this ice cream and giant slice of cake in front of me. They sang to me, even though my birthday is in March. Frankie leaned in with that grin of his and whispered, "Happy Birthday Jake, don't tell anyone back home that we do this. It's our secret."

I smiled because it was a total Frankie move, subversively spreading joy.

Jake leaned forward in his seat and stared at the floor. "I'm still in shock." He looked me in the eye. "I'm sorry. You must be too."

We sat together, wordlessly grieving for Frankie. After a respectful silence, Jake stood and with a tinge of weariness, said, "Now I have to go kick off the Christmas season at midnight."

"Yeah, let's all get in the Christmas spirit."

"Full-on Christmas. Oh, and I haven't told this to anyone yet. I was planning some shtick for tonight at midnight to kick off the festivities. Last night Frankie told me he would dress as Santa and do a little cameo. Time to find someone to fill the suit."

I settled in at the desk to write my shift report, wondering how I could possibly recap this night. I typed, *Frankie Mack died at 3:55 today,* but then deleted the line. I rewrote the first line four or five times before deleting everything and closing out the program.

Jake appeared in front of me with a frown. "There's nobody who has the charisma to play Santa tonight." He stared for a moment in contemplation, before his lips parted into a smile.

I shook my head. "Sorry. No."

"You should do it."

"I don't think so."

"Come on." Jake made his pitch. "There's no script, no lines, it's a simple cameo. C'mon, you love Halloween!"

His enthusiastic pleading reminded me of my son. "Santa comes in through the front door at the stroke of midnight, slides a gift for the world under the tree and exits stage right. A simple gesture. Think about it."

I sighed and closed my eyes, my mind flooded with thoughts of the ground covered on the night. To give up, to walk away, was to let my own spirit die, to allow my world to slip into cold, foreboding darkness. I longed for a world where kids only worry about what type of candy is in the bag, where they believe in Santa, where the world is magical. I pondered the possibility of delivering joy. And then, I imagined Frankie standing with us, having this conversation, cajoling me to do it with a wink.

"Fuck it. I'm Santa."

In the model's dressing room, I found the tattered brown box filled with billowing red velvet. The Santa suit had been stuffed away at the end of last holiday season and forgotten, left to gather dust. The box smelled musty. Carrie the floor manager poked her head in the door, and I was relieved to see her.

"Hey there, can you help me out?"

"You're not..."

I picked a piece of lint off the fabric. "I am."

"Nice."

"Do you have a minute? I need some pillows."

She nodded. "Yep. We're liquidating the American Dream linens with a show at 3 a.m. Be back in a minute."

I checked the water in the clothes steamer and switched on the machine. I pulled out the Santa suit slowly, inspected it for cleanliness, and carefully draped it on a hanger. The red suit, wrinkled and worn in a few spots, was flaked with cigarette ashes. I brushed off the specks with my hand and searched through the drawers for a lint brush. I rolled the brush across the fabric before picking at the nappy white fur.

After steaming the jacket, I laid the pants on the counter and steamed out the wrinkles. The fabric was soft, plush, and comforting in my fingers. I lifted the white beard to my nose and inhaled. It smelled dank. After stripping out of my slacks and blouse, I stepped into the red pants, then sat and slipped on my shoes. Carrie knocked softly and entered, carrying two fluffy down pillows and an old white t-shirt. Without speaking, she picked up the faux black boot covers and knelt, strapping them to my ankles. We moved about the room silently, calmly, with reverence.

I stood and faced the mirror, wearing the baggy red pants and my bra. Carrie handed over the t-shirt, which I slid into. I held both pillows to my stomach, lifting them to support my breasts. Carrie reached around with a cloth belt and I cinched it, a little too tightly at first.

I was flooded with memories of my childhood, of playing dress up in my best friend Suzy's bedroom on a wintry afternoon, wearing tutus and costume ball gowns, liberally applying makeup and eye shadow to each other, giggling and dancing in each other's arms.

Carrie held out the jacket and I stepped into the red cloak and zipped up. While the outside of the suit was plush, the inside lining scratched my skin.

"How can Santa be jolly while wearing this?"

With the white beard scratching my cheeks and the cap sliding down to my eyes, I felt as though I was peeking out through a keyhole. Carrie opened the door and I slowly, deliberately, stepped into the hall.

Jake stopped in his tracks. In a little kid voice, he shouted, "It's Santa, I know him." He instructed me to stand behind the set, next to the door, and wait for my cue. Carrie guided me through the studio. Several order entry operators pointed and waved excitedly. We stepped back to the auxiliary set, which had been stunningly *Christmasized*. The tree towered above the set, the branches decorated in glittering red and yellow ornaments. A spectacular array of shiny gift boxes tumbled from underneath the tree trunk. Garland framed all the windows and the stockings lined the mantel of the lit gas fireplace that warmed the room. I'd never seen anything so beautiful in my life. Artie had outdone himself. Carrie took my hand and led me along the narrow path behind the set.

I was a voyeur now, peeking through the window of someone's home as the host and a production assistant ran through the demonstration of a fax machine. They talked and laughed, helping each other like family. Standing quietly behind the door, I imagined the transmission and how my image was like a soul and would soon be fed at the speed of light through cables and the control room, beamed into the heavens before bouncing down into viewers' homes.

A production assistant ran over to the tree and picked

up a wrapped gift. She opened the door and handed the box to me. "Walk down the steps and place this under the tree, and then exit up the stairs."

She closed the door. I looked down at the gift in my white-gloved hands. It was tightly wrapped in green and red glossy paper. The box was empty inside and so light. The gift had been labeled for Frankie. I bit my lip to stop my tears.

I felt so small inside that Santa suit, as if I had been swallowed up, consumed by something larger than myself. "Go, go, go," a voice called out. I fumbled with the latch until it finally popped and the door swung open.

TWELVE

....

SNARLING LOVE

When I opened my eyes and discovered myself face down in my living room, my forehead matted to the Teflon carpet, I questioned the long-term commitment I had made at the altar nine months before.

As the grogginess dissipated, replaced by a hammering headache, my blurred vision slowly dialed into focus. A decapitated porcelain groom rested on the rug staring into my eyes. I pieced the fragments together, recalling a screaming match with my bride Pamela, and how in one fluid super-human motion, she had picked up our wedding cake topper from the dining room hutch and hurled it at me in a fury.

I vaguely recalled the argument, though I hesitate to even call it that. Pamela roamed the condo loudly griping to nobody in particular that the milk expired, that a new client at her office was a "fucking fraud" and that my rotating shifts left her lonely at night. In my naive zest to nudge her into a positive mindset, I'd responded by paraphrasing self-help guru and frequent Shoplandia guest Robert Covert. "We are only as happy as we choose to be."

What happened next replayed in slow motion. I spied the ceramic couple, resplendent in their shellacked finery, with frozen smiles and intertwined arms, twirling through space and time. At the last moment, I dropped more than ducked, twisting my knee as I fell face forward. My temple glanced off the edge of the glass coffee table before my memory dipped to black.

Now, using the table to steady myself, I cautiously rose and squatted on the edge of the couch. I raised a quivering hand to my head and grew dizzy at the sight of my palm drenched in crimson liquid. I was overcome with nausea.

I cradled my throbbing head in bloody hands and took in the apartment's silence. I didn't hear footsteps or the neighbor's TV bleeding through the wall. In the powder room, I studied my open wound. A flap of skin was pulled away from my forehead and I cringed with the thought of needing stitches.

My relationship with Pamela was physical and passionate. During our first months, I often thought of that classic line from a movie, "this goes to eleven." I recalled it all in a brilliant hue—the fights, the drinks, the sex. It was all consuming and I'd mistaken it for love and proposed too quickly, hoping to catch it like a genie in a bottle. But the intensity couldn't last and the rope that bound us frayed quickly. After the wedding, the tautness that I once saw as amorous, lovely and inspiring started to resemble something altogether different—dangerous, hideous and deflating.

From behind the studio operations desk, a young blonde intern named Ashley flinched when she saw me. "What happened to you?"

I touched the bandage on my temple. "Oh, nothing. I sliced my head open last night. Hey, I need a favor. Can you please take Jenna McGregor's dog for a walk?"

"I... I don't know if I'm allowed."

"I *really* need you to handle this for me." I wiped my forehead. "Would you hand me the aspirin? They should be in the top desk drawer."

"I'll get in trouble if I leave the desk." Ashley reached in the drawer and handed me an over-sized plastic bottle.

I was only three hours into my ten-hour shift as a co-ordinating producer but I was already mentally exhausted. The emergency room visit the night before took three hours, and by the time I returned home it was after midnight. I'd been tempted to call out, but I needed to take my mind off the debacle. On days I'm not nursing a possible concussion I love the rush of the studio, the thrill of piecing the production puzzle together and staying a step ahead of the live show. Today though, I was running, bouncing back and forth between the green rooms, the salon and the studios of Shoplandia. All I'd worked up was a headache and a sweat.

"What's going on?" a terse voice demanded. I twisteded my throbbing head and saw Janis Kahn, the always-scowling manager of studio operations and Ashley's supervisor. I instantly recalled why Ashley was frozen in a perpetual state of terror.

"Janis, I'm glad you're here," I lied in an attempt to smooth talk the supervisor. She was a hulking brute of a woman who ruled her team like a drill sergeant. Behind her back, she was known simply as Genghis.

"What's going on here?" Janis asked again. She examined the aspirin I had sorted in my hand.

"We need your help. Jenna McGregor's new show starts in fifteen minutes. We need someone to walk her dog. I'm asking Ashley to help." I tossed down a few dry aspirin and gulped.

"It's not our job to walk dogs." Janis snorted air through her nose. I handed the aspirin bottle back to Ashley. Through the headset draped around my neck, I heard the floor manager call out, "Jake! We need you on the set!"

I held up a finger signaling Janis to wait, knowing this would only allow her annoyance to percolate. I clicked on my intercom box, "Dan, what's up?"

"Some strange dude is rearranging the set for the next show."

"I'll head out in a moment. Give me a minute." I shut off my box. "Janis, can you please help us out?"

Janis impatiently fidgeted with her pen. "We are not a dog walking service. Guests are not supposed to *even* have dogs in the green room. Our policy is clear on this. No dogs."

"Janis, do you have a minute?" I motioned for her to follow me. We walked a short way down the hall so Ashley wouldn't overhear. I sighed, conjuring up the strength within, and finally turned to Janis with a determined stare.

"We have been courting Jenna McGregor to come to Shoplandia for, what is it now, three years? We've been seducing her, telling her how great we are, designing her jewelry, signing her contracts, and dealing with her pain in the ass agent. Now we're fifteen minutes before the debut of the most important show of the year, and her people are throwing a tantrum because her little rat dog has to take a shit."

I paused to let this sink in.

"Jenna McGregor may have won an Oscar and two Emmys sometime in the last century, but believe me, her whole posse is in the green room trembling about this live TV appearance. These people are insane. When my phone rings after we open the show, and our friendly CEO asks, 'Jake, where is Jenna?' What the hell am I supposed to say? 'Well sir, look out your corner office window. She's in the parking lot walking her dog. The studio desk wouldn't help out because it wasn't in their job description.'"

Janis reflected for a moment. I saw in her eyes she was deciding if I'd really dime her out to the CEO. The hallway was so still that I heard her grinding her teeth.

I tossed Janis a conspiratorial grin. "Do you believe we both have college degrees and we're having this discussion?"

Janis pursed her lips and almost smiled. "This is a terrible precedent. We don't have staffing for this."

"Listen, I still have to check on the set, the models and the music clearance in the next ten minutes. Please handle this for me. Maybe security can walk her dog. I'm just asking so I can focus on the live show."

My headset squawked again. "Jake, this guy out here is moving the set pieces around. He's screwing up the whole damned set. You better get out there."

"It's one time..." I motioned to pat her shoulder in a show of solidarity, but then caught myself.

Janis frowned. "I'll call security, but no promises."

"Thanks." I turned before she could change her mind and walked swiftly past the studio desk, giving Ashley a wink and a thumbs up before passing through the door.

The studio at Shoplandia is as cavernous as an airplane hangar. Rows of order entry operators take orders through headsets, typing the orders into a vast computer system. A production assistant pushed a cart of teddy bears by. I hustled past the main circular stage. Backstage was roiling with the regular commotion of several half-constructed sets. Two young female set dressers rearranged flowers on a living room set. One stepped back to examine the display. On the kitchen set, two men in aprons polished an eight-piece cookware set and propped each piece in an aesthetically pleasing cascade for the cameras. Another two men in dress shirts lifted a toilet off a cart and rested the white porcelain in the middle of the garage set.

It was not hard to spot the intruder on the jewelry set. Jenna's business manager stood with arms crossed, staring blankly at the tables and chairs as if contemplating the position of furniture in his Palm Springs pad. His clean-shaven head glistened with sweat under the lights. He sported funky spectacles and a tailored suit that might have worked in Hollywood but was out of place in the leafy suburban neighborhood of Sellersburg, Pennsylvania.

"What are you doing?" I asked.

"I'd like to switch around these two photos. I would prefer we have the chairs over this way so this other photo is the backdrop." The manager motioned toward a darkened corner of the set.

"The stage has been blocked out so Jenna will look good under our lights," I explained. The agent placed his hands on his hips defiantly.

"If we move the chairs, Jenna will be in the shadows and won't look very radiant. Do you want Jenna to look like she has a five o'clock shadow?"

The manager raised his eyebrows. "Uh...no." He arched his neck to examine the light grid as though he'd just comprehended the importance of lighting in television production. "I would prefer that photo be behind her, not that photo." He pointed at the two oversized portraits hanging from the back of the set.

The enlarged photos showed the screen idol Jenna McGregor from a bygone era, her glory days when she appeared in the lighthearted romance movies of the fifties and sixties. In the first photo, her hair was swept back and her eyes pierced the camera. Her smile was both subversive and sexy, and she sported emerald earrings that matched a drop necklace replicated in her new collection. The second photo showed Jenna looking gorgeous in vibrant color. Again, her hair was swept back.

She was adorned with stunning pearl earrings and a matching choker. She wore a black off-the-shoulder dress, surely some type of ball gown. The radiant blue of her eyes popped off the canvas, and her lips were pure crimson.

"Hold on." I clicked on my headset. "Artie, we need you on the set ASAP."

My cell phone chirped and I flipped it open. "What's up?" I flashed the fidgety manager the "hold" index finger as opposed to my middle finger.

"It's Joanie from Legal. The clearinghouse just approved the Celine Dion music for Jenna's show. There's a stipulation though."

"What's that?"

"We can only use the music twice in the hour, and no more than 30 seconds each time."

"Okay. We can do that." Artie walked in and slapped his cell phone shut on his thigh.

"Artie, can you switch out these two hanging photos before the show? Just swap their spots? Do you have time?"

"Dude, I was on my lunch break." Artie picked food out of his teeth with his pinky.

"I'm jealous. I am so hungry. Sorry to interrupt lunch. Can you help us out?"

Artie stared up at the photos. "She was quite a looker, eh?"

"Yeah. She was stunning." Artie and I stood in admiration for a moment. "Can you switch them around for me?"

"Yeah, I guess so. Just because I like you. How much time do we have?"

"Eight minutes."

"I got you covered. You owe me though."

"Thanks."

I took the manager by the arm and led him back to the green room, giving him the good news about the music. "During the show, you want to watch sales on the computer screens in the green room. It's best not to be in the studio." As we passed through to the hallway, I clicked on my headset. "Who's in the audio booth?"

"Skippy reporting for duty, sir."

"Listen, that Celine Dion love song for next hour? We can only play it twice in the hour, and it cannot, *cannot* run longer than 30 seconds each time we play it. Copy?"

"Copy that, sir."

I entered the green room with a warm smile for Jenna McGregor. I was surprised how crowded the room was now, though I also was relieved to see the dog was not present. About fifteen of her people stood about mingling with a few shopping channel executives. It was like a scene from a New York cocktail party, sans cocktails. Of course, none of *them* could take the little rat dog for a walk? They were all too busy fawning over the old time movie star. I suppressed the urge to shout out, "*Don't you have any work to do?*"

"Jenna. Are you mic'd up? Are you ready? It's show time!" I held my arm out as if she was my prom date and was struck with a flashback, sitting on the living room floor of my childhood home with my two sisters watching Jenna on TV. Burt Lancaster drove her around town in a convertible. She wore flowing dresses and a string of pearls and spouted melodramatic lines such as, "Thomas, we mustn't think those sorts of things." The story was silly, a love story, but I was glued to the TV because Jenna was so stunning. I must have been nine or ten at the time, but I fell for her smile and vivid blue eyes. It wasn't until I was in college that I realized the movie had been made twenty years before I was born.

As Jenna stood to take my arm, the microphone popped off her blazer. I fished for the cord until I retrieved the dangling mic. Facing her, I pinched open the mic clip and carefully placed it on her lapel as though I was placing a corsage on my date. I felt a light touch on my cheek and looked up to find Jenna staring with a flirtatious smile.

"Oh, you're injured. Are you okay?"

"Just a cut. I'm fine. Thanks."

She looped her arm through mine and laughed nervously as I escorted her toward the door. Her people gave the standard Hollywood salutations, "Good luck Jenna, Go get 'em Jenna!" The entourage applauded. I noticed a tremor in Jenna's arm and placed my other hand on her arm to steady her. The suits parted like the Red Sea. As we passed through the crowd, Jenna joked, "It's been too long since I've been escorted by a young gentleman. Such a good looking man too."

When the door to the green room shut and we were alone in the hallway, Jenna spouted, "Thank God you saved me. I couldn't take another minute in there. It's all such utter bullshit."

I laughed and we unlocked our arms but Jenna clasped my hand and my temperature rose. I was holding hands with one of the most adored movie stars of all time, even though she was nearing eighty years old.

"I think you'll have fun during the show. Karen is easy to work with."

"You are a handsome young man. Are you married?"

"Uh, yeah. Right now I am."

"I'm sorry. Trouble in paradise?"

I hadn't said anything to anyone and was surprised at her directness. "Yeah, I think we're starting the process."

"Is it mutual?"

"Uh, it's been... it's still sinking in..."

"I'm sorry. You know, Richard Garrison broke my heart once. I was devastated for such a long time, but then I found out he was fucking Liz the whole time anyway. It was just awful."

I led her around the corner. As we passed the reception desk, Ashley clinked down the phone and leapt up. "Good luck!"

Jenna reached out to shake Ashley's hand. "Thank you so much dear."

I opened the door into the studio and held it for Jenna.

"I'm nervous about this," she confided as we walked through. "I really don't know how I ended up here."

"I ask myself the same question every day."

She took my hand again. "You must love it here, there's such an energy."

"It's a blast. Stressful, but every day is different. You're going to be great. Just watch your language."

"Oh, I will dear," Jenna grinned. "I know it was before your time, but I was once known as America's Sweetheart. If they only knew..."

I contemplated telling Jenna she was my first crush, but instead said, "The best part will be taking phone calls from your fans. You are going to have great fun."

"You are too kind. When Alfie comes back from his walk, would you bring him out to the set?"

"Sure we will. Don't worry about a thing."

As we walked through the vast studio, a production assistant screamed out, "Rotating!" With a flip of a switch, the heavy purr of an engine started, giant gears engaged and the main stage, elevated about three feet off the ground, lurched and rotated. As the kitchen set disappeared, a patio set rotated past and a traditional beige living room swung in under the lights.

"Look at that! Just like on Broadway!" She glanced around at the space. "I can't believe the amount of sets you have. I had no idea the studio would be so vast."

We made our way through backstage to her set. I held her hand as she climbed the single step. "Here's your seat."

Jenna turned and patted my hand. "Don't worry, things will improve eventually. Love is a messy business. You hang in there."

"Thank you. I'm sure it will. Good luck with the show."

"Hello!" Karen the show host trotted around the corner wearing a red dress, coiffed hair, and a perky smile. She was accessorized with nearly every piece of the Jenna McGregor Jewelry Collection. "Okay, here we go!"

I backed off the set as the red light flickered on the camera. The control room swung another camera around and zoomed in on my bandaged head. On headsets, a voice asked, "Jake, did you get into a fight?"

Fifty-three minutes later, I stood just out of range of the camera as Karen leaned over and informed Jenna every piece sold out and the show was ending early. Jenna gasped and thanked the audience. She blew a kiss to the camera and I noticed a tear on her cheek. The director slowly zoomed in on Alfie the dog sitting stoically at Jenna's feet.

"Congratulations!" Karen quickly hugged Jenna. "I have to run to my next show. We'll see you soon!" Karen placed her finger to her earpiece and darted toward a far-off set.

I called out, "Nice job Karen!" She waved as she stepped over the camera cables. I walked onto the set and offered Jenna my hand. "Did you have fun?"

"I did!" Jenna smiled as she stood. "That was great fun talking to the customers. Time just flew by."

A floor manager stepped up and nonchalantly placed his hands up Jenna's blouse to disconnect the mic pack clipped to the back of her bra.

"Hey there, frisky. I haven't had a young man do that in ages!"

As we stepped off the set, she called back. "Alfie!

Come!"

I escorted Jenna and Alfie through the studio. As we passed the living room stage, Karen was already back on the air. She squatted and attached a hose to a vacuum cleaner as she talked into the camera. "I have some cereal spilled here to show you the suction power of this machine."

Jenna stopped behind a camera and watched Karen empty a bowl of cereal on the carpet. She crunched the Os into tiny pieces with her heels. "Straight from jewelry to cleaning appliances," Jenna remarked. "Is there anything these hosts can't do?"

When we stepped into the green room, wild applause broke out. The posse of beautiful people swarmed Jenna with hugs and accolades. I noticed on the TV monitor that Karen flipped the switch but the vacuum cleaner wasn't picking up the crumbs. Through headsets, a voice shouted, "Damn it, this thing is not plugged in." Jenna was caught up in a riptide of well-wishers and swept through to the far end of the room. Meanwhile, on the monitor, Karen held the plug in her hand with an embarrassed smile. I slipped out of the green room.

"Did we have a good night tonight?" Karen stood at the producer's desk an hour later, unbuttoning her blouse.

"I think we had a good night."

"What was wrong with Jenna?" Karen ran her hand underneath her blouse and pulled out her mic pack.

"What do you mean?"

"She was a bit shaky. One moment she was fine, and then she'd have the shakes for like five minutes and then it would disappear." Karen wrapped the cord around the pack.

"You know, her hand shook a bit when I was walking her into the studio. I just figured it was age."

"I don't know. Seemed more than nerves or age. Oh well. It was a good night. I'm ordering takeout and watching a movie. Nice job today, kiddo."

"Thanks, Karen. You too."

I pulled into my condo parking space and shut off the ignition to my car. No lights were on in the window and I exhaled with relief. It took the better part of the day for the greater sin to sink in. Pamela was not callous for hurling the wedding topper, but for fleeing the scene afterward, leaving me face down on the floor. I climbed the two steps and unlocked the front door. Did she think I was dead and flee in panic? I pondered how anyone would do that, let alone the woman I had chosen to marry. I clicked the light switch by the door and dropped my satchel. The overhead light revealed a ransacked, nearly barren room. Only the television sat on the floor in one corner, and a single folding chair leaned against an opposite wall.

Three months later, I furnished the condo with a single mattress, a recliner and a television stand. Each week I made another purchase and began reassembling my life: a toaster, an end table, a couch. I carried a letter in my satchel from the law firm of Graham, Brennan and Bloh. My cell phone was cluttered with voicemails from one of the attorneys urging me to call "so we can bring resolution to the situation, for the benefit of all involved." Like that was going to happen. The only other voicemail was from my mother, who confided she "never quite trusted that girl."

At the shared desk near the entrance to the studio, I scanned the program schedule on the bulletin board and noted Jenna McGregor was returning for a live audience show. When I booted up my computer, an email from my boss Tony popped up. The heading was simply titled *Your Decision.* I clicked through.

Jake -

This is your show next week. Think through if you would like to do this and get back to this kid. I'm okay either way, just keep it short.

I scrolled down and read the attached email.

Dear Sirs -

My girlfriend and I are attending your live audience show for the Jenna McGregor Collection. We have been dating for three years and Daisy is very fond of your jewelry and fashion shows. I have been looking for a way to propose to Daisy. Is it possible to propose to the love of my life during your live television show? Please let me know. It would mean the world to us.

Daisy is a big fan of Shoplandia. Thank you so much.

Sincerely,

Tom Turner

I sat back in my chair and sighed, tempted to tell the guy to run the other way. I grinned at the thought of sending a cataclysmic email, scaring this kid off for his own good.

After a moment, I closed the email, stood and stretched, reminding myself to be professional and to think from a producer's perspective. With eyes shut tight, I visualized what the proposal might look like on air, and thought through the possibilities of what could go wrong. What's the worst thing that could happen? She might say no or slap the guy. Maybe she would run out of the studio. An incident like that might drag Shoplandia down to the level of a *Jerry Springer* episode. This could be dangerous. This could be fun.

In the production meeting, I laid out my plan to the crew. "We will seat the couple on the end of the third row. I think we go to the audience for a question about twenty minutes in. We'll give Tom the mic and when Karen introduces him, he'll drop to his knee, or whatever the hell he wants to do."

"You know Karen is going to screw this up," the audio operator declared. "She can't keep a secret."

"No, she won't. I haven't told her. This is going to be

a surprise to both her and Jenna."

The crew laughed.

"Nice."

"I like how you think."

"Brilliant."

The director leaned forward. "I have an idea. What if we do a double box shot? We can show the proposal in one box with Karen and Jenna's reaction in the other."

"That would be stellar. Can we fit both Jenna and Karen?"

"I'll work it out." The director leaned back. "Love is in the air."

After the production meeting, I walked out to the perch above the audience lobby, leaned on the railing and scanned the gathering crowd. I tried to pick out the lovebirds, but the audience (as usual) was ninety percent women, and it looked as if the few men scattered throughout were in their fifties and sixties, and had been dragged along by their wives for the past several decades.

Guest ambassador Molly appeared. "Do you see them?"

"No."

"Don't worry, I'll check off everyone against the guest list and find them. They'll be seated in the right spot. Third row. End of the row."

"Thanks. I have to go meet Jenna. I'll see you in the studio."

"This is so romantic. We're going to need some tissues for the audience!"

"Let's hope that's all we need."

"Aw, it's gonna be awesome."

"Just call me the Matchmaker."

Jenna McGregor's return was met with much less fanfare from those inside the building. I walked into a nearly empty green room, a stark contrast to the standing room only crowd at her premiere. Jenna sat on the couch watching the show while Alfie rested under the coffee table. Jenna's eyes lit up and she held her hands out. I leaned down to peck her on the cheek.

"Welcome back. Round two? Are you excited?"

"I am excited! It was great fun last time. I was hoping I'd work with you again." She reached for my hand and Alfie sniffed my pant leg.

Jenna's fingers trembled in my hand. "Are you nervous?"

"I'm always a little nervous, my dear."

"I read that you are presenting an award at the New York Fashion Designers show. That looks like quite a show?"

"Oh yes. Both Tommy and Calvin insisted. I can't say no to those two. It's nice to still feel wanted." Jenna smiled. "And how are you these days?" She lifted her fingers over my scar. "It's healing nicely?"

I smiled when I realized she was talking about Pamela. "I'm fine, thanks. She's gone. I came home to find she'd cleaned out the apartment."

"Oh no. A true bitch."

I shrugged. "We were crazy and in love. But after we

got married, I discovered she was just crazy."

Jenna shook her head. "Well, I don't believe there's such a thing as one true love. I've been married four times and I loved each one of those bastards."

The little dog yelped and Jenna looked down. "Yes Alfie. You are my one true love." The dog jumped on her lap and nuzzled against her. "Alfie will always be loyal." She looked up. "Well, you are still a young man. You have so many loves ahead of you. And there are so many pretty women working here. Aren't I right?"

"You are definitely right about that."

The door swung open and Merchandising VP Bob Payne sauntered into the room with his broad smile. "Emma McGregor, my dear!" I stood and moved over to check sales on the computer, giving Payne a moment to chat with Jenna. Alfie leapt from Jenna's lap as Payne leaned in and kissed the movie star on the cheek. Alfie yelped and sniffed at Payne's trousers.

"How are you? You look amazing, of course, " Payne asked. I admired Payne's capacity to smoothly enter and exit a green room. The man was so quick and light in these appearances. Like a magician, he escaped without having to tend to any business matters or resolve any issues. He was the epitome of schmooze.

"I snuck out of a meeting to see you my dear, so I only have a minute..."

Jenna giggled at the thought. Payne guided the conversation deftly, asking about her recent visit to the Riviera and her appearance on *The Tonight Show*. For these few minutes Payne was totally in the moment, making

Jenna the center of his world. As he turned to scurry out, Payne shot me a wink and a smile to indicate he appreciated the absurdity of it all, the ingratiating ass-kissing aspect of the whole business.

At the door, Payne glanced down at Alfie. The little terrier jumped up and down excitedly, as though he expected Payne to take him for a walk. Payne bent to stroke the dog, but Alfie viciously snapped and bit deeply into Payne's hand.

"Shit!" Payne pulled back his hand and examined the puncture wounds. He shook his hand. "Damn it!" For a brief moment, Payne stepped back and cocked his leg like a field goal kicker. I winced, expecting a yelp and flying fur.

"Bad Alfie!" Jenna stood and walked toward the dog, and then she said softly to Payne, "I'm so sorry Bob, are you okay?"

Payne feigned a smile as he studied his injured hand again. Blood trickled down his wrist onto his white shirtsleeve. "I'll be fine. Good luck tonight with the show. Knock them dead." He opened the door with his left hand and exited, but before the door shut, Payne blurted a stream of expletives into the hallway.

Jenna turned to me. "Do you think he's okay? I feel terrible about this."

"I'm sure he'll be fine." I stepped to the door and noticed a trail of blood splotches on the carpet. "I hope he'll be okay."

Alfie ran to Jenna's feet with his tongue panting. She picked up the dog in her arms, cradling the pooch like a baby. "You are such a bad little dog. What am I going to do with you?"

"I'll see if I can catch Bob and double check on him. I'll be back in a few moments and we'll get you mic'd up."

I found Payne seated in the waiting area, being treated by one of the security guards with a first aid kit. The guard wrapped Payne's hand in gauze.

"Are you okay?"

Payne looked up in disgust. "That damn dog got me good."

"I thought you were going to kick it across the room."

"I almost did that, didn't I?" He grinned.

The guard started packing up the first aid kit. "I don't think you need stitches, but you should make sure you are up on your shots."

"Yeah, I'll get right on that."

The security guard stood and looked at me. "I thought we had a no dog policy in the green rooms."

"Oh, I wouldn't know. I'm just the producer." I shrugged. "I suggest you follow up with Janis Kahn."

I heard the buzz before I even entered the live audience theater. The side door led directly to the stage, and I looked up at the tiered seats of the packed house. Women chatted away, pointing up at the current show, which was displayed on monitors hung from the ceiling.

I was surprised at who was seated in the chairs assigned for the lovebirds. A couple in their sixties were seated at the end of the third row. The man was bald and plump, dressed in a plaid dress shirt and brown slacks. He fidgeted and glanced around nervously. Beside him was a woman in a bright patch-worked sweater, adorned with red hearts. Her curly blonde hair was streaked with gray. She tapped the man's arm and pointed up at the monitor.

Molly touched my shoulder. "Yeah, that's really the couple."

"Definitely not the young love I was expecting. This will be interesting."

"Aw, it's still so sweet. Let me warm up this audience." She stepped forward and clicked on her wireless mic. "Hello and welcome to Shoplandia! My name is Molly. Quick question - how many of you have been to see a live show with us before?" Hands shot in the air with the enthusiasm of a kindergarten class.

Twenty minutes into the show, I stood on the side of the set with my headset on. Molly whispered to Tom Turner and gave him a microphone. He wiped his hand across his glistening forehead and waited nervously. Daisy twisted in her chair and grinned at her boyfriend.

Show host Karen said, "I understand we have a question from the audience. Who is out there? Hi, what's your name?"

The monitor now showed Tom who held the mic a little too far away from his mouth. "Hi Karen. Hi Jenna. My girlfriend Daisy and I drove here from Missouri just to see this show."

"You drove from Missouri? Wow!"

Jenna touched her hand to her heart and smiled.

"Thank you so much."

Tom paused. "Daisy loves Shoplandia and we both grew up watching Jenna in the movies. Anyway, we're both widows, er, I'm a widower..."

"Tom, what's your question for Jenna?"

Through headsets, someone yelled, "Put up the double box!"

Tom froze for a second and blinked at the camera, then powered through. "Actually, my question is for Daisy..." He stepped into the aisle, turned to Daisy and dropped to his knee. The audience gasped.

Karen grinned and Jenna covered her mouth.

"Daisy, you make me so happy and I want to spend my life with you. Will you marry me?"

Daisy sat frozen. Her eyes were as big as glistening cubic zirconia stones. Silence swelled in the studio first, then flowed through the electrical current to the control room where each of the staff held their collective breath, before the signal beamed up to a satellite and bounced back down into the homes of millions of shoppers across North America.

Just when I thought I could no longer hold my breath, Daisy nodded her head up and down, and her chest convulsed in waves. Both Karen and Jenna smiled broadly and dabbed at their tears while trying not to smudge their makeup.

Through headsets, a voice said, "Holy shit. I didn't know what she was going to do." A voice in the control room proclaimed, "Bring us champagne!"

After the show, Karen popped out of her seat and

called out to the audience. "Thanks so much for coming today!" She leaned in and pecked Jenna on the cheek. "I had a great time, dear. Thanks so much."

"Oh dear, you are off and running. The pleasure is mine."

Karen dashed off the set as I took Jenna's hand. "Nice job today, were you surprised by the proposal?"

"You have no idea. It was just glorious. How exciting was that?" She twisted and called out, "Come on Alfie."

When we reached the hall, I asked, "Do you mind greeting the newly engaged couple?"

"I'd love to."

Molly held open the door and the couple ducked into the hallway.

Daisy shrieked, "Jenna McGregor, I am so excited."

Jenna took Daisy's hand into hers.

"Congratulations, my dear," Jenna declared. "You have had an exciting day. And to think you drove all the way from Missouri." She turned to Tom. "And you are a scheming little devil, aren't you? Who says romance is dead? Bravo to you for pulling this off. You are a Romeo!"

Tom blushed. "Thank you." He held up a camera. "Can I get a photo of you two?"

"Let me take it. You both should be in it."

Tom hesitated for a second, but handed me the camera and pointed out the flash button.

Alfie barked and Jenna bent down. "Come here, Alfie. You want your photo taken also, don't you?" She picked up the dog and held him against her. Tom lined up and smiled as the camera flashed.

After their goodbyes, Jenna placed Alfie on the floor. "Which way are we heading?"

"Here, we'll take a shortcut." I held open a metal door and we entered backstage of the main studio. Two set dressers struggled with a cart holding a massive framed wall. They dodged us and the set piece teetered.

"That was just delightful," Jenna took my hand.

Suddenly, a voice called out, "Watch it!" A thunderous slam made Jenna jump and startled the hell out of me. The giant set piece had tumbled to the floor and splintered into fragments. Alfie barked and scampered away.

The floor manager shouted "Rotating!" and I felt my stomach knot. I twisted around just as the frightened Alfie disappeared into the underbelly of the circular stage. The floor manager shouted again, "Rootaatiing!"

The huge gears lurched into motion and we heard a yelp, followed by a low painful whimper that escalated into a shrieking, terrifying series of yaps. The set only spun a few inches and abruptly ground to a halt. The floor manager quickly smacked the emergency button. On the living room set, a bowl of water sloshed over the sides.

I tossed back my head and turned to see if Jenna grasped what had just happened. She clenched my arm and whispered Alfie's name. It felt as if the air had been sucked out of the studio. Jenna collapsed to the floor and started wailing.

"Can somebody call security? We have an issue." I

flicked off my intercom box and bent down to Jenna, who was weeping violently. "My Alfie, my poor Alfie."

"Let's get you back to the green room." I placed my arm under hers and lifted her to her feet. Jenna continued to wail and a production assistant ran over with a box of tissues.

I escorted Jenna past the front section of the stage that overlooked the producer's desk and the order entry arena. A buzz of whispering among the order entry operators halted as Jenna and I passed through. I guided Jenna to the green room with my arm around her, and I didn't let go until she was safely seated. She had stopped sobbing, but appeared to be in a state of shock. She stared blankly at the wall across the room and I brought her a glass of water.

"I'm so sorry, Jenna." The television monitor showed Karen holding up a blue and white big shirt as she described the array of colors, "one for every occasion." I picked up the remote and powered down the show. Unsure what to do, I simply sat and held her hand in silence.

After a few moments, I heard a soft knock and the door slowly opened. The floor manager held a shipping box emblazoned with the Shoplandia logo in his hands.

"Don't bring that in here," I cringed, but Jenna motioned for him to place the box in front of her on the coffee table. He lowered the box and back-pedaled out of the room. Before I could stop Jenna, she peeked inside the box. "Oh, my poor baby," she whispered and began a fresh wave of sobbing.

Before I could comfort her, Bob Payne burst through the door, waving his bandaged hand. "Congratulations! That was a fabulous show..." He stopped at the sight of Jenna in tears. "What's the matter?"

I tilted my head at the box. The VP stepped up to the coffee table and lifted the lid a few inches.

"Oh my."

I slowly added items to my condo over the following few months. I drank at the Square Bar with the crew, and confided details of my disastrous marriage to friends. The blur of work carried me away from the debacle that was my personal life, providing distance and perspective. One afternoon as I walked past the host lounge, Karen bolted out the door and nearly ran me down.

"Hey! I was thinking about you!"

"What's up?"

"I'm running to makeup, where are you headed?"

"Into the studio."

"Did you hear about Jenna?"

"No. What's up?"

"Do you remember she had the shakes?"

"Yeah, of course."

"Well, according to *Entertainment Tonight*, she has Parkinson's."

"No."

"Some gossip columnist reported she stumbled at the fashion awards show and accused her of being drunk. She wanted people to know the truth. It's so sad."

I leaned back on the wall and felt a chill. The times I'd been holding her hand, asking if she was nervous, I thought she was simply aging. I sensed a shifting of the floor and placed the palm of my hand against the wall to steady myself. "Wow, what a shame."

Two hours later, I grabbed a chair and pushed myself into the desk at the mouth of the studio. I was listening on headsets to ensure there was no emergency. I Googled "Jenna McGregor." Hundreds of images of the actress popped on the screen and I clicked through to a few, examining her photos and a few freeze frames from movies.

"Jake, do you have a moment?" I looked up to see my boss Tony on the other side of the desk.

"Sure." I closed the Google page quickly. "What's up?"

Tony folded himself into a chair and leaned forward. "I'm sure you've heard about Jenna McGregor."

I nodded. "I just heard about it, it's so sad. I'm stunned."

"Well, she isn't able to fly out here and join us any longer. It's apparently too much. Within another few months she won't be making any public appearances. It's been a slow decline, absolutely horrible. We want to keep the jewelry line running and Jenna is supportive of us doing this with a new on-air guest."

I sat back and reflected. "How can I help?"

"We would like to somehow have Jenna's presence felt during the shows. We just got off the phone with her and the vendor. We want to shoot an interview with her so we can use clips during her shows."

"That would be a nice touch."

Tony nodded. "We have a remote show in Los Angeles next week, so I was hoping to have someone go over and shoot the interview."

"That sounds like a good idea."

"Well, Jenna specifically requested you."

I sat back.

"Buke was supposed to go on the remote, but I'd like to switch you and he out. You can work the remote and then you have the next morning to visit her in Encino with a videographer and shoot an interview."

Jenna's home was a modest little rancher with a nicely manicured lawn, still glittering from the morning sprinklers. I walked up under the carport and knocked on the side door. A gentleman, a few years younger than Jenna, with a pencil thin mustache, appeared at the entrance. He wore a dress shirt with the top three buttons undone and a gold chain with an eagle draped against his copper skin.

"Jake?"

"Yes. Hello."

The man stuck out his meaty hand. "I'm Ray, Jenna's ex-husband, one of them anyways." He provided a reassuring grip and I instantly felt comforted. "Jenna has told me so much about you, she's a big fan. Thanks for coming out."

Ray led me through a den, a kitchen and into a living room. The rooms were shaded and cool, the wallpaper in calming greens and browns. In the living room, Jenna smiled from her wheelchair.

"My boyfriend, Jake."

I leaned down, placed my arm around her and kissed her on the cheek. "Jenna, how are you?"

She reached up and held my hand. "I'm doing as well as can be expected. This disease is a bastard, but I've rested up for your visit."

I stepped back and scanned the room. Mementos from Jenna's movie days were everywhere. Framed photos of Jenna with Frank, Elvis, Marlon. Trinkets and movie props were neatly aligned on a set of shelves. I walked closer to study the photos.

"How are you healing?" she asked.

"The scar will remain, but I think I'll survive."

"You are young, with your whole life ahead of you." She sighed. "If only I was fifty years younger."

I smiled, but my eyes suddenly welled up. "If only I was fifty years older."

I followed Ray through the kitchen and into the backyard. A shaded porch led out to a small swimming pool, shaped like an egg, with brilliant blue water. The backyard was an oasis, with flowering shrubs and palm trees perched in the corners of the fenced-in yard.

"I'd like to shoot the interview here. Will she be okay in the sun?"

"I imagine she will."

The videographer studied the sun's location and suggested we set up on the backside of the pool, away from the house. "We can have the pool over her shoulder."

As Ray wheeled Jenna out, she commented, "I don't want to sit in this contraption during the interview."

"We have you taken care of dear."

He locked her wheelchair in position and stretched out his hand. I stepped forward and took her other hand. She shuffled over and lowered herself into a poolside chair.

I dragged over a patio chair and sat across from her. "I'll ask you questions, you just take your time and give us your thoughts. Okay?"

"Of course it is. I'm ready to recount my life story."

I asked her about her jewelry, about her love of the merchandise. I asked her about the movies and the actors she starred with over the years. She responded with energetic and clean anecdotes, as if she was still that young starlet under contract with the studio. After thirty minutes or so, as I wound up my questions, I sensed a weariness setting in.

"Hey Mike, I think we're done here. Can you let me sit alone with Jenna for a bit?"

"That's cool. I'd like some more of that iced tea." He walked around the pool and headed under the shaded porch, where Ray escorted him inside. I scooted my chair closer. Gentle ripples moved across the surface of the pool.

"I guess this is it."

"Jake, I've lived such a blessed life. I have nothing but gratitude for every moment, for every love I've had. And I've had some good ones. Sometimes, I wonder. Is it selfish to want more?"

"Let me ask you a question, if you don't mind."

"Of course, I don't mind."

"Out of your four husbands, which one was your true love?"

"The one I was with at the time."

"No, really now. One must have been your true love?"

"I'm not falling for that," she grinned. "Three of them have died, and I cried each time. Thank God Ray is still here to help me." She shifted in her chair and looked out over the pool. "I'm so fortunate to have lived this life. My life. Look at this glorious day, I'm here in this beautiful Southern California weather—poolside, in the company of a handsome young man."

I blushed and reached out, taking her fingers in mine.

"There is so much that is lovely in this universe, but it flies by in a mind-whirring blur. My only regret is that I remember so little."

On the red-eye flight home, I tried to nap but turned restlessly. When the flight attendant offered me a tray of food, I waved her away. I occasionally slept in short fits but woke each time in a sweat, as though a fever was breaking.

In the airport parking garage, I walked by my car twice in a daze before realizing which vehicle it was. The sun was peeking over the horizon when I arrived outside my condo, and I was looking forward to two days off. With my bag over my shoulder, I unlocked the front door and pushed it open. Before stepping inside, I stuck my hand in the mailbox and pulled out a few circulars and letters. A letter from the State of Pennsylvania certified that my divorce was final. I tossed the mail on the kitchen table and dropped my bag on the floor.

I was suddenly overcome with hunger and realized I'd not eaten since early the day before. I opened the refrigerator and saw it was barren—nothing of sustenance—just a few bottles of beer, orange juice and a couple pears. I opened the freezer and spied a stack of frozen dinners and a box of waffles. I tugged at a plastic wrapped container in the back of the freezer. *Wedding cake* was scrawled across the lid in black marker. I pulled out the container and unwrapped a giant wedge of butter pound cake covered in white fondant icing.

After dropping the wedge onto a plate, I tossed it into the microwave and tapped a few buttons. I pulled a beer out of the fridge, cracked it open and took a long swig before rummaging through the silverware drawer for a fork. My stomach rumbled as I watched the cake wedge spin. As the icing slowly pooled onto the plate, I realized just how famished I was.

THIRTEEN

....

FAN LETTER

September 23, 1989

Dear Jackson Carter,

This may be a bit forward, but I've enclosed a photo of my daughter Clarissa for you. I just know from having seen you so many nights on the air that you and Clarissa would be a match made in heaven. Just like you, Clarissa loves the grape leaf design in the Rushmore Gold jewelry you present on Tuesday nights at 9 p.m.

Clarissa doesn't watch Shoplandia as often as I do, but she thinks you are cute. She acts nonchalant about the whole thing, but because she is my daughter I can tell that she is smitten with you. (She can't bear to watch that Calabrese guy.)

You and Clarissa have so many similar tastes. You are always talking about dressing up and going out for an elegant meal, and when you look into the camera and say, "Go ahead and pick this bracelet up, you're worth it,"

I can see you are talking directly to my Clarissa.

Just like you, Clarissa loves watching sunsets, sleeping in on weekends and eating banana walnut pancakes with extra maple syrup. And just like you, Clarissa works in retail sales, doing her best to make sure her customers are happy.

Now I don't pay any attention to my husband Earl. He says some awful things at times, and he doesn't believe a man should be dressed up in suits, selling jewelry and figurines on television. Earl is a bit old-fashioned, and when he says things like you're a little light in your loafers I always defend you because I believe you are straight and honest. Earl is just a crotchety old man, but he's the best I could do under the circumstances. Just between you and me, I want Clarissa to do better.

Last night when I saw you selling the Karaoke machine and you sang Clarissa's all-time favorite song, *Unchained Melody*, I shouted Clarissa's name and started weeping with joy. Your voice was so glorious, it was as if the heavens had opened up. I'm sure it was a sign from the Almighty above that you and Clarissa are destined to be together. Unfortunately, Clarissa was out, working her night shift at Walgreen's down in Carthage, and I fumbled with the VHS tapes, trying to find a blank one so I could record your beautiful rendition, but I was afraid I'd mistakenly tape over *Jake and the Fatman*, which Earl had not yet watched because it was poker night with the boys.

Then last night, I had a dream that Shoplandia announced they were coming to do a production from our town, you know, at the Precious Moments Chapel nearby, and in my dream, you showed up at Walgreen's, searching down each aisle until you found my Clarissa. She was replenishing the anti-fungal creams in aisle six and as soon as she saw you, she knew, she just knew! And this dream was so vivid, cable television vivid, that I thought surely this must be a sign from the great Lord above. That's when I knew I would write you today.

Sincerely,

Ellen Marie Marstan

FOURTEEN

....

TEMPERANCE

"Here's video of the legendary Jackson Carter." War-ren Matthews waved a videotape over his head as he walked into Johnny Wake's office.

"Finally, it's here!" Johnny swirled away from his computer screen. "I was beginning to think he never really existed." He pointed at the VCR. "Throw it in."

"Wait until you see the production quality," Warren snickered as he fiddled with the VCR. "Everything about the show was terrible back in the day." He clicked play and faded video popped up, grainy streaks across the screen, the colors bleeding into each other. The camera sat on a wide shot of a beige backdrop. An antiquated logo on the back wall read Shoplandia.

Johnny Wake cringed. "Atrocious." He leaned in to examine the screen. "You have to love cable program-ming from the old days."

"Wait until you see the graphics." Warren stared at the screen as if anticipating a train wreck. A man in a tuxedo walked confidently onto the set, paused in the center of the stage and smiled directly into the camera with a flirtatious eye.

"Hello, I am Jackson Carter, and this is the Jewelry Showcase." The man was slim and his tuxedo looked as though it had been fitted moments ago. His light brown hair was parted in the middle, not a strand out of place.

"That is some helmet hair!"

Warren laughed. "It's almost a mullet!"

Jackson smiled into the camera and reverently picked up a bracelet. Within moments, the camera cut to a close up of the gold links twirling between his manicured fingers. A graphic with boxy, antiquated letters appeared on the screen. J-405 8-inch bracelet, 14k, Introductory Price $297.83

"What kind of font is that?"

"Fugly Bold."

Johnny snickered. He had landed at Shoplandia only three years ago, but he'd heard the stories of how the channel had started; how they built a small studio on a shoestring budget back in the early eighties and talked upstart cable operators into carrying the channel by offering a percentage of sales from customers. Now, nearly twenty years later, Shoplandia was a slick, multi-billion dollar cash cow with the finest studios and technical equipment available.

His first week on the job, someone had handed Johnny a found letter from a customer, and then he started hearing the stories of this infamous Jackson Carter. The customers adored him, but those in the studio were clear in their disdain. "I'd change my shift so I wouldn't have to deal with him," a technical director told

Johnny.

"It's amazing how much has changed," Johnny said.

On the screen, Jackson Carter introduced the bracelet as if it were the object of every woman's desire. As he rolled it in his fingers, the bracelet glistened under the studio lights. He described the buttery texture and the quality craftsmanship that went into each link as he held the bracelet with the utmost respect.

"When you walk into a room with this on your wrist, people will notice you. I can assure you of that! I would notice you." Jackson winked. He sat straight, his slim body perfectly aligned in his chair. Jackson's suit was impeccable, as though he'd lint brushed it clean between each airing. Everything about the man focused on perfection.

Johnny sat mesmerized. "This guy was good."

Warren nodded. "He supposedly created issues behind the scenes." The two men fell silent watching as Jackson flirted with Edna from Nyack on the phone.

"You'll just love this. I guarantee it."

"I just know I will. I can't believe I'm talking to you," Edna giggled.

Jackson smiled into the camera. "Now Edna, let me ask you a question. Is this for a special occasion?"

"My husband is sitting on the couch here. He said I could buy it for our anniversary, which is coming up next week. It will be his gift to me."

"Your husband is a smart man. What's his name?"

"His name is Herbert," and then she yelled out, "Herbert, you should say hello to Jackson."

A gruff voice called out in the background, "Hello there."

"Hello Herbert!" Jackson waved and smiled. Johnny noticed just the smallest hint of condescension in Jackson's smirk. "Well, I think Herbert's going to get himself something real special for his anniversary after buying you this, am I right Edna?"

Edna laughed as if she was blushing at the thought. Over the phone in the background, Herbert shouted, "I darn well better!"

"Herbert!" She replied in a shocked voice.

Jackson laughed out loud. "Herbert, you are a good man! Well Edna, I hope you and Herbert have a great anniversary and I hope he takes you someplace real special so you can show off this bracelet. You should get it in seven to ten days!"

"Brilliant," Johnny muttered. "Warren, leave the tape with me. I want to watch the whole thing."

That night, Johnny Wake stayed in the office and watched another two hours of Jackson's shift. He scribbled the details that set Jackson apart as a show host, noting how Jackson's smile reached into the camera as if he was in the viewer's living room. Johnny rewound the tape and watched certain segments repeatedly, studying how the camera stayed on Jackson as he flirted. Yet there was something else too. Under scrutiny, Jackson's attitude often bordered on patronizing and he reveled in pushing the envelope without callers catching on. The t-callers who fawned over him also sounded like older women, and they made offers.

"Oh, Jackson, I do wish you could meet my daughter!"

"Jackson, my daughter would be perfect for you."

But then something made Johnny cringe.

Jackson smiled into the camera. "We have another phone call. Hello?" There was no caller on the line. "Hel-looo?" Jackson asked again, and then he looked off camera in the direction of the producer's desk. "Kenneth, oh Kenneth. There's no caller on the line." Jackson tried to maintain his smile, but he was visibly irked that no caller was to be had.

"Kenneth is my producer today," Jackson said into the camera. "Kenneth will soon be working the overnight shift for a very long time." Jackson gave a condescending smile off camera and nodded before continuing with his presentation. For the final few moments, Jackson's on-air demeanor was tense, as though he was seething underneath.

Johnny leaned back in his chair. "Jackson Carter has a bit of a temper."

The next morning, Johnny Wake had his weekly one-on-one with the big boss. As the CEO of Shoplandia, Gordon Creosote's second floor corner office was perched as if it was in the trees, with floor to ceiling glass on two sides. The view overlooked the woods and the executive parking lot and since their meeting was an 8 a.m. standing appointment, they watched as the first of the office employees began streaming in like worker bees. Johnny sat across from Creosote in a high-back leather chair as they reviewed the current projects.

"One other idea I'd like to throw out there," Johnny

suggested.

"Shoot."

"There appears to be a cult following for this former host named Jackson Carter. Our research shows we have many long-time customers who miss this guy. They're always asking in chat rooms, what ever happened to Jackson?"

"I heard the guy was nothing but trouble behind the scenes."

"That's what I've heard from some of the studio crew. The guy apparently had an ego the size of Montana. Anyway, it seems as though he fell off the face of the earth."

"He was fired, if I recall correctly. I heard he was a monster."

"Yeah, that's what I heard. Anyway, he's been off the air for over ten years, yet the customers are still asking about him. I've been watching tapes of the guy. He had this on-air persona that was very charismatic. I really think he knew what he was doing. I can see how he had built this cult following."

Creosote shifted in his chair. "What's your thought here?"

Johnny sensed he was losing Creosote's attention. "Well, I've asked a few of my guys to try and track him down, just to find out if he's alive and lucid. If we find he's alive and stable, maybe it's worth trying to bring him back, even if just for our anniversary show. Of course, if he's in an asylum, we'll pass."

Creosote spun his chair around and looked into the

trees. Johnny endured the silence for a few moments. "I'd proceed cautiously on this one," Creosote finally said. "I don't know much about this guy, but I know he was considered a loose cannon."

By the end of the day, Warren returned to Johnny Wake's office with several leads.

"Johnny, here's what we found out. There are a ton of Jackson Carters out there. We've Googled, Yahoo'd, Facebooked, Myspaced him. Based on the information we have, we believe he returned to the Toledo, Ohio area. He grew up there. There are four Jackson Carters living within a fifty mile radius of Toledo."

Johnny pushed a buzzer on the intercom and called for his assistant Tina. When she showed up at the door, he announced, "I'm going to Toledo. Book me a flight out there. Warren, send me a copy of the addresses. If you can find out where each of these guys works, I'll take that info also. But I do not want him tipped off."

Warren headed toward the door. Johnny called out, "Warren!"

"Yeah boss?"

"See if there's an archived headshot I can take with me."

"Will do."

Johnny sat back in his chair and wondered for a brief moment if his obsession had gone a bit too far. He couldn't shake this idea of bringing Jackson Carter back on the air, even if it was for a ten second appearance in a straight jacket. The promotional possibilities, the buzz that could be created among the devotees was limitless. He envisioned the headlines splashed across the tabloids. He imagined the free press. But there was also something deeper driving Johnny's obsession.

Johnny's plane touched down in Toledo on a crisp morning. He hopped in a rental car and reviewed his directions for a Jackson Carter who lived on the north side. Thirty minutes later, Johnny pulled up to a small ranch home with a landscaped lawn. He knocked on the door. An elderly man answered with one hand resting against a cane for support.

"Jackson Carter ?"

"Yes," the man responded with a quizzical look.

"I'm sorry, I'm looking for a different Jackson Carter ."

As Johnny pulled up to the next location, he double-checked his papers. The address was correct, but the building was Saint Peter's Homeless Shelter. Johnny walked into the reception area—a dingy, musty waiting room with peeling paint and dog-eared posters about God's love, HIV warnings and the importance of good behavior. In the corner, a bearded man sat back with his head reclined and mouth open. He wore a red knit cap, filthy jeans, boots, and a brown and orange flannel jacket.

Johnny stood inside the front door for a moment, debating whether or not to leave, when he realized someone was moving behind a receptionist's window. He approached the petite woman. "Hi. I have this listed as the address for Jackson Carter ?"

"We don't really confirm who is staying with us. May I ask who you are?"

"I'm Johnny Wake, an old friend of Jackson's."

"Jackson has not been here for a few weeks. He was staying here but apparently had a relapse."

"Relapse?"

"Look, these residents come and go. Many get used to living on the streets. They may come in to warm up when it is freezing, but they prefer to live on their own."

Johnny turned slowly, but twisted back to the woman suddenly, flashing the photo of Jackson in her face.

"Is this Jackson?"

She glanced at the photo and her eyes widened. She nearly laughed. Johnny knew he had her. She stiffened and looked away.

"I really can't confirm or deny your question. I'm not at liberty to discuss any more. We're bound to uphold our client's privacy."

When she turned back, Johnny was already out the door with his answer. He was about to hop in the rental car when he noticed the bearded man had followed him. Johnny raised his eyes to acknowledge the man.

"I know where he is," the man called out in a raspy voice. He wore several layers of sweatshirts under his flannel, and the sole of his left boot flapped open like a crocodile's snout.

Johnny stood with the driver's side door open. "Will you take me to him?"

"It'll cost you."

"How much?"

"Fifty bucks."

"Okay, get in."

The man's stench permeated the car. Johnny rolled down the window, relieved it was only a rental.

"I'm Johnny."

"I'm Cliff. Got any cigarettes?"

"No. Sorry. Which way do we go?"

Cliff signaled to take a right. After a few more blocks, he pointed left. On their right, past some type of refinery, Johnny noticed a massive body of water.

"What lake is that?"

"That's Lake Erie, man." After a few seconds of silence, Cliff declared, "There's something out there. In the water."

Johnny craned his neck. "Where? I don't see it."

"Not now." Cliff glanced at Johnny. "It's not there now. But it's out there. Believe me."

"What is? What's out there?"

"I've heard folks describe it in all different ways, some say it is a giant eel. I met a guy who saw it once, he drew it out on a bar napkin and it looked like a giant squid, er, what's the word?"

"Octopus?"

"No. That ain't it." Silence filled the car. Cliff slapped the dashboard. "It's a kraken. That's what it is."

Johnny Wake nodded. "Have you ever seen it?"

"No. I don't need to see it. I can feel it."

As he drove, it dawned on Johnny that he was taking a risk, driving around in a desolate section of a strange city with a homeless, possible deranged, man. He pictured a gruesome scene on Toledo's local news—authorities dredging Lake Erie searching for his decayed body.

Cliff muttered directions every few minutes. The scenes out the window grew bleak. The twins and row homes grew smaller, several were boarded up and crumbling. Weeds sprouted through the cracks in the sidewalks.

"How long have you known Jackson?"

"For a bit." Cliff looked out the window. "He's a bastard."

The seedy neighborhood slowly changed into a series of industrial sites that lined Lake Erie. Cliff told him to take a right and they merged onto a highway, with a sign reading Michigan. Johnny grew alarmed.

"Where the hell are you taking me?"

"Jackson ain't on the streets. That bitch don't know nothing. Jackson lives in Temperance." Cliff looked over. "Don't worry. I ain't gonna do nothing."

After a short ride on the highway, Johnny saw a sign for Temperance and Cliff nodded to take the exit. At the bottom of the ramp, they stopped at a traffic light. Johnny looked at a dilapidated gas station across the street. One block later, they turned down a small side street lined with ramshackle white clapboard houses on small fenced lots.

"Park here." Cliff put out his hand. "I need the money now, before we go in."

Johnny fished through his pockets and pulled out the cash. For a split second, he thought of asking for a receipt for his expense report.

"You aren't fucking with me – are you?"

"No. I ain't fucking with you." Johnny looked at Cliff's craggy face and unkempt beard, and studied the man's bloodshot eyes.

Johnny and Cliff climbed out of the car and into the sunlight. Johnny felt as if he had stepped into some 1970s buddy detective television show, some strange alternate world.

He studied the neighborhood. The yards were barren. A rusted Mercedes sat on blocks in the yard of the decaying house. The shutters were falling apart, paint peeling, the dead winter lawn and shrubs had not been maintained. The shades were drawn on all the windows. In the distance, Johnny heard a menacing dog's growl and the rattling of a chain.

Cliff knocked and a ghost of a young woman pulled back the door. She was young, a faded tank top covered a scrawny shell of a body.

"Hey Cliff." The girl wiped her nose with the palm of her hand. "Who's he?" She pointed at Johnny. "I don't think Jackson wants a visitor today."

Cliff pushed open the door and walked past her. Johnny followed into the darkened room.

After a moment, the girl sighed. "He's in the back."

Cliff told Johnny, "Wait here."

Johnny scanned the surroundings. The room was litter strewn; two stained couches rested along each wall with cushions missing. Other cushions had been slit open with foam stuffing oozing out. A coffee table sat in

248

front of the one couch, littered with Pepsi cans, a Jack Daniels bottle, porn magazines. Graffiti had been scrawled on the walls, sporadically broken up by holes that had been kicked or punched. Newspapers and trash were strewn about the stained carpet.

The pale young girl sat on the couch and eyed up Johnny Wake. He shifted his weight from one foot to the other.

"Is that Dolce & Gabbana?"

Johnny glanced down at his jacket. He ran his finger over the gray wool, and then looked back at the girl. For the first time in his life, Johnny Wake was at a loss for words.

"Your jacket. Is that Dolce & Gabbana?"

Johnny had to pull open his jacket and check the label.

"It is," he said, surprised.

"I'll trade me for it," the young girl offered.

At first, Johnny thought he'd misheard the girl. He studied her frail frame. She sniffled and again rubbed her nose with the back of her hand. It slowly sunk in what she'd meant, what she'd offered. Before Johnny could respond, Cliff appeared from the darkened hallway. "He'll see you now."

Cliff held a tiny packet with white crystals in his hand as he pointed to the back room. Johnny looked down the darkened hall, and then glanced back at the girl on the couch. She stared at him as she scratched her inner thigh.

"Down there," Cliff pointed again and Johnny

thought he had no choice. He'd set this wheel in motion. He walked down the hallway until he came to a door slightly open on his left. He took a deep breath before easing the door open with his palm.

The room was dark with just the faint red glow of the sun trying to break through the curtains. A large mattress and box spring rested in a corner. On the other side of the room, three people were settled into a dilapidated floral couch. Two pale young women flanked a bloated, bearded man dressed in a ratty silk robe.

The coffee table was cluttered with paraphernalia. Soda cans, a whiskey bottle, a scale, baggies, white powder on a mirror, ashtray, cigarettes, a pack of Mentos. A boxy, antiquated television off to the side played video of a much younger Jackson Carter in a navy blue suit, perched behind a desk on the set of Shoplandia.

"Have a seat," the man on the couch said.

Johnny brushed off the cushion of a dirty chair and sat on the edge. He studied the TV for a few seconds, watched the young Carter on the screen, and then looked at what he'd become.

"Jackson Carter?"

"The one and only." He sipped a drink from a tumbler. "How much do you want?"

"I'm not here to make a purchase."

Jackson furrowed his brow. The girls gazed across the room.

Johnny took a deep breath. "My name is Johnny Wake, and I work at Shoplandia."

Jackson tilted his head and squinted one eye. He appeared to be brought back to reality from whatever high he'd been on. "I see. Can I get you a drink Mr. Wake?"

"No thanks. I just wanted to see what you've been working on since you left the network."

As Jackson rose up and walked across the room, his robe fell open, revealing dirty silk boxers and a stained tank top. He peeled a curtain back and peeked through the window.

"America has gone to hell in a hand basket." Jackson dropped the drapes back in place and paced back and forth. Johnny noticed a worn path in the old, orange shag carpet under Jackson's feet.

"You were quite the show host back in the day," Johnny said. "You had a lot of fans. What was your secret? What's the secret?"

Jackson halted mid-stride and glared at his guest. Red streaks coursed through his eyes. His pupils were dilated. He finally put his head down and started pacing again. Johnny shifted in his chair.

Jackson began to bellow. "The secret? Run away from the pain and toward the pleasure. Make them feel like if they don't have the next great thing, their lives will be hell and they will be ostracized, their lives meaningless." He turned on his heels and stopped in front of Johnny. "But if they attain it, if they purchase it, if they part with their hard earned money for a chunk of metal in some fancy fucking design, then they will become a god. They will be desired, they will be loooooved. If you own this, you will be worthy!"

Jackson spit out the last word. A girl on the couch

sniffled. "There are only two things that matter in this world. Everything hinges on only two things." Jackson stopped pacing and looked directly at Johnny Wake. "Do you know what they are?"

"No," Johnny replied. He sat on the edge of the seat, expectant. His heart palpitated as if the Holy Grail was about to be revealed to him.

Jackson walked up to Johnny and slowly leaned in, so close that Johnny smelled the stench of liquor on his breath, so close Johnny thought Jackson might smack kiss him. Jackson's lips brushed against Johnny's ear as he whispered, "Getting tail and snorting blow."

Jackson stepped back and grinned, and then he reached out and lightly caressed Johnny's face with the back of his hand. "That's the whole fucking secret."

Johnny shivered and glanced at the two frail girls on the couch. One had dozed off, curled up in the fetal position. Johnny thought somebody should check her pulse. The other smoked a cigarette and watched the impeccable Jackson Carter on TV flirt with a caller. The bloated Jackson walked to the curtain and glanced out the window again.

When Johnny went to stand, his knees buckled and he caught himself. He stumbled into the hallway in a daze, and followed the wall with his hand to steady himself. The momentum carried him toward the door. In the front room, Cliff and the young woman leaned over a coffee table shaping the powder into lines.

The woman grasped at Johnny's pant leg as he stumbled past them. "So we got a deal?"

Johnny yanked his leg away and pulled open the door in one movement. Children were laughing in the distance. The girl rolled off the couch and clambered after him.

"Come on, do we got a deal?"

As he stepped outside, Johnny turned toward the young voices, and saw grade school kids with backpacks and lunch boxes streaming off a school bus at the corner. Their voices floated along with the breeze.

"You loser!" the woman called after him, but he was out in the Michigan sunlight.

....

FIFTEEN

SO MANY BOXES, SO MUCH STUFF

Karen leans forward and examines her face in the salon mirror. She isn't fond of this substitute makeup artist, Charlene, who moves rapidly, chews gum and skimps on foundation. Maxine, her usual makeup artist, understands Karen's personal desires and the need to lighten up around her aging, baggy eyes. Only Maxine understands that Mocha works better than Cocoa Number 4.

When Karen started as a host at the fledgling Shoplandia, she quickly and expertly applied her own makeup. At the time, she was twenty-six years old with fair, clear skin. Back then, her jaw line didn't require expert contouring. She just dabbed powder on and was ready for air, but over the years, the process to make her camera ready has grown more complicated.

"All done." Charlene takes a step back to eyeball her work.

Karen lifts herself and leans in to the lighted mirror, debating whether or not to ask Charlene for more concealer. Hell, what she really wants to do is tell Charlene to start over, to start from scratch. Instead, she swallows the percolating rage and mutters, "Thanks, dear," as she exits the salon.

It's already been a strange day. An hour ago as she climbed the broad wide steps to the front entrance of Shoplandia World Headquarters, she realized her employee badge was sitting at home on her kitchen counter. Too late to return, she heaved open the towering glass door and entered the white marbled lobby. Gerry, the usual security guard, was not stationed at the desk. Instead, a new kid with short blonde hair and a bulldog nose glanced up.

"I forgot my badge." She impatiently adjusted her massive Dior shoulder bag, delivering a subtle hint that she was in a hurry.

The kid asked, "Your name?"

"Karen Loftus."

He turned his attention to the computer screen and pecked on the keyboard. "What department do you work in?"

She sighed. "Broadcasting."

He clicked the mouse and typed again. After a moment, he squinted at the screen and scrolled through the directory.

"Sorry, Ma'am. I don't see your name here."

She rolled her eyes and grinned. "Do you ever watch the show? That show over there?" She pointed to a massive television monitor that ran the length of the far wall. The security guard peered over as if he was viewing it for the first time. On the air, a woman in an apron pulled a cooked goose out of the oven and set it on the kitchen island.

"Not really." He gave Karen a blank stare.

She bit her lower lip. "I'm a show host. I've been on the air four nights a week for the past 19 years." As soon as she uttered the sentence, Karen wished she could retract it. A sense of heaviness settled on her and she lifted the bag off her shoulder and plopped it on the glass counter. She suddenly shuddered. What if she's been laid off? Maybe an HR processing glitch deleted her prematurely from the computer?

The kid squinted. "Wait, aren't hosts in a department called Talent?" He navigated to another page. "There you are. I have it now." He jostled the printer until it spewed out a temporary badge that he handed to Karen. "Have a good night."

Karen slung her bag over her shoulder and walked briskly down the hall, as if the confusion at the front desk had sent her tightly packed schedule into frenetic disarray. But it hadn't. Her agitation faded and her pace slowed. She let out a faint smile at her own fleeting paranoia. As she entered the atrium, she looked up and said aloud, "Oh, for God's sake."

A sprawling, freshly printed white banner hung from the wall featuring a giant headshot of America's new favorite Shoplandia show host, Renee. The young host's slender forearm was set near her face at a bizarre angle, her wrist adorned with a series of gold bangles. The suits had recently hired this bubbly host to freshen the face of the network. Renee's trademark was her natural patter, punctuated by a laugh that reminded Karen of a howling creature. Corporate fast-tracked Renee through training, and each subsequent release of the show host schedule showed her rising in the ranks, being given more opportunities in prime time.

Karen dropped her gaze, but she felt her gut knotted with a sense of dread. The suits upstairs kept searching for new talent, young slim women with chirpy voices, eager-to-please types with perpetual smiles and triple pierced ears. Though Karen still hosted prime time, she sensed the top brass was closely examining her shows. She imagined small flocks of suits sitting behind closed doors, pecking at the show host schedule like hungry vultures, eager to implement change and boost sales.

With hair and makeup now in place, she opens the door to the host lounge and hears the unmistakable chorus of professional broadcast voices. The booming operatic Tanya shouts out, followed by a counter-punch, the snarky laugh of Henry and the giggle of Renee.

The door slams shut behind Karen as she makes her way through to the shared open space, and all three hosts turn as their laughter fades.

"Hi Karen," Renee perks up. She holds a Big Gulp in her hands, the straw smeared with her cherry red lipstick.

"Hello," Karen replies. "Sounds like I missed the party."

Tanya says, "We were just telling Renee how much

we loved her banner in the atrium. Did you see it? It's gorgeous."

Karen hesitates for a moment and then makes her way to a workstation. "I must have missed it. I'll have to check it out."

"It's a great photo," Henry exclaims.

Renee cringes. "You guys are too kind. You can tell they photoshopped my wrist into the photo. I think it is an odd angle. It looks like someone else's hand."

Tanya scoffs. "Nobody can notice that."

"Ah, don't worry about it," Henry replies. "You should see what they will be doing with our body parts next."

There's silence as all three women anticipate a dirty joke to ensue, but Henry remains straight-faced. "No, I'm serious."

Karen leans in, fires up the computer at her workstation, and sits down to listen. "What are they working on?" she asks to pop the awkward moment, though she is only marginally interested.

Tanya glances over at Henry and he just shakes his head. "Have you heard how engineering has taken over studio 3C for some special top secret project?"

"No," Karen replies.

"Evidently they are working on some type of holographic background. They can put a host in front of a green screen and create a 3D background using animation with these powerful new computers."

"It's kind of crazy," Tanya marvels. "The idea we'd be selling a product and not be in a physical space."

"Yeah, but here's the crazy part." Henry suddenly

stands and walks to the door to the conference room. He pokes his head through to see if anyone might be listening, then closes the door and returns to his seat, before leaning in toward the women.

"Have you seen the video from that festival out west where they showed a rapper on stage? They created a holograph of that dead rapper, Sixpacks, that dude who was shot, and he was resurrected on stage in front of a live audience."

"I saw that on *Entertainment Tonight*," Renee chirps.

"Well, according to Bernie, have you met Bernie? He's our chief engineer."

Renee nods and sips from her Big Gulp.

"Well, Creosote called Bernie into his office right after this holographic rapper hit the news. Creosote is apparently obsessed with this technology. He was asking Bernie how we might use it here at the network."

Tanya squints. "So we can keep selling after we're dead?"

"We could bring Frankie Mack back?" Renee asks.

Henry shakes his head. "No."

Silence swells as they recall their deceased friend for a moment.

Finally, Karen gasps, "to replace us?"

Henry raises his hands and shrugs. "I don't know. I guess that's what he's thinking, but it seems kind of sci-fi. The holographic images are scripted and pre-programmed."

The four hosts sit silently, pondering the thought that their jobs might someday be outsourced to the geeks in Information Technology.

Tanya crinkles her nose and shoos Henry. "Yeah, there's no way to do that live." She stares blankly for a moment, and then asks reflectively, "Is there?"

"I really don't know, maybe in the future," Henry replies. "Anyway, Bernie says right now the holographic imaging is too expensive and the software is still cumbersome. He thinks we're years away. But Creosote asked him all these questions. He asked Bernie to invite the design company to visit. He suggested trying a holograph with a model."

Karen has been sucked in now, her eyes are wide with worry. "How would you put a piece of jewelry on a holographic model?"

Renee pipes up. "Sixpacks was wearing a big gold rope in that concert. I remember watching it sway around." She takes a sip on her straw and the room is filled with a slurping echo.

At the Studio Desk, the intern silently points to the green room and Karen heads in to meet with a guest.

Two men in tired looking suit jackets stand at the far end of the room while a third man sits stoically on the couch with his legs crossed. The seated man is tanned and relaxed in a pair of khakis and a blue polo shirt. Karen determines he must be the on-air guest, George. Upon seeing her, he rises with hopeful expectation.

"Hi. Sorry I'm late. It's been a crazy day. I had to get my makeup on."

"The old war paint," he replies with a grin.

She stares at him oddly as they shake hands.

"That's what my dad used to call it. Nice to meet you. I'm George. Meet Lawrence and TJ." She shakes their hands and swivels back to George.

"Can we review the product out on the set?" George asks. "It's a grout cleaning kit. We've built a prop for the demonstration. It's a really revolutionary product!"

"Let's do it," she replies and turns to head out to the set. She rolls the word revolutionary around in her head. Nothing in her shows, or in her life, is revolutionary anymore.

Karen had come from a small news station in Western Maryland, where she was the writer, the producer and the host of the morning newscast. She barely earned enough for her apartment—an in-law suite on a farmstead off the Chesapeake Bay. She had been in the news business for six years out of college, and was gaining no traction, so she auditioned for this new type of channel that sold stuff on air. At her audition, she picked up a fork and talked about it for three minutes, describing the sharpness of the tines and the balance of the weighted piece. She described the shine on the metal and delicately explained that, with a little buffing, it would be as good as new and was an essential tool for bringing happiness to one's life.

In the early days, her presentations were dreadful. Each product had a blue card printed out with the item number and a description. She would carefully handprint her own notes on each card, detailed remarks so she could speak fluently about the item for eight to ten minutes. She included personal anecdotes, explaining how her mother used a similar fry pan to make flapjacks on snowy mornings or how her father had once had a bird feeder in the backyard that brought her brothers and sisters great joy.

Eventually, she weaned herself off the carefully blocked notes. She developed the ability to chat off the cuff about anything, at any time, with a smile and a pleasant attitude. She enjoyed presenting items in a friendly manner, and when she took phone calls on air, she felt as though she was out shopping with girlfriends, encouraging them to make a splurge. When management decided to start scheduling guests on the air, it proved to be a mixed blessing. Sometimes she wouldn't get more than a few introductory words in before being run over by a loquacious guest who had rehearsed an infomercial script for the last two weeks, spewing out over-the-top phrases that made her think they surely must either be paid on commission or by the word.

Now, she stands on the garage set facing an immense blue-and-white tiled faux shower and bath unit, complete with a sliding glass door smeared in mud. The prop is atrocious. Karen is sure that Dottie, today's coordinating producer, must have had a fit when this mammoth piece rolled through the back loading dock like a Trojan horse.

"Isn't it great?" George pronounces with a sense of pride.

Karen notices one of the dowdy vendors has tagged

along while holding a brown box under his arm like a loaf of bread. George moves to a small table where the grout cleaning kit is displayed. "Here's what comes with the kit: three brushes, each with a unique angle and brush softness, and two grout cleaners. One is a paste and the other is granular. It's all very exciting."

She picks up one of the brushes and runs her fingers through the bristles. The head of the brush is cocked at a severe angle. She imagines scrubbing her shower with this brush. For the last ten years, she has used a cleaning service and can't recall the last time she vacuumed a rug, mopped a floor or cleaned her bathroom. Twice a month, she returns home to find her townhouse sparkles, the maid just another piece of her autopilot life.

George explains how he would like to see the presentation unfold, the points he hopes to make and the demonstration he is prepared to show. Karen simply nods, only half-listening.

"How does that sound?" George asks.

"Sounds fine."

"I'm sorry," George says as he steps back. "Here we are, launching into our thoughts and we didn't ask what you think customers will respond to? After all, you are the expert. You've been doing this much longer than we have."

She eyes him carefully. Is he implying she is old? After a moment, she decides not. "No. I think you have it covered. I think the key is to not move too quickly when you are demonstrating. Show the brush scrubbing the grout."

"I've only done this at trade shows, not on live TV."

She points to the robotic cameras. "We need to be sure our camera is on a tight shot as you scrub away. That's the moment it clicks in the customer's mind that she has to have it. We call it the money shot."

"The money shot?"

"Yep. If you are moving too fast, I'll ask you to slow down or pause for a minute. Think of this presentation like a dance," she smiles slyly, "except I'm in the lead."

George nods with understanding. "I shall follow your lead," he says respectfully.

"Wait until the red light is on the camera before you clean the grout."

"Understood."

"If there's nothing else, I need to go."

The vendor steps forward and offers the box to Karen as if he is making an offering.

George says, "Oh, we wanted to give you a product sample to take home and try."

Karen takes the box. "Thank you, gentlemen." She looks at George. He is in his late forties, with graying sideburns and a weathered face. He is a good-looking man with a strong chin. She likes this about him.

Two hours later, she is back at the outhouse on wheels. George stands completely still, stiffly holding his grout cleaner as though he is posing in American Gothic.

"Just relax," Karen reassures him. "Everything will be fine."

After describing what is included in the kit, Karen opens the sliding glass door of the shower unit. The inside has been aggressively smeared with mud and the ridiculous sight makes her snicker. As the handheld cameraman steps in, Karen jokes, "Evidently, this shower belongs to a pig farmer. George, muck it out."

Throughout the presentation, George moves slowly and awkwardly. He is hesitant to clean any section until she prods him along. His natural charm from their meeting has dissipated. He doesn't want to make a move without her. She has to continually point out sections of the shower stall and ask, "Can you clean this for us?"

When she asks him to scrub a section over the soap rest, he replies, "Are you ready for the money shot?"

Karen winces. "You can wipe it now."

As George swipes the mud off the tiles, the line producer exclaims in Karen's ear, "He shouldn't be calling it the money shot! What the fuck?" Karen glances at the monitors to make sure she is off camera and then she turns up her palms and shrugs.

George finishes wiping the tile. "It's really magical, isn't it?" The camera focuses on the white stripe left in the wake of the sponged hand.

"Revolutionary," she replies, the word slipping out before she can stop herself.

As the presentation comes to a close, Dottie appears behind the cameras with her hands on her hips. A voice in Karen's ear instructs her to head to the living room to present a police scanner. As she steps off the set, Dottie rushes in and admonishes the guest.

"We don't talk about the money shot on the air. That is an inside term, do you understand?"

Karen glances back and sees George standing like a school boy being disciplined. Dottie is waving her arms to drive home her point.

"There are certain things that we don't talk about on the air, and the money shot is one of them!"

When she arrives home exhausted, anxious to slip her aching feet out of their high heels, Karen pulls her Lexus into the garage of her townhouse slowly, eyeing the tennis ball that hangs on a string from the ceiling. Years ago, her father had hung the tennis ball at the precise spot she should stop before hitting the wall, yet be tucked in enough so the garage door will close behind her. Still sitting inside the car, she clicks the remote and listens to the garage door close. She cuts the engine just as the door taps the concrete.

She lifts the sealed brown box off the passenger seat and holds it under her arm as she unlocks the door and enters her basement, which resembles a scaled down version of Shoplandia's stocked warehouse. Boxes of various sizes are stacked from floor to ceiling, resembling a towering game of Jenga that might topple at any moment. She lifts the sealed brown box and carefully rests it on top of a pile that's taller than she is. She releases her hands slowly, prepared to catch the box if it falls, but the carton is well centered on top.

Scanning the cramped space, she wonders what she will do with all this dead weight. Most of the boxes are unmarked and unopened. Others show their contents through a combination of bright, happy images and pithy marketing language. The boxes hold a wide range of items she has presented over the years—pots and pans, shoes, purses, radar detectors, shower faucet heads, porcelain figurines, hair dryers, autographed baseballs, makeup kits, even a grotto statue of the Virgin Mary.

Barely a day has gone by when she hasn't brought her work home with her, and with the sight of certain boxes, her mind floats back to a specific moment in time.

Covert's condescending smile on his 5-CD *Empower Your Cortex* reminds her of his electric presentation in the audience theatre. The limited edition McAdoo horse dung lawn ornament (shaped like a bullfrog) represents the day of an investors' meeting, when shareholders crawled through the studio like flies. With each glance of the vibrant assortment of oranges, bananas and apples on the Ottoman 2000 Juicer box, she recalls her deceased friend, Frankie Mack.

She hasn't used these items, but instead has buried them in their shells. They've become accumulated markers that reflect the arc of her career. She winds through the narrow goat path, cautious not to knock over any of the towers, and climbs the stairs.

Despite the subterranean clutter, the first and second floors of her townhouse are immaculate, thanks to the cleaning company. Karen barely ever cooks at home. She opens the nearly empty fridge, pulls out a bottle of Chardonnay and pours a glass. After a sip, she tops the glass off and returns the bottle to the fridge. She carries the wine up to her bedroom.

Standing at the foot of her bed, she slides off each layer—her royal blue silk blouse and skirt, her bra and her Spanx—before taking her wine glass into her bathroom. In the mirror, she studies her reflection. "War paint," she mutters. She'd not heard the expression in years and it unnerves her.

With a twist of the faucet, warm water runs over her wrists. She opens a washcloth and lets the water soak through it and over her hands. She wrings the excess moisture out and smothers her entire face, wiping off her eyeliner and her base. After rinsing the towel under the water one more time she cleans her face until there is no trace of her war paint. Only age spots remain.

In the morning, Karen laces up her Reeboks and heads out for her morning walk. As she returns, she notices a man hammering a lawn sign into the ground at the entrance to the townhouse development. *Multi-family Yard Sale Saturday, 8 a.m. - Noon.* The man stands up straight, smiles and waves, and Karen returns the gesture.

Stuck in the handle of her front door is a yellow flyer. *The more the merrier. De-clutter your life.* The pamphlet gives details of the Saturday yard sale. While sliding her key into the lock, Karen senses a tingle pass through her body, and she immediately knows. She will unload herself on Saturday. She will sell what she can, lighten her burden, free up her basement.

Inside the front door, Karen grabs a key off the credenza and walks down to the cluster of mailboxes in the cul de sac. Halfway to the boxes, she spies one of her neighbors, a woman who is involved in the association and always has the latest gossip. "Hi Shelly, I see we are having a garage sale?"

"Good morning, Karen. Yes we are! Will you be joining us?" The woman is short and round, wears wire-rimmed glasses and a velour pantsuit that Karen thinks might be sold on a competing shopping channel.

"I just might," Karen replies. "I have a few things I could clean out of the house."

"I bet you do! I'd love to see what you have for sale."

Karen cocks her head, surprised at the woman's enthusiastic response.

"I saw you on TV last night, cleaning the bathroom with that good looking gentleman."

Karen laughs, "Oh, that. It's all part of the job."

"I wish I could find a man to do my cleaning. I can't get Clark to put a single dinner plate in the dishwasher."

Karen grins. "That's funny Shelly. What's the news in the cul de sac?"

When Shelly returns home, she bolts right to the kitchen, picks up her phone and dials her sister Thelma, who shuffles paperwork at a local doctor's office. "Karen Loftus is going to take part in our community yard sale!"

"No, really? Get out of here!" Thelma leans out of her cubicle to see if anyone is eavesdropping, and she determines all is clear.

"I just talked with her. She said she is in."

"Did she say what she has?"

"No, but I was in her basement once. She has so much stuff."

"Wait, you were in her house? Did I know that?"

"Well, just her basement," Shelly clarifies. "Last spring I found a letter she had dropped at the mailbox. I walked it over and I went into her garage. Her basement door was open." Shelly pauses for full effect. "Thelma, she must have every product she has ever sold in there. I was going to yell up the steps but there were so many unopened boxes, so much stuff: cookware, vacuum cleaners, handbags, a bread-maker."

"A bread-maker? Get out of here."

"I'm telling you, it was a lot of stuff. I just stepped inside and called her name, but she didn't answer, so I left the letter on a box. Her basement is crammed to the ceiling. I'm telling you Thelma, she must have one of everything she's ever sold."

Thelma hangs up the phone and once again wheels her chair back and checks for traffic in the aisle. Once she determines all is quiet, she pulls her chair back in, collapses the medical billing program on her computer screen, and logs onto her favorite website, *Shoppophile!* She scans through the threads of conversations from the cult of shopping channel fans:

My storage bags leak air...

Has anyone tried the Covert Tapes?

We Love Renee!

What Host Phrases Annoy You The Most?

RIP Frankie Mack

My Diamonelle stone popped out. How's yours?

Thelma clicks to start a new thread, and types out, *Shoplandia Host Holds Major Yard Sale.*

On Saturday morning, Karen's alarm clock sounds softly at first, but gains in intensity until she can ignore it no longer. She covers her eyes and stretches her legs until it registers that she needs to move fast.

After slipping into old jeans and a t-shirt, she makes her way down the basement stairs. Surrounded by the towering stacks of boxes, she wonders how much she can clean out in an hour, and wishes she had time for a cup of coffee. She opens the door from the basement into the garage and suddenly hears voices from outside, on the other side of the roll up door. After a moment, she smacks the pad. As the door rolls up, feet and legs become visible. A few dozen strangers are gathered in her driveway.

She stands at the entrance to her garage and scans the crowd. A few are nestled in lawn chairs, others are chatting among themselves. It's as if they are in line, waiting for Rolling Stones tickets to go on sale. The voices stop and all eyes fall on Karen. A woman taps her friend on the shoulder, "Look! It's really her!"

"What are you all doing here?" Karen asks.

"We're here for the yard sale," a man sitting in a lawn chair with a magazine on his lap responds. The crowd stands hushed, in anticipation of Karen's next move.

Karen nods slowly. "If you don't mind, I need to pull my car out to the curb. Can you give me some room?" The crowd parts amongst whispers. As she turns to get in her car, she hears the scrape of lawn chairs being dragged across her driveway, and then a voice exclaims, "She looks different without makeup."

Karen slides into the car seat. Her hand trembles as she starts the ignition. After checking her rearview mirror twice, she slowly backs out the car. Several vehicles are parked along the curb so she has to drive halfway down the block to find a parking spot. It's a beautiful morning, sunny and cool. Although this is to be a community yard sale, and she notices a few neighbors setting up, a crowd has formed only in her driveway. Walking back to her house, Karen notices license plates not just from Pennsylvania, but also representing Delaware, Maryland and New Jersey. The eyes follow her as she walks up her driveway.

"What do you have today?"

"What are you selling?"

"I've watched you for years!"

"You'll just have to wait and see." Karen tries to maintain a smile. Once inside the garage, she hits the pad and turns around to watch the people disappear as the door slowly descends. The door taps the ground, but she stands frozen.

After setting up two folding tables, she spends her remaining time lugging boxes from the basement to the garage. The plan was to sticker each item as she brings it out but she decides to just carry out as much as possible. Many of the boxes have never been opened, and she has no memory of what is inside. She slices the tape, removes the extra cardboard and the packing peanuts. The process takes longer than she has planned.

She wipes a bead of sweat from her brow with the back of her hand. She wishes she could roll up the garage door for a breeze, but doesn't want to work under the eyes of the gathering crowd. She works quickly, chipping a fingernail and slicing her finger with a box cutter. According to her watch it's 7:54 and she has barely made a dent in the basement. The voices outside grow as she stacks her boxes.

Exactly at 8:00, the voices intensify and she feels she has no choice but to open the door. She wishes she had asked a girlfriend to help, to stand guard. As the door rolls up, she sees the mob has swelled. For a brief silent moment, they stand in her driveway with the morning sun at their backs, cast in an eerie silhouette. All she hears is the chirping of a bird. One woman steps into her garage, and then there is a surge, they swarm, sorting through Karen's personal items, and she is bombarded with a series of questions.

"How much for the Precious Moments figurine?"

"What's in this box?"

"Are the prices marked?"

"Can we open these boxes?"

"Is this all there is?"

She has mistakenly left the door into the house open and people are now floating into her basement examining items. Empty boxes sit in one corner and people have ripped through them, as though she has hidden something at the bottom of each stack.

As Karen haggles the price of a Belleek ceramic salt and pepper shaker set with a man who resembles a bodybuilder, a petite white haired woman carrying a cane pokes at her.

"I talked to you once before on TV, like three years ago during a *Jewelry Showcase*, do you remember?"

Karen isn't sure whether to laugh or be indignant that the woman tapped her with the cane. "I've taken thousands of calls through the years. I'm sorry."

The woman lets out a huff. "We talked about my granddaughter getting married."

"Oh, that's nice." Karen feels a hand on her shoulder and she swivels to see someone holding up an eight-outlet surge protector. "How much do you want?"

"Two dollars."

A gaunt man approaches wearing a cap with a Navy insignia. He has gray stubble and wears black-rimmed glasses. "Hey, we've been wondering. Whatever happened to that Jackson Carter?" A plump woman with red-dyed hair and a pink fleece jacket runs over to his side and loops her arm in his. "Yeah, I sure do miss him. He was so sweet."

"I honestly don't know. He seems to have disappeared." She envisions Jackson reincarnated as a hologram, standing straight and tall in a tuxedo with a smirk on his face.

At first she thinks she should stand at the garage door to keep people from walking out without paying, but once people enter her basement she has to keep checking inside. When she returns to the garage, it looks as though a few of her items are missing, but she can't recall which objects they might be.

Karen hasn't labeled the products, but she continually hears people estimating how much each item sold for on the live show, and how much they are willing to pay for the item this morning. It strikes her that everything will go for the right price.

"I'll give you $15!"

"Will you take $12?"

"Do you have item L-50493?"

To complicate matters, many of the people just want to talk to Karen. They feel like she is a friend from watching her over the years. Karen tries to be polite, but she is unnerved at the need to put on her professional face unexpectedly and so early in the morning. She watches people walk down her driveway with products they haven't paid for, and she experiences the strange sensation of being dismembered.

"Excuse me," she calls out. The bodybuilder doesn't turn around.

Both pockets of her jeans are stuffed with bills and she holds a wad of cash in her hand. She craves a shower and wants to end the whole scene but the bargain hunters continue to stream into her garage. Across the way, a few neighbors stand in their empty yards, staring over at the flurry of activity. Their own tables are set up with odds and ends, untouched in the sun.

By the time she is approached by a man in a gray polo shirt and dirty jeans, with an unlit cigarette dangling from his mouth, she is fed up with the situation, and decides to ignite a match of her own.

"How much for the sprinkler thingy?"

Exasperated, she declares, "Everything is free."

"What?" The man's cigarette falls from his lips.

"Everything is free. Take it all."

She backs up a few steps and cups her hands around her lips. "Everything in my garage and basement is free! Help yourself! Please take it all." For a moment, silence falls over the garage. People stare until she mutters again, "Seriously, this stuff is free." The crowd rushes the garage. Her basement transforms into a mosh pit of pushing and shoving people. With boxes under their arms and over their heads, people beeline to their cars, and then run back to the garage. One young man snaps photos of the scene with his cell phone. People don't know what's inside the boxes, and apparently they don't care.

Along the wall of the garage, she notices nobody has taken her large blue Coleman Cooler on wheels, probably because she has Loftus scrawled in marker on the white lid. She plops herself down on it, leans back against the cool cinder block wall and observes the mayhem. She is reminded of walking through a bustling Grand Central Station a few weeks earlier, and noticing a panhandler standing by the wall, ignored by the masses.

Across the garage, through the frenetic foraging, a young teen girl stands perfectly still, staring at Karen, though not with the usual grin of recognition. Karen glances at the girl, but isn't brave enough to challenge the teen's glare. People stream by between them, carrying boxes, like it's a bustling city sidewalk on Christmas Eve. With courage, Karen glances back at the girl. Although the girl's eyes are still fixed on the show host, it becomes clear that the teen no longer sees her. Karen tingles with the sensation that she has shrunken and disappeared amid the mayhem. A shiver shoots through her and she doesn't look the girl in the eye again.

The eruption of a shouting match shakes Karen out of her daze. A tall woman in jeans and a purple shirt pulls on one arm of a collectible Bernice Ball rag doll while a short stout woman leans back holding the doll's other arm in a tug of war.

"I saw it first."

"No way. I called it."

"I'm not letting go."

"Well, neither am I."

"You bitch!"

The tall woman stops leaning back. She instantly lunges forward and with one fell swoop of her long bony arm, she slaps the small woman's face. The little round woman lets go of the doll and wobbles. The tall woman picks up the fallen doll with both hands, folds it under her arm and runs out of the garage, passing two men in police blues who are walking up the driveway. The officers watch as the mob feasts on the remaining boxes and one officer steps up to Karen.

"Ma'am, we have reports of some type of problem here, a possible riot."

Karen looks up at the officers. "Oh, I think it's just about over."

The older officer scans the scene, while the younger officer walks to the basement door and is nearly knocked down by a woman exiting with a large unmarked box.

"Ma'am, are you giving your items away?"

"Yes, that's all it is, not a riot. Help yourself, though I think everything is about cleaned up."

Karen rises from the cooler and steps toward the officer, surprised at the lightness in her step.

SIXTEEN

....

LAUGH TRACK

Years after his fateful indiscretion, Ron Calabrese now sits in a musky editing studio on the outskirts of East Hollywood. His sole job is to add the laugh track to a series of sitcoms, none of which he finds funny in the least. Ten hours a day, he sits on a ragged pleather chair, which has cracked to show the charred inners, and watches as young, feral 20-year old actors repeat foul tepid lines while slacking in fake coffee shops and loft apartments.

The live audience doesn't chortle at the appropriate moment. Their guffaws are ill-timed and forced. Calabrese views these shows without laughing at all, without even smiling. Sitcoms without humor. Yet he "sweetens" them, as the term is called in the business.

Calabrese's toolbox includes a series of sixteen different laugh tracks. There is *raucous laugh* and *light chuckles*. One of the tracks can only be used sparingly. *Hyena woman* is named as such because a high-pitched squeal can be heard exactly seven seconds into the track.

The room in which he spends ten hours a day is

poorly lit and the video monitors hang above a series of dials and buttons that are his editing system. The red shag rug, which covers both the floor and walls, whiffs of cigarettes and mold. The cleaning ladies haven't vacuumed, or even dusted, in the last fifteen years. He's become proficient at his purgatorial pursuit, laying in the proper laugh tracks for a half hour show (twenty-two minutes in entirety) in about two-and-a-half to three hours. The repeated watching of these shows, re-racking each scene multiple times to determine which track to use, slowly grates at his synapses as if they are worn cartilage. An x-ray of his soul would reveal bone now scrapes on bone.

When he first arrived here, it being the only job he could find after being fired from Shoplandia for groping a model on live TV, Calabrese thought he could at least view female actresses on the screen, freeze frame them in certain poses, examine their ears, imagine what they would be like if they were to visit him in his third-floor rented room that overlooks the back alley of a Vietnamese restaurant.

But now, at fifty-six, his sexual prowess has died out. He has squeezed off one too many, his glasses are like Coke bottles, and he senses his testicles are permanently depleted. Calabrese's boss, a massive balding ogre who sports a rat tail wrapped in a rubber band, stops by once a week to check on progress. The boss drives a dinged up red vintage Jaguar with a license plate that reads LAFF. He hasn't offered a review or a raise, and Calabrese hasn't asked. He has come to understand this is his penance, and the routine of watching and knowing when to add the laugh track and how to dip it underneath has come to be second nature. He does his task mindlessly, stopping only to smoke a cigarette or to step into the hallway to retrieve a cola out of the vending machine located across from the Holistic Healing Clinic and down the hall from the Jehovah's Witness suite that is only used on Sundays.

The repeated watching of sitcoms weighs him down, watching the beautiful people ironically chat about their pride, their drinking, their sex lives and their gluttony. The characters only desire other beautiful people, Caribbean vacations, pay raises and flashy cars.

The hills beyond Los Angeles are smoldering with wildfires, and when the wind is just right, the smoke drifts low over the valley. Interstate 5 has been on the news due to a series of fatal accidents, and homes in the hills have been evacuated. When Calabrese walks to his rusted-out Hyundai at night, he smells the soot and watches the ashes float through the sky, swirling in the Pacific trade winds. At night, when he looks to the east, over the mountains, he witnesses an orange glow beyond the hills. But then the rain comes. A cold, cleansing rain. He has trouble driving through the raindrops, the windshield wipers don't pivot fast enough and he catches himself, excited as he senses the rust bucket hydroplane across the lanes of the deserted highway. He could ease up now and save himself, but it's too late for that. He shuts his eyes, releases the steering wheel, and breathes in a deep whiff of that sweet, sweet rain.

SEVENTEEN

....

SHOPLANDIA

It was the muggiest of days in a summer where the studio had turned into a perpetual circus, and I had my usual pre-shift jitters. The tingling in my arms started as I made my way from the office to the studio, as if I was preparing to make an entrance onto the stage of a play. Deep down, I knew once my shows began, I would slip into my role and feel a sense of purpose, serving the irascible hosts, placating the on-air guests and vendors, and cajoling the backstage crew. I'd recently been feeling more comfortable in the role of producer than as myself.

It had been over a year since Pamela had left me, having cleaned out both our condo and our bank account in one fell swoop. I'd had the unlikeliest of rebound crushes on the aging Hollywood star Jenna McGregor, and her poolside words of encouragement had given me a dash of hope, though not necessarily the courage, to put myself on the line, to make myself vulnerable again.

Meanwhile in the studio, the summer had brought a drought in our sales. In the green rooms, vendors implored the buyers to give their products a second airing.

"It's like planting a seed. You've got to give it time," they pleaded. Up in the offices, a sense of unease radiated from the suits. This pressure to hit the sales numbers often tugged at our efforts to serve the customers first, and the tension infested our psyches. Down in the studio, we wrestled with how to stay true to ourselves, and after our prime-time shift, we often found ourselves quenching our thirst and losing ourselves at the Square Bar. But I'm getting ahead of myself here, as the story of finding my courage really began as I started my shift that day.

I had just turned the corner of the hallway when I caught sight of one of my show hosts for the night, Tanya, stumbling out of the salon. Her hair had been teased and coiffed into what resembled a frightening birds' nest. With eyes red and watery, she placed her hand along the hallway wall to guide herself.

"Hey Tanya," I called out, but she stumbled by in a state of shock. No "Hi Jake," or "Hey Meecham." She scanned her badge and slipped into the safety of the show host lounge. I made a mental note to give her time to decompress. I would need to ease her out of her cocoon before airtime.

The operations desk sat spookily empty for this time in the afternoon, as though the crew had retreated quickly, leaving the outpost abandoned. I opened the door into the studio, and heard the sounds of life. Buke sat at the coordinating producer's station as Henry the show host hovered over him. Henry spun and his eyes lit up.

"Jake, wait until you hear this," He said. "You know how the executives have been reviewing videos of our shows, putting the hosts under the microscope?"

I nodded as I dropped my satchel. Buke shot me a grin.

"Well, Looter has been leaving us voicemails, reminding us that during each product presentation we have to, you know, make the turn."

Making the Turn (*phrase*) - *to formally conclude a sales presentation by asking for a commitment. After explaining the features and benefits of the product, directing the customer to pick up the phone and place an order. To close the deal.*

"He must be getting pressure, because today he brought in a motivational psychologist to talk to the whole team of hosts. This doctor supposedly works for pharmaceutical companies, psyching their sales teams up to go out and close deals. He gave us this whole psychological jujitsu about how salesmen are afraid to make the turn because of, get this, our fear of rejection. He wants us to meet with this quack to try and overcome our fears..."

"You mean, through hypnosis?" I asked.

Without looking up, Buke added, "Next week, he's going to bring in a voodoo doctor."

Henry snorted with laughter just as the floor manager popped his head around the corner. "Henry, we need you on the set." Henry checked his watch. "Shoot, I'm late. Gotta go!"

After a moment, Buke looked up from the computer to ensure Henry had left. "God bless Henry. What would we do without him? I'm glad you are here." Sarcasm dripped from his voice. "You're in for a helluva night."

"You think? How was today? Any prank calls?"

"No. We made it through unscathed. Your girl Andrea was down here asking for you."

That stopped me cold. "I wouldn't call her my girl. Besides, is nothing private anymore?"

Buke just smiled. "Nothing is private in the studio. You know that."

I acknowledged that sad fact with a sigh.

"Besides you might have some competition with Dmitri tonight."

The truth is I've always liked Andrea. She's the entertainment buyer, bringing in such novelty items as Siegfried and Roy DVDs, Snooki novels, Jack Hanna DVDs, David Cassidy CDs, or the complete James Bond Collection on Blu-ray, often with an accompanying fading star as the on air guest. She is down to earth and funny.

A few months ago, she asked me to sit in on a conference call with the self-proclaimed memory expert Svengali. She wanted a producer's thoughts on how we could present his *Memory Madness* Kit. Svengali boasted that his kit would improve a person's memory power in seven days, and he pitched the idea of a live audience show where he would recall and recite each audience member's name. The project sounded interesting, but at the end of our forty-minute call, Svengali mistakenly referred to Andrea as Donna and then asked me to repeat my name, and I told him it was Spridel. Andrea guffawed so loudly she had to walk away from her cubicle. After we hung up, she raised her palms in the air and we laughed at the absurdity. She never placed the purchase order.

About two weeks after that, Andrea was back in the studio with the famed exercise guru and anti-fat fanatic Simon Rakoff, you know, the guy who wears those little striped shirts and tank tops and sings Broadway tunes to women. The production crew was heading out to the Square Bar that night after our shift, so I half-jokingly suggested to Simon and Andrea that they come out for a nightcap. Simon stared at me, unsure if I was serious or teasing him. Honestly, I wasn't sure myself. After a moment he took a single step back and belted out the refrain from "That's Amore", knowing this was going to be picked up by the open microphones in the studio.

Simon didn't show up at the Square Bar that night, but Andrea did. As I sometimes did after working a ten-hour shift, and since my divorce, I drank hard. In a whirlwind of draft beers and Jagermeister shots, I gossiped with Andrea about hosts, guests and co-workers. Later, as we sat alone together in a booth, Andrea detailed how she had fled the city for a fresh start after her own messy, sordid divorce. She had been persuaded by her old boss Bob Payne to come work at Shoplandia. She mimicked Payne, "You won't believe how many people buy from their TV! Watching the sales screen is intense, like mainlining capitalism directly into your veins. I'm telling you, this Shoplandia is an alternate universe."

After last call, I found myself back at Andrea's apartment, where I spent the night in her bed. As dawn broke, I awoke with a swelling headache, a parched tongue, and a panicked sense of awkwardness. I tip-toed into her living room with my clothes, and under the spying eyes of her cat, stepped into my jeans and slipped out while she slept.

At the time, I'd considered this rendezvous a private matter and had not mentioned this fling to anyone, but the crew evidently knew. With constant headset chatter and the nagging urge to stave off boredom in our 24-7 world of tchotchkes, word had spread like a kitten video on Youtube.

After gathering my papers and checking in with Dylan at the line producer's desk, I stopped back out at the operations desk to grab a headset box. A rush of voices suddenly filled the hallway and an entourage swept through, with the man known only as Dmitri at the center. I have to admit that the sight of this legend took my breath away. Dmitri was not as tall as one might have expected, but he was broad shouldered and tan, his muscular physique offset by a billowing white shirt. I had seen Dmitri's gaze before on the countless romance novel covers that lined the checkout aisle of the Fresh Shop, and in occasional TV commercials pitched to lonely housewives. The male model's hair flowed down his back, a golden lion's main. Dark eyebrows and a serene smile framed his chiseled face.

"Oh, Jake! Are you on tonight?" asked Andrea. She was one of those in the constellation swirling around Dmitri and I hadn't even noticed her.

"Hi, I am. We're having some good times. Welcome to the show." Andrea now guided the entourage my way, and the mythic Dmitri stood before me. "Dmitri, this is our producer Jake. Jake, meet Dmitri."

I shook Dmitri's warm and comforting hand, and realized Dmitri was staring into my eyes with a piercing calm. Not that I'd been thinking about it much, but I had expected the world's sexiest man—and romance book cover icon—to be a bit arrogant. Although this legend could theoretically bed practically any woman he desired, he carried himself with a surprising humility.

"Welcome to Shoplandia," I nodded, embarrassed when I realized I had kind of bobbed my head as if meeting royalty.

"I'm happy to be here. Everyone has been so kind."

"Our host Tanya is anxious to meet you."

"And I, her."

Andrea asked, "Do you know which green room we're in?"

"The operations desk will help you out." I leaned in to Andrea, and in my best producer's voice, whispered, "I'll stop by in a little bit to see what we need for the show."

"I chatted with Tanya yesterday, so I think she should be okay to go."

"Nice to meet you sir," I said to Dmitri.

The sex symbol silently bowed and smiled, and the entourage glided down the hall.

Back in the studio, I spied Tanya at the side of the set. Her coiffed Bridezilla hair was flattened out to a non-threatening style so she no longer looked like a cast member from *The Rocky Horror Picture Show*. As soon as Tanya saw me, she tapped the microphone clipped on her blouse to ensure it was off, a sure sign she was about to speak her mind.

"This has been one fucked up day and I'm not even on the air yet."

"What's up? Maurice?"

She sighed. "Him and the fucking big hair phenomenon." She looked at me as if faintly recalling she had passed me in the hallway, and said in a pleading tone, "Oh Jake, I just couldn't go on the air like that. I do enough for this company. I'm happy to make the turn, ask for the money, whatever the hell they want, but I can't make a fool of myself with that big hair. Some lines I won't cross."

I patted her on the shoulder. "Believe me, I understand. Don't worry about it. Has Maurice seen you since?"

"No, but I don't care. He'll have to deal with it."

"It's going to be all right. Here's something to brighten you up. Dmitri is in the building," I added with a bit of levity.

Tanya grinned like a mischievous teenage girl. She looked out over the order entry operators, trying to sneak a peek through the green room window. In a wistful tone, she asked, "I wonder, is Dmitri married?"

"No, but you are."

She turned, startled and blushed. "Oh right. Thanks for the reminder. You know, working with Dmitri is the only reason I didn't call out sick tonight. Will he be shirtless on the air?"

"Sorry. Not if I have a say in the matter."

My name echoed through headsets, "Jake? We have a situation."

"What's up?" I asked into my mic.

"The ops desk needs you."

"I'm on it." I clicked off the box. "I have to run."

As I turned, she called out, "Hey Jake."

"What's up?"

"Break a leg."

The operations desk was buzzing. Maurice's assistant, What's Her Name, leaned in on the counter berating our intern. "Maurice can't get his work done and he is very, very angry." The poor intern's face was frozen, on the verge of tears.

In Maurice Maillard, we had created a monster. Two years ago we had debuted the Maurice Shampoo and Conditioner line of products after one of our buyers "discovered" the young handsome stylist teasing hair in a salon on the Left Bank. The show was an immediate success and we debated whether it was Maurice's good looks or whether the 1980s towering hair was truly coming back in style. We couldn't keep the shampoo in stock. And then *People* magazine ran a piece titled the Big Hair Phenomenon and the Frenchman's ego had swelled to "proportions grandes." Down in the studio, we referred to this as the Big Head Phenomenom.

"How's it going?" I asked with a glance, inserting myself in the conversation.

What's Her Name just stared blankly for a moment, the set of her jaw led me to think she was grinding her teeth.

"I'm the coordinating producer tonight. What's going on?"

"The sink in the salon is clogged. Maurice has to rinse and wash the hair of several models for his show and he can't do it. We're screwed!"

An image floated through my mind. The flamboyant pony-tailed hairstylist tossing out French epithets in a rage, sending What's Her Name into a tizzy.

"Okay. Let's go check it out."

The escalating voices could be heard from the hallway. I opened the door to find Maurice theatrically insulting two scruffy maintenance workers with a colorful mix of broken English-French curse words. A handful of shocked models watched the scene in horror.

Maurice yelled, "Debouchez l'evier! Je ne peux pas travailler comme ceci. Debouchez l'evier!"

I put up my hands. "Everyone relax. We'll get this figured out."

"Vous devez deboucher l'evier foutu!"

"Watch your mouth, there are ladies present."

Maurice's eyes opened wide. He was tall and lean, dressed in a black sweater and faded jeans, his hair pulled back in his trademark ponytail. I turned to the maintenance guys. "What's the deal?"

"We tried plunging but it didn't work. We've tried the liquid plumber, but no go. We need to take the pipe under the sink apart."

The salon manager fidgeted nervously with a pencil.

"Natalie, do you think we can use the bathroom in the host lounge?"

"I don't know. Joe Looter said we're not supposed to be in there. He tells us it is only for hosts." She said this as though the words came down the mountain on a tablet, as if the host lounge is some type of sacred territory.

The clock on the wall read that it was twenty minutes past five. "Looter's gone for the day," I stated, eyes raised, insinuating we have no time for dealing with bullshit.

She blinked and meekly offered, "I can go see if anyone is in there."

"Good idea. Don't ask for permission. Just scout it out and see if it is empty."

She scurried out, happy for the reprieve.

"Maurice, if you need to wash hair we will get you another sink somewhere in the building. Are there any models who don't absolutely have to have their hair washed?"

The Frenchman turned to his assistant stylist. They spoke rapidly in French and pointed at a few models with shorter hair. Maurice walked over and ran his hand through a model's locks.

"These three, we save to last. No time, no wash. Okay?"

"Okay."

Natalie returned and said timidly, "There's nobody in the host lounge. I propped open the back hallway door."

"Great, thanks." I took a deep breath. "Now, we are going to follow Natalie to the show host lounge, which has a sink. The lounge is supposed to be off limits to guests, so please be quiet in there so we don't get kicked out. If we behave, everything will be fine."

The models sighed and started moving their lanky, undernourished frames, closing their gossip magazines, placing their nail files in their purses and shutting down their cell phones. Maurice's assistants gathered up their hair dryers, brushes, curling irons, combs, clippers, towels, gels, shampoos and conditioners, and tossed them into their Louis Vuitton bags. The displaced hair posse walked single file down the hall like a group of refugees kicked out of their homeland.

Back at the coordinating producer's desk, I felt the urge to check in on the outside world. I logged on the computer and clicked through a few news websites to see if the outside world had collapsed into massive sinkholes, or been consumed by wildfires or North Korean missiles or a zombie apocalypse. Some days I was convinced that if something like this happened, we would be forgotten in our windowless studio, and we'd go on selling bangle bracelets, eye creams and 100% pure beef patties as Armageddon raged beyond our walls. I imagined spending my final hour on earth checking the overhead camera angle for a Kitchen Aid bread bakery presentation or verifying we had all three cuts of video for an Ab Sculpting demonstration. After this horrific momentary insight that I would die alone while in the studio, I was relieved to look up and see Andrea quietly standing a few feet away.

"Are you okay?" Her smile was tempered with a look of true concern.

"Oh, yeah." I shut down the browser. "This place consumes me. Sometimes I need to see what is happening in the real world."

She asked in wonderment, "Wait, there's a world outside Shoplandia?"

I grinned. "Amazing, isn't it? How's Dmitri? Is he your new boyfriend?"

She blushed just a little bit and playfully punched me on the shoulder. "Um, no. You're so funny." She was laughing now with that contagious smile and I realized she was the bright spot of my day, of my summer. After our first time together, we had one other night, a deja vu of sorts where we once again connected amongst the bustle of the crew at the bar. We made out in the parking lot and ended up back at her apartment under the watchful gaze of her cat. In the morning, I once again slipped out without facing her. Now laughing with her at this moment, I asked myself why.

She fidgeted for a moment. "So Dmitri's folks are asking if we can have him surrounded by women during his presentation."

"What?"

"They want it to look like Dmitri attracts women

wherever he goes. The legend follows the man sort of thing."

"A chick magnet?"

She laughed. "Yeah, I guess."

I leaned back and closed my eyes, trying to visualize the on air presentation. "Do they want cover models?"

"No. They realize it's last minute."

I just sighed.

Andrea snickered. "It will be tough, but I'll go on air. I can take one for the team."

"I bet you will." I grinned.

"Can you stop back and chat with them?"

"For you? Sure I can."

She raised her eyes and chuckled.

"Okay, I'll stop back there in a bit."

Just as I turned back to the computer, What's Her Name appeared, hovering over the workstation.

"Hey, I'm sorry about Maurice," she said softly. "He's really wound up tonight. He's worried that his new agave conditioner won't sell, and he is mad that he has to sleep in the green room because of the 5 a.m. show, and I'm not sure how long I can take this. This has been the worst job of my life." What's Her Name leaned into the desk and wiped a tear from her eye. "I just wanted to say I'm sorry. For him and for me. I'm not usually like this."

"It's okay," I replied, suddenly feeling awkward that I didn't know her name, that nobody in the studio had bothered to remember her name. "Don't worry about it. You have a tough job." I stared at her and my face felt flush. Unsure what else to do, I stood and asked, "Would you like to go on the air with Dmitri?"

Out on the main rotating stage, Tanya stood at stage left, talking into the camera while holding a pain reliever wand. Dylan sat back in his chair, chatting through headsets with the control room. I checked out the scene in order entry, scanning for women who might want to be on air with Dmitri. I figured if I could rally three more women I'd be set. The supervisor stood three rows down, chatting with an operator. As she walked back up to her desk, I interrupted. "Rachel, I have a question."

"What's up?"

"We have Dmitri on the air tonight..."

Her eyes lit up like candles. "I know. I'm so excited." She clasped her hands together.

"Well, his people want to show Dmitri surrounded by women, but of course, they just mentioned this now."

"You want me to go on air with Dmitri?"

"If you'd like. Could you round up maybe three or four women to hop off the phones and join you? Just for a few minutes, I promise." Rachel tilted her head and looked over the rows of operators. I hesitated, wanting to be careful how I phrased the next comment. "You know, women that look nice, dressed for on-air. They need to be airworthy."

Airworthy *(adj.) A person who is presentable; dressed appropriately, meets certain standards of dress and attitude that won't be objectionable to viewers. A person the producer is com-*

fortable putting on live television.

Rachel continued to scan the floor of the order entry arena. Eight rows deep, with six operators on each side of the row, meant ninety-six operators. Some were men, so we crossed them out. I knew several women would be too shy. Rachel bit her lip and finally said, "Let me see what I can do."

"Be discreet," I advised.

I stepped into Dmitri's green room and Andrea introduced me to the manager, a man named Victor, who was the antithesis of Dmitri. Small and squat, wearing a suit jacket and an open collared dress shirt which revealed a hairy chest, he resembled a used car salesman who had latched onto a good thing.

Victor began his request before we had even shook hands. "We want to have Dmitri surrounded by gorgeous women."

"We don't have any models booked for your show."

Victor looked at the screen, in which Maurice was teasing out the locks of a gorgeous blonde model. "There doesn't appear to be a shortage of lookers for this show."

"Yes, but they were scheduled and paid for by the vendor, and they were only hired for this specific hour."

Victor nodded, his lips pursed. "We're trying to sell the dream here, you know what I mean Bud? It's all about the fantasy of being wrapped in Dmitri's arms."

"Andrea has been gracious enough to volunteer and I'm working on a few more women from our order entry arena to join Dmitri at the end of the presentation."

Victor glanced at Andrea. With a sigh, he said, "I guess beggars can't be choosey."

"What? What do you mean by that?"

Victor put up his hands, palms out and shrugged. "Whoa! That came out the wrong way. I didn't mean it like that."

"Listen, this is live television. We don't airbrush and photoshop at Shoplandia. We'll round up a few women for the end of the presentation." I shook my head in disgust as I pivoted out of the room. The door behind me didn't swing shut, and I sensed someone had followed me into the hall.

"Hey." It was Andrea, and she grinned like the day the memory expert couldn't recall her name. She wasn't upset, just surprised and concerned. It was an odd moment, because my outburst could have been construed as either a defense of Andrea or a general defense of women, and it felt like a sliver of both. "Are you okay?" She asked.

"Yeah. That was just a bit rude."

"I don't think he meant it that way, but thanks." She touched my arm for a moment, and held her hand there just long enough for me to look into her eyes. As I did, my anger dissipated.

"Thanks. I'll see you out at the set in a few minutes. I want to check out who we have rounded up for Dmitri's on-stage fan club."

In front of the producer's desk, at the foot of the stage, the women had gathered, gazing dreamily at

Dmitri. These were not the curvaceous models with taut stomachs who graced the covers of the romance novels. These were authentic suburban women from Sellersburg, Pennsylvania. These were real-life moms who supplemented their family incomes by answering the phones part-time to put gas in their mini-vans and make their kids' orthodontist payments. Dmitri might be selling every woman's dream on the cover of his romance novels, but here in the suburban studio of Shoplandia, our lives are a little more grounded in reality.

Andrea and I stood behind Dylan as he massaged the presentation, adding and dropping a quantity counter as needed, feeding Tanya phone calls, suggesting the control room shoot close ups of the ten-book collection, each one showing Dmitri in a state of undress, his bulging arms wrapped tightly around a photo-shopped and airbrushed voluptuous woman.

Suddenly, Dmitri surprised us all by proclaiming he would read a passage from one of the books, *Left Breathless*. Through headsets, Clancy expressed skepticism that Dmitri could actually read.

The legend picked up the paperback and thumbed through it. After a dramatic silence, he started reading from a random page. The camera zoomed into a tight shot of his chiseled face. He read steadily and eloquently, but it wasn't how he read that made me hold my breath.

"She unzipped his jeans..."

"Oh, Christ." Tanya stood just off camera. She shot me a glance, her eyes wide with surprise.

"He slid his hand down between her thighs..."

Dylan cringed, "Um, I don't think he should be reading this."

"She opened herself to him like a flower..."

The women at the foot of the stage stared intently at Dmitri. One woman fanned herself with her hand, a woman giggled, and another held her hand over her heart. Then I watched as one woman, a white-haired ex-nun named Angela, fainted face first into a camera tripod. It happened in slow motion. Everyone heard the thud when she hit the floor except Dmitri, who was so focused on his reading that he didn't notice the commotion. "She shivered as his fingertips traced a trail along her skin..."

"Oh shit." I immediately dialed security. "We have someone down in the studio. We need first aid."

Dylan jumped into Tanya's ear. "Please stop him from reading any more. Tell him we have a t-caller."

Dan the floor manager cradled Angela's head as distraught women surrounded them. Poor Angela's glazed stare was fixed on the ceiling. A large slice of skin dangled on her forehead and blood dribbled down her cheek. Dan blotted tenderly at the gash with a paper towel.

On the stage, Dmitri answered the caller's questions with ease and grace. His piercing brown eyes sparkled in the camera and his smile pierced the hearts of women across the country. The phones started to ring in order entry. The control room, unaware of the off-camera commotion, called for the women to join Dmitri and

Tanya.

A security guard moved in with a medical bag and knelt down to Angela as I shepherded the women. "It is time to take the stage." A production assistant waved the women up the steps and posed them around the bronzed hunk. A second security guard moved in so I stepped back to the producer's desk and joined Dylan, who had stood to peer over his desk at the unfolding spectacle.

On the monitor, we watched the camera pan across several book covers from the collection. Rogue pirate Dmitri perched on the edge of a cliff with his guns wrapped around a busty brunette beauty. Frontiersman Dmitri dipped a busty blonde beauty backward, a log cabin and rugged mountains in the distance. Royal Dmitri stood boldly with two busty black-haired beauties on either side of him, a castle and a Rolls Royce behind them. And then we were live on the set, Dmitri and Tanya surrounded by nervous suburban moms and grandmothers, dressed in sweatshirts and sweaters. The sight flooded my heart with joy.

"Can we get them to look like they are having fun?" Dylan asked into headsets. The production assistant stepped gingerly to the side of the camera, placed his fingers to his cheeks and stretched his mouth into a smile. The women responded with nervous grins.

I turned to Dylan. "Between you and me, this may be my finest moment as a coordinating producer."

Dylan laughed. "The glamorous world of television."

"Nah dude. It's just the real world."

When Tanya finished her shift, she insisted I snap a photo of her and Dmitri. Together we stepped into the green room to find Andrea leaning over the computer monitor checking sales. She looked up as we entered, "What happened to that poor woman?"

"Security ran her to the hospital," I replied. "She probably needs stitches. They think she might have a concussion."

Dmitri's eyes arched with confusion. "What happened?"

"One of the women passed out while coming up on stage," Andrea replied.

Dmitri broke into a pained grimace, as if we had told him his own mother had taken ill.

"She was coming to the stage? To see me?" Dmitri swiveled from me to Andrea, and then back, his mouth open with true concern.

"Yes, she was about to take the stage. To be on the air with you." The poor guy was so shaken that I thought it was best not to tell him she had fainted from his erotic reading.

Dmitri turned to Victor. "We must go visit her."

Victor scoffed. "We're not doing that."

"We must. She was injured for me."

"Dmitri, it's ten o'clock at night. Do you know the bedlam you'd set off if you walked into the emergency room? Not to mention, we have a three hour drive back to New York and you are on *Kelly Live* in the morning."

Dmitri paced the room with his head down in thought. Victor dropped his face into his hands and moaned, as if he couldn't believe this predicament. He sighed and looked up. "I keep telling him that the brand of Dmitri stands for eros - erotic love. That's where the money is, but he wants to broaden the brand to agape love. Honestly, I think it dilutes the brand."

Dmitri halted in the center of the room and announced, "We will send a bouquet of flowers."

"The operations desk should have the number for a florist," I said. Someone called my name on headsets. I clicked on and asked them to hold for a moment.

Andrea offered, "I can get the florist's number. You go ahead."

"Thanks. I have to run, but it was nice meeting you." I shook Dmitri's hand and then stepped over and clasped the manager's hand also. At that precise moment, Clancy from the control room asked on headsets, "I think I need a drink tonight. Who's in for a nightcap?" A few voices enthusiastically agreed.

I was feeling a bit thirsty myself. While exiting the green room, I clicked on my box. "I'm in."

When I arrived at the Square Bar, several members of the control room were already gathered, halfway through their first bottles and laughing off the stress of the night. We joined the crew and the beers flowed. Clancy was in rare form, joking about the show hosts and the last Simon Rakoff appearance. After picking up a beer, I saw Dan come through the door with What's Her Name.

As he passed by, Dan leaned in and whispered, "Her

name is Lynn."

I grinned and greeted her, "Welcome to our watering hole, Lynn."

She smiled. Outside of the studio, without frenetic nerves from mediating between Maurice and our crews, she looked unburdened. A minute later, I understood why.

She shouted over the noise, "I quit tonight!"

At first, I thought I had misheard her. "Wait, you quit?"

"Yes I did. I couldn't deal with him anymore." Dan handed her a beer and she held it up for a toast. "Good riddance to Maurice." The three of us clinked bottles. "I feel so light and free right now." She took a big swig from her beer, gulping half the bottle. Dan's eyes popped and he laughed.

"Fuck Maurice," Lynn burped. "That man will drag you down."

"Lynn, let me introduce you to some of the folks from the control room."

We joined the crew and the beers flowed. When I looked over, Dan and Lynn were downing shots of tequila. I'm not sure who first said it, though I recall a voice echoing throughout the bar. "Somebody needs to cut off that man's pony tail." Clancy made a snipping motion, moving his two fingers like scissors through the air.

Dan grinned, hoisted his beer bottle and chanted, "Bring me the ponytail of Maurice Maillard."

Lynn laughed and pulled Dan close to her. She carved

out a niche where they could lean on the bar. The phrase caught on, and every few moments, when there was a momentary lull in the conversation, Clancy or Lynn or some stranger would chant, "Bring me the ponytail of Maurice Maillard!" At one point, Dan wrapped an arm around her and left it there.

After my second beer, someone tapped me on the shoulder. Andrea stood before me with a warming smile.

"Have I got a story for you," she said as I handed her a beer. "Evidently, there aren't any florists open at ten o'clock at night so Dmitri stopped at the hospital and saw Angela. He insisted he didn't feel right not going. He kept saying it was the right thing to do. So finally, Victor relented. I figured I better go with them, just in case. They stopped at the SuperSaver and bought supermarket roses. Well, you should have seen Angela's face when Dmitri showed up. I thought she was going to pass out again. He took her hand and told her that he was sorry and that he hoped she would heal quickly."

We clinked beer bottles and I introduced Andrea to some of the crew she hadn't met. At one point, as Andrea chatted with Dan, a graphics operator from the control room pointed to me, silently inquiring if she and I were together. I smiled slightly and turned up my palms, as if I was noncommittal, and he raised his beer toward me. A moment later, Andrea raised her beer bottle and exclaimed, "Bring me the ponytail of Maurice Maillard!"

In the morning, I awakened in Andrea's darkened, air-conditioned bedroom. As my eyes adjusted to the morning light, I noticed my jeans and dress shirt scattered on the floor. The strangest sight made my heart stop. A ponytail was sticking out from underneath my shirt. I shut my eyes and tried to recall what might have happened after the bar, but my brain was rebooting too slowly. I blinked my eyes and focused. The dress shirt wiggled and Andrea's cat emerged from underneath. I held my hand out in relief. The cat slinked over and sniffed at my palm. After a few strokes, she drifted away as I let my fingers smooth down her tail.

For the first time, this bedroom felt safe and secure. I slowly rolled over and watched Andrea sleeping under the covers. Her tousled hair and rhythmic breathing reassured me, and as I studied her for a few moments, she smiled in her sleep. I closed my eyes and licked my lips. The night before returned slowly. For the first time in a year, I sensed a calmness that didn't emanate from work or drink. I imagined Dmitri standing up in a Manhattan green room, greeting that tiny blonde Kelly with a giant bear hug, and then waving to a sea of women in the audience as he walked out onto the set. I wondered if What's Her Name - Lynn - was waking up beside Dan this morning. I thought of Angela resting comfortably in a hospital bed with her bandaged head, the room filled with the fragrance of Dmitri's red roses. I was flooded with a certainty that this woman beside me was worth the effort and that this was my moment to make the turn. Andrea stirred and opened her eyes for the briefest moment before closing them again. And then she smiled.

ACKNOWLEDGEMENTS

For their monthly inspiration and editorial guidance, thank you to Carla Sarett, Virginia Beards, Eli Silberman, Mark Mitchell, Laura Tamakoshi, Jennifer Jansen, Earl Wilcox, Henry Pashkow, and Sara O'Connor. For her diligent editing, thanks to editor Sue Gregson. For reading early drafts and providing feedback, thanks to Robb Cadigan and Terry Heyman.

Special thanks to graphic designer Larry Geiger for his creative book cover designs and collaborative efforts. Check out his awesome work at larrygeigerdesign.com. Thank you to Gary Colyer Jr. for the photo.

Writing is a solitary pursuit, so I appreciate meetings with friends at the Brandywine Valley Writers Group, the Main Line Writers Group, and the Philadelphia Writers Group. Also big thanks to my friends on Facebook and Twitter who provide everyday laughs at the virtual water cooler.

Thanks to Jeannine, Jay, and Brendan Breslin for putting up with my obsessions and idiosyncrasies.

Some of these stories have appeared in slightly different form in the following journals: "Damn Yankees" was published in *Turk's Head Review*. "Laugh Track" was published in *The Molotov Cocktail*.

ABOUT THE AUTHOR

Jim Breslin's first collection, *Elephant: Short Stories and Flash Fiction*, was published in 2011. He has been published in *Turk's Head Review, The Molotov Cocktail, Metazen, Think Journal*, and *Schuylkill Valley Journal*. He was nominated in 2011 for a Pushcart Prize. Jim is the founder of the West Chester Story Slam and Delco Story Slam, monthly storytelling events. For seventeen years, he worked as a television producer at the home shopping giant QVC. He lives in West Chester, PA.

For more information on Jim Breslin and his writing, visit jimbreslin.com.

ALSO FROM OERMEAD PRESS

Exit Pursued By A Bear and Others
Poetry by Virginia Beards
(2014)

"*Exit Pursued by a Bear* is original and delightful, a remarkable debut."

    - Daisy Fried, *My Brother is Getting Arrested Again*

Chester County Fiction
Anthology
(2011)

Sixteen stories from authors who live and work in Chester County, Pennsylvania. Tales of love and loss, violence and heartbreak. Stories by Virginia Beards, Jim Breslin, Robb Cadigan, Wayne Anthony Conaway, Peter Cunniffe, Michael Dolan, Ronald D. Giles, Terry Heyman, Joan Hill, Nicole Valentine, Jacob Asher Michael, Eli Silberman and Christine Yurick.

Elephant: Short Stories and Flash Fiction
By Jim Breslin
(2011)

In this debut collection of stories, Jim Breslin explores the soul of suburbia; the disenfranchised and the desperate. Sometimes funny, often sad, the unsettling stories in Elephant portray the suburban landscape of loneliness and hope.

Made in the USA
San Bernardino, CA
30 December 2015